I don't believe this, P9-BZX-732 arrived at a West Hollywood safe house maintained by Sloane. *It's bad enough that I have to take orders from Arvin Sloane again. Now I have to make nice with another ruthless killer from my past?*

She found Maya Rao in the living room, watched over by a pair of armed guards employed by APO. The Indian assassin was sprawled on the sofa reading the latest issue of *Wired* when Sydney entered. Her lustrous black hair and flawless brown skin gave Maya the look of a lounging Bollywood movie star. Unlike Sydney, who had changed into her most severe black suit for the occasion, Maya was dressed casually in a midriff-baring tank top and loose sweatpants.

The cozy domestic setting struck Sydney as profoundly wrong. She would have preferred to conduct this meeting in a CIA interrogation cell. Then again, she didn't work for the CIA anymore . . . officially.

"Sydney Bristow!" Maya greeted her, rising from the couch. The guards tensed for action, just in case, but Maya was careful to avoid any sudden movements. Perverse amusement gleamed in her dark eyes. "Long time no see, as you Americans say."

Also available from
SIMON SPOTLIGHT ENTERTAINMENT

THE

SERIES

FAINA

ALIAS™

THE

SERIES

TWO OF A KIND?

ALIAS™

THE

SERIES

TWO OF A KIND?

GREG COX

An original novel based on the
hit TV series created by J. J. Abrams

SSE

SIMON SPOTLIGHT ENTERTAINMENT

New York   London   Toronto   Sydney

SSE

SIMON SPOTLIGHT ENTERTAINMENT
An imprint of Simon & Schuster
1230 Avenue of the Americas, New York, New York 10020
Text and cover art copyright © 2005 by Touchstone Television
All rights reserved, including the right of reproduction in whole or in part in any form.
SIMON SPOTLIGHT ENTERTAINMENT and related logo are trademarks of Simon & Schuster, Inc.
Manufactured in the United States of America
                10 9 8 7 6 5 4 3 2
Library of Congress Control Number 2004115764
ISBN 1-4169-0213-9

WHITE SANDS MISSILE RANGE
LAS CRUCES, NEW MEXICO

A solitary tank rumbled across the desert. Dunes of sparkling white gypsum sand reflected the sunlight beating down upon the Tularosa basin, a desolate valley ringed by rocky gray mountains. Stubborn stalks of yucca sprang up around the fringes of the ever shifting dunes, defying the harsh, inhospitable conditions.

The sun beat down on Hayden Chase as well, making her pine for her air-conditioned office back in Langley. A middle-aged black woman in a severe but stylish business suit, the senior director of the Central Intelligence Agency refused to let the

1

oppressive heat and glare compromise her steely demeanor. *Let's just hope today's demonstration proves worth the trip,* she thought.

Chase peered at the tank through a pair of binoculars. She stood at the foot of four rows of bleachers stacked at a safe distance from the testing range. A vinyl canopy provided a degree of shade for the seated observers, which included a number of top Pentagon brass, a smattering of senators, a few nervous Boeing executives, and other dignitaries. No press, though; attendance for this particular demonstration had been granted on a strictly need-to-know basis.

"I'm glad you could make it today, Madam Director," a hearty voice addressed her.

Chase lowered the binoculars and turned to face Gen. Josiah "Hot Rod" Harrison. A stocky man with a florid red complexion, Harrison was a few inches shorter than Chase herself. Four brightly polished stars adorned the epaulets of the man's dress uniform. A successful test today was his ticket to a fifth star.

"I think you'll be very impressed by what you're about to see," he enthused, talking up the project. "Kestrel represents the next generation in UCAV technology." Chase recognized the acronym for "uninhabited combat air vehicle." "Properly deployed, it could allow us to carry out multiple air strikes on enemy targets without putting a single American pilot at risk."

"The CIA has been using unmanned drone planes for some time now," Chase reminded him politely. A gust of hot, dry wind blew against her face, and she took a sip from a plastic water bottle before continuing. "I'm certainly familiar with the concept."

"Ah, but Kestrel is absolutely state-of-the-art. Unlike early unmanned aircraft, which required an operator to be in the line of sight of the drone, Kestrel has a unique cybernetic brain that allows it to adapt to changing conditions in pursuit of its mission. It can engage or evade enemy air defenses, use both air-to-air and air-to-surface missiles, and penetrate areas contaminated by either biological or chemical weapons. And because there's no need to accommodate a human pilot, Kestrel can fly faster and farther than any manned aircraft." Harrison beamed with pride, as though extolling the accomplishments of his favorite child. "It's capable of vertical or horizontal takeoffs. It's practically impervious to the elements . . . trust me, Ms. Chase, you're about to witness the future of military aviation."

"I certainly hope so," she said, fully aware of just how much time and money the Pentagon had put into developing Kestrel. "The last thing we need is any American fighter pilots taken hostage by the enemy."

"A thing of the past," the general assured her. He pointed toward a fortified concrete blockhouse several yards away from the bleachers. This, Chase knew, was the command center for Kestrel, packed full of technicians and costly computer equipment. "That's where the UCAV is piloted, so to speak. You can't get much safer than that."

"Perhaps," Chase conceded cautiously. She hadn't gotten to where she was by making rash assumptions. Still, the initial reports on Kestrel *had* been promising.

The roar of an approaching aircraft intruded upon the conversation. She glanced at her wristwatch. In theory the prototype had taken off a few moments earlier from a runway elsewhere within the sprawling test facility.

Right on time, she thought.

An expectant hush fell over the spectators. Raising a hand to shield her eyes from the glare, Chase scanned the sky for a first glimpse at today's featured performer.

"Here she comes," the general said redundantly.

A second later Kestrel emerged into view. The soaring delta-winged prototype resembled a stealth fighter, only smaller and more streamlined, with no need for a cockpit. About the size of a small Cessna, roughly thirty feet in length, the UCAV circled once above the sunbaked basin in order to give the audience below a good look at the aircraft. Like its avian namesake, Kestrel had blue-gray wings and one wide black band on its tail.

Pretty sleek looking, Chase thought, recognizing the basic design from various classified reports, *but can it live up to the hype?* The prototype alone, she knew, had cost more than fifteen million dollars.

She turned her attention back to the distant tank, which, like the UCAV itself, was being navigated by remote control. Any moment now Kestrel was supposed to fire a Hellfire missile at the tank; if things went according to plan, the surplus vehicle would soon be history.

The crowd held its collective breath as Kestrel swooped in toward its target. At the last minute, however, the prototype suddenly deviated from its course. Executing a hairpin turn at a g-force that would have killed any human pilot, the UCAV accelerated toward the open sky above the San Andres mountain range.

What the hell? Chase thought. All around her the other observers reacted in confusion and alarm. Startled gasps sounded from the bleachers, while a few panicked attendees began running for shelter, just in case the AWOL aircraft turned around and targeted the spectator area. Chase briefly considered making a break for the blockhouse herself.

Next to her, Harrison had completely lost it. "What do you mean you can't control it?" he shouted into a walkie-talkie, oblivious to Chase's presence. His outraged face went from red to purple in about thirty seconds. "Scramble the fighters! Shoot it down if you have to, but don't let it get away!"

But it was already too late. Chase watched grimly as Kestrel disappeared into the horizon. If nothing else, the general had clearly not exaggerated the aircraft's speed and maneuverability. Given its head start, she sincerely doubted that any manned aircraft would be able to catch up with Kestrel before the rogue UCAV vanished completely.

The top secret prototype had just been stolen right before their very eyes.

CHAPTER 1

LOS ANGELES

"I still can't belicve you'd never seen the dancing alligators before!" Michael Vaughn teased Sydney as they rode the subway together. With her sister out of town on a mission, he had spent the night at her place, where, among other things, he had been shocked to discover this gaping hole in her cultural literacy.

"Hey, can I help it if I didn't exactly have the archetypal American childhood?" she defended herself. "You've met my parents. Can you really imagine Jack Bristow at a Saturday matinee of *Fantasia*?"

"You've got me there," he admitted.

They sat side by side on the speeding subway train. Rush hour was over, so finding seats together had not been a problem. Sydney basked in the tranquil moment, knowing better than to take it for granted. If there was one thing her career in espionage had taught her, besides being *very* careful about whom one trusted, it was to savor such cozy respites when they arose, because you never knew how long they would last. *This time tomorrow,* she reflected, *I could be in a firefight in Madagascar—or a torture chamber in Beirut.*

Vaughn must have been thinking along the same lines. "So, what do you think Sloane is calling us in for?" he asked her. A slender young man with wavy brown hair, he was dressed casually in a sport jacket, T-shirt, and jeans. A hint of a five o'clock shadow gave him a slightly raffish look.

"Nothing good," Sydney predicted. Like Vaughn, she wasn't exactly dressed for the office. She'd thrown on a cream-colored tank top, khaki shorts, and sneakers. Her straight brown hair fell loosely past her shoulders. "This is Sloane we're talking about, not the prize patrol."

Despite her glib tone, her mood darkened. The

last thing she wanted to do on a sunny Saturday afternoon was deal with Arvin Sloane and whatever dire emergency had prompted his summons. She exchanged an apprehensive look with Vaughn. "I guess we'll find out what's up soon enough."

The train slowed to a halt, and Sydney glanced out the window at the platform outside. *This is our stop,* she confirmed, rising from her seat. Together she and Vaughn exited the train, along with a handful of other passengers. The air-conditioned Metro station, located along the system's Red Line, held only a modest crowd of pedestrians waiting to board the train.

As the rest of the exiting passengers headed left for the stairs and escalators at the far end of the platform, Sydney and Vaughn hung back until they had the platform to themselves, then headed briskly in the opposite direction. Their footsteps echoed in the subterranean station, while the wind from the departing train stirred up the candy wrappers and Styrofoam cups littering the platform. Loudspeakers conveyed service information through a buzz of static.

At this end of the platform, the farthest point from the entrance, was a reinforced metal door bearing the inscription AUTHORIZED PERSONNEL ONLY.

An overhead security camera kept watch over the scuffed, unprepossessing door, which appeared to guard nothing more exciting than a maintenance closet or service tunnel. The average commuter passing through the station would never give the door a second thought.

Which was precisely the idea.

"Care to do the honors?" Vaughn asked.

"I don't mind if I do," Sydney replied lightly, trying to hold on to their relaxed mood for a little while longer. She hoped it didn't sound too forced.

A grubby-looking card reader was mounted to the wall next to the door. Sydney reached into her purse and fished out a white plastic key card. The blank card bore no corporate logos or any other identifying marks, only a black magnetic strip on its underside.

She automatically looked around to make sure no one was watching, then slid the card through the reader. A locking mechanism clicked open. Sydney pushed open the door and stepped quickly inside. Vaughn followed her, closing the door behind them.

They proceeded into what appeared to be an electrical junction room, approximately ten square feet in dimension. At least two dozen brightly painted fuse boxes lined the dingy concrete walls. A printed sign warned: CAUTION! HIGH VOLTAGE.

Sydney barely noticed the sign anymore.

Working in unison, she and Vaughn each approached a different fuse box, one firehouse red, the other a lurid shade of green. Without fear of electrocution Sydney opened the red box, exposing two columns of switches inside. She flicked three of the switches in exactly the right order; at this point she knew the sequence by heart.

"Your turn," she instructed Vaughn.

"Right on it," he said.

He opened the green box and flicked four more switches in sequence, then nodded at Sydney, who continued the process by walking over to a blue box and performing a similar operation. She hesitated briefly before flicking the final switch, knowing that once she did so, her romantic weekend with Vaughn was officially over.

Duty calls, she acknowledged reluctantly, *whether we like it or not.*

She flicked the last fuse.

K-klang-ksshh!

A harsh metallic ring emanated from behind the fuse boxes, followed by a hiss of compressed air being released. A seemingly solid wall swung open, revealing an open doorway.

Open sesame, Sydney thought. There was always something inherently cool about a secret door, no matter how many times you had occasion to operate one. And to think that this particular passageway was only a few yards away from a public subway platform. . . .

Not exactly as chic as Credit Dauphine, she thought of the dingy junction room, *but effective camouflage nonetheless.*

"Excellent teamwork, Ms. Bristow," Vaughn said, a boyish grin on his face. He chivalrously stepped away from the doorway to let her pass. "Ladies first."

"Thank you, Mr. Vaughn," she replied. "Your cooperation, and courtesy, are greatly appreciated."

Their playful banter brought a smile to her lips. At moments like this she really believed that she and Vaughn could make things work this time, despite everything that had come between them over the past few years.

Lauren, for example.

Sydney forced herself to concentrate on the present.

In contrast to the run-down appearance of the junction room, the corridor beyond was sleek and pristine, all polished reflective surfaces and expensive fixtures. Only a few rusty pipes and concrete buttresses betrayed the underground passageway's humbler origins, from before the abandoned tunnel got its extreme makeover.

They walked down the hallway, passing an elevator and another closed metal door, until they reached the end, where yet another reinforced steel door awaited them. This one swung open readily, admitting them into a cavernous chamber abuzz with activity.

Serious-looking men and women wearing dark business suits moved purposefully through a maze of cubicles and workstations, while their seated colleagues manned computer terminals and secure phone lines. The hum of urgent conversations greeted Sydney's ears. The air-conditioning made her shiver, and for a second she longed for the summer heat outside.

The scene reminded Sydney of a busy day at the L.A. offices of the CIA, except on a much smaller scale. At most, no more than twenty-five employees peopled the general bull pen area of the underground sanctuary, which had started out as a class-five bomb shelter back during the bad old days of the Cold War. Thoroughly refurbished and updated, the bunker now served as the top secret headquarters of a covert intelligence unit code-named APO, short for "Authorized Personnel Only." Organized along the lines of the now defunct SD-6, APO was a secret black-ops unit accountable only to themselves—and Hayden Chase of the CIA.

A unit that, officially, did not exist.

A transparent wall separated the bull pen from Arvin Sloane's personal office. Sydney braced herself as she and Vaughn approached the door of the office. Although she didn't know what the subject of today's briefing was going to be, she knew who was going to be in charge. And she didn't like it.

Back into the serpent's lair . . .

"Okay, as far as we can tell," Marshall Flinkman began, "somebody hacked into Kestrel's navigational system and reprogrammed its CPU once it was in the air . . . which is supposed to be impossible, but since when has that stopped anyone?" He grinned sheepishly and shrugged his diminutive shoulders. "I have to admit, at first I was kind of hoping that the UCAV's cybernetic brain had achieved self-awareness and rebelled against its creators, 'cause that would have been extremely cool. Like in the *Terminator* movies or even *Short Circuit.* You know, 'Number Five is alive!'" he chirped, doing his best impression of a chatty robot. "But the hacker scenario is a little more plausible, since true artificial intelligence is still a couple of decades away at least. Although there's been some interesting progress in the development of quantum processing and parallel—"

"Thank you, Marshall," Sloane interrupted. The older man's slight frame belied his air of authority. He had close-cropped salt-and-pepper hair and a neatly trimmed white beard that was almost invisible against his narrow face. "That will be all."

Marshall gulped and sank back into one of the plush chairs occupying the lounge area in Sloane's spacious office. Sydney gave him a consoling smile from her own chair a few feet away, hoping to take away some of the sting from Sloane's brusque dismissal. *Marshall is always so eager to please,* she thought. *So what if he tends to ramble sometimes?*

Along with her and Vaughn, most of APO's major field agents had gathered in the lounge for a briefing on the stolen experimental aircraft.

Glancing around the room, Sydney spotted her father and Dixon. As was usually the case, the older men, including Sloane, were dressed less casually than Sydney and Vaughn; APO had a looser dress code than the CIA, but Jack Bristow and his contemporaries still preferred dark, conservative suits and ties. Marshall tried for the same look but ended up with a more rumpled effect.

A couple of familiar faces were missing, since Nadia and Weiss were in the final stages of a mission in Guatemala at the moment. Sydney took a second to hope that both agents would be safely back in Los Angeles before long.

Having Nadia move in with me was a good idea, she mused, looking forward to her sister's return. *We should do something fun together when she gets back.*

Her smile evaporated as Sloane began to speak. "Naturally, the CIA, as well as military intelligence, are making their own efforts to locate Kestrel," he told them, "but Director Chase has also instructed us to make this our number one priority. It is vital that we recover the prototype—or, at the very least, keep it from falling into the hands of America's enemies."

Which, up till a few months ago, would have included you, Sydney thought bitterly. Even after all these weeks she still couldn't get used to the idea of working for Sloane again. Not that she wanted to; the day she forgot what a murderous SOB Arvin Sloane really was would be the day her soul died beyond all hope of resuscitation. She owed it to Danny and Francie and all of Sloane's innumerable other victims never to get too comfortable dealing with the man, no matter how useful he might be when it came to running black-ops units like APO.

"Captured electronic chatter," Sloane continued, "reveals that whoever stole Kestrel intends to sell the prototype to the highest bidder." Dapper as ever, in a tailored black suit, he strolled around the lounge handing out briefing folders to Sydney and the other agents. She repressed a shudder as he walked behind her chair. "Needless to say, we cannot allow this transaction to take place."

He came to a halt directly across from Sydney. "Fortunately, we already have a lead. Via some of my more dubious contacts I've been approached by an individual who claims to have been involved in the theft of the UCAV." He smiled cryptically at

Sydney in a way that made her skin crawl. "An old acquaintance of yours, Sydney, who insists on dealing with you alone."

Uh-oh, Sydney thought. *I don't like the sound of this.* Whom was Sloane referring to—Sark? Allison Doren? Aunt Katya? She tensed in anticipation of whatever bomb Sloane was about to drop. "Who?"

He didn't even bother trying to conceal his amusement.

"Maya Rao."

CHAPTER 2

RAJASTHAN, INDIA
TEN YEARS AGO

The annual Pushkar camel fair was in full swing, transforming the small temple town, nestled on the fringe of the Thar Desert, in northwestern India, into the site of an enormous and almost overwhelming spectacle. The yearly event, timed to coincide with the religious festival of Kartik Poornima, drew more than two hundred thousand people, not to mention some fifty thousand camels, for five days of furious trading, racing, and festivities. Hundreds of tents and stalls dotted the barren plain west of Pushkar, which teemed with native tribesmen, traders, and tourists. The brightly hued turbans and colorful tie-dyed garments of the people gathered for the event added to the festive nature of the scene.

Disguised as a local Rajasthani woman, Sydney strolled through the fair in a deceptively casual manner. Makeup darkened her usually fair complexion, while an ornate veil, embroidered with dozens of tiny mirrors, helped conceal her features. A brilliantly red scarf, the same color as her pleated, ankle-length skirt, covered the long black wig she wore over her own hair. Ivory bangles circled her arms from her wrists to her shoulders. A delicate silver anklet tinkled with every step. *Good thing I'm not trying to sneak up on anybody,* she thought; the jangling jewelry served to help her blend in with the local women, who had donned their best clothes and finery for the occasion.

Rows of stalls, selling everything from perfume to pots, lined a dusty path leading through the fairgrounds. Food vendors hawked chai, pakoras, and freshly squeezed sugarcane juice, along with numerous other enticing treats. All strictly vegetarian and nonalcoholic, of course, given the religious nature of the festival. The smoke from dozens of cooking fires rose toward the clear blue sky.

The tantalizing aromas made Sydney's mouth water as she worked her way through the crowded bazaar, feigning interest in the various goods on display. In truth, there was so much to see and hear that Sydney had to make an effort not to be distracted by the sheer sensory overload. Acrobats and musicians performed for the fairgoers milling around, along with roaming mystics and magicians. A sacred cow wandered freely through the fair. A bony, half-starved fakir, wearing only a saffron loincloth, meditated while standing immobile upon one leg; a horizontal metal spike transfixed his cheeks. Sydney winced just looking at him.

Keep your mind on the job, she reminded herself, doing her best to focus on the mission at hand. She whispered into her mirrored veil, which contained a concealed microphone, "Little Princess to Taj Mahal. Do you read me?"

"Roger that, Little Princess," a familiar deep voice spoke into her ear. "I have you in sight."

She glanced around the crowded bazaar. In the bustling confusion she couldn't immediately locate the other agent. "Okay, I give. Where are you?"

"Look behind you. Roughly seven o'clock."

Pretending to examine a pair of embroidered

slippers, she paused and sneaked a peek to her left. Sure enough, she quickly spotted the exotic figure of what appeared to be a sadhu, an ascetic Hindu holy man. A matted white beard fell halfway down the man's chest, contrasting sharply with the figure's saffron robe. A thick layer of gray ash was smudged over his face, hands, and feet. A serene expression upon his face, he roamed the bazaar holding out a clay begging bowl before him.

Sydney grinned behind her veil. Dixon certainly looked convincing in the role of a wandering sadhu. "How are the offerings going today?" she teased.

"Not bad." He shook his bowl so that she could hear the coins rattling inside. "Not quite enough to cover our expenses, but it should make a nice donation to the nearest temple." His voice took on a more businesslike tone. "So far, so good. You don't seem to have picked up a tail."

Music to my ears, she thought. Although she and Dixon had been partners for only about six months now, she had already learned to rely on his judgment and skill. She couldn't think of anyone she'd rather have watching her back.

Except, maybe, for Noah . . .

A pang of emotion stabbed at her heart, but

she forcefully pushed the feeling aside. Now was not the time.

Their mission today was to extract one Nasir Azad, a chemist employed by Zero Defense, an international terrorist organization. Through intermediaries Dr. Azad had convinced the CIA of his desire to defect, and it had fallen upon SD-6 to bring the man to safety—in exchange for whatever information he could provide regarding the internal workings of Zero Defense. The sprawling camel fair, which attracted visitors from all over the world, had seemed like the perfect opportunity to snatch Azad under the cover of the raucous celebrations.

At least that's the plan, Sydney thought apprehensively. While the swarming hordes offered a welcome degree of anonymity, she was only too aware that the crowd could also hide a multitude of enemies. *Let's hope that everything goes just as smoothly as anticipated.*

"Good to know," she acknowledged, resuming her leisurely trek through the fair. An elderly tattoo artist called out to her, aggressively trying to lure her into his stall, but Sydney raised her hands to reveal that both her palms were already covered with elaborate henna designs. "I haven't spotted any sign of the opposition either," she informed Dixon.

With luck, Zero Defense had no idea that Azad intended to defect. Still, Sydney had been in the spy game long enough to know that sometimes even the most elaborate covers could be blown; for all she knew, the fairgrounds had already been infiltrated by assassins determined to keep Azad from spilling the terrorists' secrets.

"Not even Maya?" Dixon asked.

Sydney frowned at the name. Maya Rao was Zero Defense's top agent—and a cold-blooded killer second to none. Born an untouchable in an obscure Indian village, she had defied her lowly roots to become a notorious bandit queen, preying on the rural countryside, before being recruited by Zero Defense two or three years ago—about the same time that Sydney was enlisted by SD-6. She and Sydney had clashed numerous times over the past few years—in Calcutta, Zurich, Rio, and Nepal—with inconclusive results. Sydney looked forward to bringing her down someday, but not right now. Her mission this afternoon was to get Azad out of here in one piece, not to settle scores with a dangerous adversary.

"*Especially* not Maya," she assured Dixon.

Several yards ahead, beyond the overflowing bazaar, a rickety steel Ferris wheel towered above the plain. The spinning amusement park ride, which was dwarfed in turn by the rocky mountains lying to the north, was Sydney's ultimate destination: her rendezvous point with Azad, assuming that Maya and her murderous cohorts hadn't gotten to him first.

Time to find out.

Confident that Dixon was not far behind her, she headed slowly but surely toward the distant Ferris wheel. Reaching the end of the merchants' aisle, she stepped out of the relative shade of the canopied stalls into the clear November sunshine. Mercifully, the cool season was upon them, so it was only seventy-five degrees out; Sydney was silently grateful that the festival did not take place during the sweltering heat of the Indian summer, when the temperature might well have exceeded one hundred degrees.

The arid field between her and the Ferris wheel was jam-packed with both people and livestock. Countless camels occupied the open plain, squatting on the ground or grazing on whatever scant greenery was available. Rajasthani tribesmen, sporting prodigious black mustaches, watched over their herds while extolling the virtues of individual camels to prospective buyers. Sydney noted with amusement that, if anything, many of the camels were even more extravagantly groomed and ornamented than the bejeweled and bangled women dressed in their holiday best. Gleaming mirrors, beads, and cowries adorned the beasts' intricately embroidered saddles, reins, and back covers, which flaunted a variety of brilliant colors in the true Rajput style. Jewelry and perfume, intended specifically for the camels themselves, were laid out on blankets by another battalion of eager salesmen. The contrast between the homely pack animals and their gaudy trappings could not have been more extreme; the camels looked to Sydney as though they were decked out for Mardi Gras.

Cattle and sheep were also being traded, she observed, but they could hardly compete, in either numbers or ostentation, with the humpbacked stars of the festival.

In general, the menfolk seemed more interested in the camels and their accoutrements than the women were. *Must be a guy thing,* Sydney concluded, which gave her a good excuse not to linger amid the growling and spitting camels as she closed in on the Ferris wheel. Wincing at the sight of a young camel getting its nose pierced, she glanced at a wristwatch tucked in between her bracelets. *Almost there,* she thought. *Right on schedule.*

She kept her eyes peeled for Maya Rao but quickly realized that the odds were against her. Trying to spot one particular Indian woman in the middle of the Pushkar camel fair was like looking for a specific drag queen at a gay-pride parade. *Maybe this wasn't such a great idea after all.*

Searching for Maya, or any other suspicious activity around her, Sydney found her gaze drawn to a young couple ambling hand in hand a few yards away. Their baseball caps, khaki shorts, and souvenir T-shirts marked them as American tourists. They were smiling and laughing and clearly very much in love. *On their honeymoon,* Sydney wondered, *or just a romantic vacation abroad?*

A fresh pang of heartsickness got past her defenses. It had been more than six months since Noah Hicks had disappeared into a deep-cover assignment without even saying good-bye. She had waited avidly for him to contact her somehow, to let her know that what they'd had together still mattered, but . . . nothing. *If he wanted to reach me,* she thought woefully, *he would have found a way by now.* Her throat tightened at the thought that she might never see Noah again, which was apparently just the way he wanted it. *Serves me right for falling for a fellow agent. Remind me never to do that again. . . .*

Arriving at the foot of the Ferris wheel, she looked around for Azad. In the crush of the crowd it took her a second to zero in on a pudgy, middle-aged man standing to one side of the line for the ride. Eyeglasses rested on the man's nose, above a neatly trimmed black beard lightly flecked with gray. His tan Nehru jacket coordinated with the cap on his head.

The man, who matched her description of Azad, appeared to be waiting for someone. He glanced repeatedly at his watch, while anxiously searching the mob around him. Unlike the other fairgoers, he seemed disinterested in the festival's diverse attractions.

Bingo, Sydney thought, moving in for a closer look. Her eyes focused on the bright red ribbon wrapped around the man's left wrist. Such ribbons, humorously referred to as Pushkar passports, testified that the stranger had already paid for a priest's blessing at nearby Pushkar Lake, known throughout the world for its sacred waters. Unlike the many other pilgrims attending the festival, however, the bearded man wore the ribbon on his left wrist instead of the right—just as arranged.

Taking no chances, Sydney carefully scoped out the crowd before approaching Azad. The would-be defector didn't appear to be under surveillance, although it was hard to tell, given the thronging humanity. It seemed as though the entire subcontinent had descended on Pushkar.

Here goes nothing. Weaving her way through the crowd, she walked up to Azad. *"Namaste,"* she greeted him in Hindi, holding her palms pressed together before her.

He blinked in surprise, as if not expecting his CIA contact to take the form of a veiled Rajasthani beauty. *"Vanakkam,"* he replied in Tamil, completing the exchange of passwords. So far, everything was going according to plan.

To further confirm her identity, she pressed her palm against Azad's, transferring the henna design to his own flesh. He inspected his new tattoo through the thick lenses of his glasses, then drew a folded piece of paper from the pocket of his jacket. Opening the paper to reveal a printed pattern, he compared the tattoo with the illustration.

Sydney winced at the sight of the paper; Azad was supposed to have memorized the design, not kept a copy of it. Obviously the man was a better chemist than field agent. *This is what happens when you deal with amateurs,* she thought, sighing inwardly. Politely but firmly she plucked the paper from Azad's fingers and ripped it to shreds before his eyes. She could only hope that the scientist's carelessness had not fatally compromised her mission.

Satisfied that the tattoo patterns matched, he looked at Sydney imploringly. "Now what?" he asked with a tremor in his voice; she could tell that he was extremely frightened. *I don't blame him,* she thought. *If Zero Defense knows what he's up to, they'll never let him leave Pushkar alive.*

"Not here," she instructed him, raising a finger in front of her mirrored veil. Despite the general hub-bub of the fair, there were too many ears nearby. They needed a more private place to confer. She pointed at the towering Ferris wheel, whose highest car wobbled more than one hundred feet above the crowd. "Up there."

After purchasing tickets, they waited in line until an empty car stopped in front of them. Sydney eyed the creaky apparatus warily; the entire ride looked as though it had seen better days. Its faded paint job was chipped and peeling. Duct tape covered gashes in the padded seats, prompting Sydney to wonder how often the decrepit Ferris wheel was inspected for safety. It would be pretty ironic if, after surviving umpteen battles with enemy spies and terrorists, she was ultimately done in by a broken-down carnival ride. *That wasn't in the SD-6 training manual!*

Then again, the ride had already conveyed hundreds of delighted fairgoers without incident. Taking her life in her hands, Sydney got into the car with Azad. She swallowed hard as the Ferris wheel lurched into motion. Metal struts squealed alarmingly as their car rocked gently above the fairgrounds. An Indian pop song blared over the growl of the ride's straining engine.

She waited until they were a quarter of the way through their first revolution before addressing Azad again. "There's a jeep waiting outside the fair that will take us into the desert, where a helicopter will fly us to Jaipur. From there we can catch a plane to the States. You'll be safe in Los Angeles in a little more than thirty-five hours."

Azad nodded nervously. He was perspiring heavily, and not from the heat. Bloodshot eyes with dark shadows underneath hinted at many sleepless nights. "Are you positive it's safe?"

Too late for second thoughts now, Doctor. "That depends," she answered. "Do you have any reason to believe that you were followed here? Or that Zero Defense suspects you might be planning to defect?"

She didn't want to scare the jittery scientist, but it was important to know where they stood. If there was any chance that Maya Rao or her associates were nearby, she needed to be ready for them.

"No! Of course not!" Azad insisted. "I've taken every precaution."

Except for shredding that tattoo design, Sydney thought, but she kept her mouth shut. There was no point in scolding Azad about that now.

"Please," he entreated. "You have to protect me. I'm taking a terrible risk here!"

"Don't worry," she assured him. "You're in good hands."

Just as they reached the top of the Ferris wheel, however, a gunshot rang out, refuting

Sydney's confident assertion. She looked down to see two armed strangers manning the platform below, in lieu of the ride's operator, who now lay on the ground with a bullet hole in his skull. Blood streamed from the dead man's head, turning the dusty ground into crimson mud. Screams rose from panicked fairgoers, who fled from the scene as fast as their legs could carry them. Trapped on the revolving Ferris wheel, the other passengers found themselves caught in the middle of the attack, with nowhere to go except straight down.

Damn! Sydney stared at the gun-wielding intruders on the platform. There were two of them, a man and a woman. She didn't recognize the man, a burly, steroid-enhanced goonda who struck her as hired muscle, but she had a pretty good idea who the woman was. Wrapped in a vibrant lime green sari, the woman took control of the Ferris wheel while her thuggish partner stood guard over the platform, clutching a smoking automatic pistol. Tipping her head back, the female invader grinned up at Sydney. Dark eyes, strikingly rimmed with kohl, gleamed from an exotically beautiful face worthy of a fabled Rajput princess. A crimson bindi dot adorned her smooth brown forehead, and her sleek black hair was pulled away from her face, held back by a golden chain. Silver hoops dangled from her earlobes, matching a silver stud in her nose. Her pearly white teeth flashed with malicious glee.

Maya Rao, in the flesh.

No, Sydney thought, reaching for the Beretta concealed beneath her skirt. *Not her. Not now.*

"Allah preserve me!" Azad shrieked. He grabbed on to Sydney, interfering with her efforts to draw her gun. His terrified eyes bulged from their sockets. Spittle sprayed from his lips. "You've got to stop her! She's here to kill me!"

"Not if I can help it," Sydney muttered. She shoved Azad away from her in order to get at the Beretta. Her fingers closed on the grip of the weapon.

Their car had already begun its descent. Maya took hold of the brake lever and yanked it hard, causing the gigantic wheel to come to a sudden, jarring halt. The car rocked back and forth wildly, halfway between the ground and the top of the Ferris wheel. Sydney realized that they were stuck hanging in midair, just the way Maya wanted them.

"Hello, Sydney!" she shouted. "Ride's over!"

She took aim at Azad while Sydney was still trying to adjust to the motion of the car swaying beneath her. The muzzle of Maya's Glock flared, and Sydney threw herself in front of Azad, determined to take the bullet instead. A vicious impact slammed into her ribs, knocking the breath from her body.

Thank God for Kevlar, she thought. The body armor beneath the tie-dyed fabric had saved her life, if only for the moment. *We're way too exposed up here.*

"Help! Somebody help us!" Azad screamed, too consumed with mortal terror to thank Sydney for saving his life. He dropped to the floor of the car and buried his head beneath his hands. He tried to get as low as possible, sprawling across Sydney's feet. "I knew this was a mistake! I'm going to die!"

Ignoring Azad's hysterics, as well as the pain from her bruised ribs, Sydney fired back at Maya, but the rocking of the car sent her shots astray. Ducking behind the far side of the loading platform, Maya exchanged fire with Sydney, missing her intended target but wounding an innocent passenger in another car. Sydney heard the unlucky victim cry out, fueling the horrified screams of the other stranded passengers.

Time to get my feet back on the ground.

Turning her aim away from Maya, she targeted the abandoned braking lever instead. She squeezed the trigger, and nine millimeters of hot lead slammed into the lever, blasting it free.

The wheel started turning again. Sydney felt her car drop toward the platform below with precipitous speed. "Get ready to bail!" she shouted at Azad, unhooking the safety bar in front of them. A bullet ricocheted off the back of the car, striking sparks from the rusty metal, and Sydney fired back at Maya to keep her busy.

C'mon, Dixon, she thought urgently. *Where the heck are you?*

Maya's nameless accomplice turned to fire at Sydney as well, only to stiffen as a bullet ploughed into his back. He crumpled to the ground, not far from the body of the murdered ride operator. Sydney saw a gun-wielding sadhu force his way through the crowd running from the Ferris wheel. "Hang on, Sydney!" he called out. "I'm coming!"

Maya realized she was outnumbered. She peeled off her sari to reveal a tight-fitting Lycra bodysuit underneath. She raced toward the merchant stalls, firing back over her shoulder.

Sydney's car neared the loading platform. With no way to stop the ride, she grabbed on to Azad and threw them both out of the moving car. They hit the platform with a bump, then rolled onto the dirt below. Sydney sprang instantly to her feet, while Azad cowered in a fetal position. "Merciful Allah!" he prayed feverishly. "Spare your unworthy servant!"

Dixon rushed to her side. "Are you all right?" he asked, yanking off his fake white beard. "It was difficult to get a clean shot with so many people in the way."

"I'm okay," she said quickly. She nodded at Azad, still sprawled in the dust beside them. "You take care of him. I'm going after Maya!"

He didn't argue with her. "Be careful!"

Sydney felt a twinge of sympathy for the unfortunate people still stuck on the spinning Ferris wheel, but they were no longer in any immediate danger; presumably somebody would be along to take charge of the ride soon. In the meantime Maya was getting away.

Bangles jangling and ribs aching, Sydney sprinted after the Indian assassin. Her head scarf went flying behind her, exposing her faux black hair. *No way are you giving me the slip again,* Sydney vowed, her heart and legs pounding. *This time you're going to pay for your crimes.*

With her American rival hot on her heels, Maya dashed into the heart of the overpopulated camel market, where a number of lavishly festooned animals were preparing to take part in the traditional camel beauty festival. Provoking startled shouts from onlookers, she leaped onto the sequined saddle of a squatting dromedary and took hold of the reins.

The surprised camel clambered to its feet, and Maya dug her heels into its sides. "Hut-hut!" she hollered, striking its flank with the butt of her gun for emphasis. Realizing that the crazy woman on its back meant business, the camel took off with surprising speed. An irate desert nomad shouted in protest as Maya absconded with his precious livestock.

Great, Sydney thought sarcastically, watching her nemesis get away from her. She glanced dubiously at another nearby camel, whose sandy brown hide was decked out with spangles and polished seashells. The truculent beast spit a disgusting wad of brownish glop onto Sydney's feet, as if sensing her intentions. *Oh, well,* she resolved, *when in Pushkar . . .*

Following Maya's lead, she hopped onto the back of the noxious spitter. The camel's owner ran forward angrily, until he spotted the metallic black Beretta in Sydney's hand, at which point he backed away in a hurry. He held up empty hands as he pleaded for his life in Hindi.

"Kshamaa kijiyeh!" she apologized hastily with more than a touch of guilt; a good camel was worth tens of thousands of rupees. Ending Maya Rao's murderous career was worth even more, however, so she seized the camel's reins, which were attached to a peg going through the animal's nostrils, and urged the camel to its feet. It rose with a sudden swaying motion that nearly threw Sydney from the saddle, but she managed to hang on by clamping her legs around the camel's ribs. "Giddyup!" she commanded, and fired her gun into the air.

The Beretta's sharp report startled the camel, which bolted for the desert at top speed. Sydney bounced atop the embroidered saddle, tossed from side to side by the camel's rolling gait. *My butt is never going to be the same,* she thought wryly, but at least the pain in her posterior helped to distract her from her bullet-bruised ribs. *The things I do for SD-6 . . .*

Pulling on the camel's reins, she galloped after Maya, who was creating a trail of havoc as she drove her own mount headlong through the teeming festival. Men, women, and children ran for safety as Maya's camel barreled into the crowd, trampling over blankets spread with pots, shoes, textiles, and other wares. A trio of musicians dropped their instruments and dived out of the way barely in time; the camel's hooves reduced the fragile drums and sitar to splinters. A second later the animal's shoulder clipped the corner of a jewelry stall, toppling it over. Hairpins, chains, nose rings, and anklets spilled onto the dusty ground.

"Give it up, Maya!" Sydney yelled, hoping to end this before anyone else got hurt. "It's over!"

A gust of cool wind carried Maya's mocking laughter back to Sydney, making her blood boil. "I've heard that before!"

Sitting atop the rushing camel was like standing on the deck of an ocean liner being tossed about by heavy waves. Grasping the reins with one hand, Sydney succeeded in firing off a couple shots from her Beretta but missed Maya by a mile. *Damn it,* Sydney thought in frustration as the turbulent ride forced her to take the reins with both hands again. She couldn't risk shooting an innocent bystander by mistake.

Like Maya had.

The Pushkar valley was bordered by hills on three sides and sand dunes on the fourth. Maya seemed to be heading for the desert. The shifting dunes beckoned on the horizon. The golden sand shimmered beneath the sun. The vast Thar Desert, Sydney knew, was full of small villages and ruined Rajput fortresses, into which Maya could easily disappear if she got the chance.

Forget it, Sydney thought. *I'll chase her all the way to the Pakistani border if I have to.*

She jabbed her heels into the camel's sides, intent on keeping Maya in sight. Adrenaline pulsed through her veins as the camel let loose with a fresh burst of speed. *That's it,* she thought, exhilarated by the camel's competitive spirit. *We're gaining on her!*

Maya must have heard the camel's hooves closing in on her, because she glanced back over her shoulder and gave Sydney a dirty look. The delicate chain holding Maya's hair back had been shaken loose by the bumpy ride, so her flowing black locks blew freely in the wind. She reached up and snatched one of the silver hoops dangling from her ears. Ripping the earring free, she hurled it at Sydney like a throwing star.

Uh-oh, Sydney thought, ducking her head to avoid the lethal accessory. But Maya hadn't been aiming at her at all; instead the razor-sharp metal hoop sliced into the foreleg of the racing camel beneath Sydney. The beast let out a yelp of pain and toppled forward at a perilous angle. Sydney tried to jump free, but her foot got caught in the stirrup. The camel crashed to the earth, taking her with it. Fifteen hundred pounds of wounded camel landed on her left leg.

Bone snapped loudly and Sydney screamed in agony. Trapped beneath the weight of the thrashing camel, she could only bite down on her lip and watch in chagrin as Maya vanished into the desert, leaving a cloud of dust and sand behind.

Sydney lay on the rocky ground for what seemed like centuries, until she heard bare feet running toward her. "Sydney!" Dixon called out, his face still partially caked with gray ash. He dropped to her side and immediately checked her vital signs.

Fighting off shock and unconsciousness, Sydney looked up at him anxiously. "Azad?" she asked.

"Safe," he assured her. He offered her a sip of water from a plastic bottle, then started looking around for some way to get the fallen camel off Sydney's leg. "You saved his life—and completed our mission."

But Maya got away . . . again. She glared angrily at the boundless desert, blaming Maya for every spasm of pain that shot through her broken leg. *Just one more thing she owes me for,* Sydney thought vengefully. *And one of these days I'm going to collect.*

You can count on it.

CHAPTER 3

I don't believe this, Sydney thought as she arrived at a West Hollywood safe house maintained by Sloane. *It's bad enough that I have to take orders from Arvin Sloane again. Now I have to make nice with another ruthless killer from my past?*

She found Maya Rao in the living room, watched over by a pair of armed guards employed by APO. The Indian assassin was sprawled on the sofa reading the latest issue of *Wired* when Sydney entered. Her lustrous black hair and flawless brown skin gave Maya the look of a lounging Bollywood

movie star. Unlike Sydney, who had changed into
her most severe black suit for the occasion, Maya
was dressed casually in a midriff-baring tank top
and loose sweatpants.

The cozy domestic setting struck Sydney as profoundly wrong. She would have preferred to conduct
this meeting in a CIA interrogation cell. Then again,
she didn't work for the CIA anymore . . . officially.

"Sydney Bristow!" Maya greeted her, rising from
the couch. The guards tensed for action, just in case,
but Maya was careful to avoid any sudden movements. Perverse amusement gleamed in her dark
eyes. "Long time no see, as you Americans say."

"This isn't a social call," Sydney informed her
coolly. She instinctively positioned herself between
Maya and the attached kitchenette, which was
stocked with knives, forks, and other potentially
lethal implements. Just because Maya had already
been searched and disarmed didn't mean she
wasn't still as dangerous as a cobra.

Keep this professional, Sydney reminded her-
self. She felt a phantom pain in her leg, where
Maya had dropped a camel on her ten years ago.
Don't let her bait or manipulate you.

"Oh, don't be such a stiff, Sydney," Maya chided

her. Her lilting voice conveyed a slight Bengali accent. "Is that any way to talk to an old friend?"

Sydney could not resist snorting in disbelief. "Last time we met, you left me for dead in Rajasthan."

"Nothing personal." Maya shrugged casually. "That was just business."

"Let's get down to business, then," Sydney insisted. She gestured for Maya to take her seat back on the couch. A half-eaten order of Indian takeout sat on a coffee table in front of the assassin. Sydney caught a whiff of curry and chicken tikka. "I understand you have information on the stolen UCAV?"

Maya glanced around the room. "I assume this entire place is under surveillance, audio *and* video?" She didn't wait for Sydney to confirm or deny her assertion. "Good. That will save me from having to repeat myself."

She settled back into the sofa, wincing slightly as she did so. "We're not talking secondhand rumors," she began. "This is the real scoop. I was directly involved with the New Mexico heist, working on behalf of the Baden Liga."

Sydney's eyes widened. The Baden Liga was a

German terrorist group with seriously deep pockets. Earlier this year they had come dangerously close to acquiring a stolen Argus supercomputer, only to be foiled at the last minute by Sydney and her fellow agents. *This sounds like their kind of operation,* she admitted reluctantly.

Part of her didn't want to believe a word Maya said, but when it came to recovering Kestrel, they needed every lead they could get, which put her in the uncomfortable position of hoping that Maya was telling them the truth. Or at least one version of it.

"How did you do it?" Sydney asked, her arms crossed atop her chest. She remained standing in order to maintain an advantage over the seated killer. "No offense, but you don't exactly strike me as the nerdy hacker type."

Maya shook her head. "Sorry. You don't get that until we have a deal. The point is that the Baden Liga double-crossed me after I delivered Kestrel to them. I barely got out of there alive, and I've had hired assassins on my tail ever since. Want proof?" She tugged down one strap of her tank top, revealing a bloodstained bandage over her left shoulder. "I had to dig the slug out myself."

Like I'm supposed to feel sorry for you? Sydney

thought. The bullet wound appeared to support Maya's story but was hardly conclusive; she certainly wouldn't be the first spy to manufacture an injury for the sake of a cover story. Sydney had done it herself on occasion.

"You were saying?" she prompted with a conspicuous lack of sympathy.

Maya took Sydney's indifference in stride. Grimacing, she inched the strap back into place. "I was on the run and pitifully short on allies. Fortunately, I'd heard rumors that you and Sloane were working freelance these days." She gave Sydney a knowing grin. "That *was* you who swiped the Shintaro sword in London, right? And impersonated Marie Gerard in France?"

A chill ran down Sydney's spine. Granted, those both had been pretty high-profile missions, complete with public shoot-outs and chases, but it still unnerved Sydney to have Maya calmly see through her various aliases. *What's the good of being a spy if the bad guys know exactly what you've been up to?*

Maya took Sydney's silence as confirmation. "Don't look so appalled," she teased. "This is a small, highly incestuous business we're in." She nibbled on her chicken tikka. "So, what ever happened to your mother, anyway?"

Sydney's nails dug into her palms as she clenched her fists. She kept her voice tightly under control as she glared down at the other woman. "What exactly do you want?" she asked coldly, sounding more like her father than she wanted to admit.

"Protection," Maya answered, recognizing it was time to get serious. "In exchange I'll help Sloane locate and capture Kestrel. He can do whatever he wants to do with it, sell it back to the Americans, put it up for auction, use it to launch air strikes on his in-laws, for all I care. Just keep me alive until I can get this goddamn contract taken off my head." She stared at a random corner of the ceiling. "You getting this, Sloane?"

Probably, Sydney thought. She had no idea where the hidden cameras were, but like Maya, she was sure they were there. *Chances are, Sloane and my dad are discussing Maya's offer at this very second.*

"Anything else?" she asked.

"Yes. There is one more thing." Maya sat up straight on the edge of the couch, ready to play hardball. "I'm going to need a partner to steal back

Kestrel. Guess who gets that assignment?" She smiled mischievously at Sydney. "I'm working with you, and nobody else, or there's no deal."

It took effort, but Sydney kept her jaw from hitting the floor. *Is she serious?* Sydney thought in dismay. "Why me?"

"I've always been impressed by your abilities in the field," Maya explained, "which I've certainly had the opportunity to observe on various occasions."

Usually while trying to kill me, Sydney observed.

"My life is at stake here, among other things," Maya added somewhat cryptically. "And I'm not about to put my fate in the hands of some unknown, and possibly expendable, minion of Sloane's. I want a partner I know I can rely on." She leaned forward and gave Sydney a conspiratorial wink. "You and I, we're two of a kind."

"I'm nothing like you!" Sydney protested, offended by the very suggestion. It occurred to her that the bindi dot on Maya's forehead made a highly tempting target. "You're a terrorist and an assassin."

"And you work for Arvin Sloane," Maya shot back. "Spare me your righteous indignation. You're not fooling anyone except maybe yourself. You lie, steal, and shoot people for a living—and you're bloody good at it. Otherwise we wouldn't be talking right now."

I'm defending my country! Sydney thought vehemently. But of course she couldn't tell Maya that; as far as the other woman knew, Sloane was running his own rogue organization, unaffiliated with the CIA. Frustration churned in Sydney's stomach as she was forced to maintain her cover story in the face of Maya's snide accusations. "It's more complicated than that," she answered lamely.

"If you say so," Maya said with a smirk.

"Okay, we have a deal," Sydney announced as she stepped back into the living room after conducting a hasty conference call with Sloane and her father. As she had expected (and feared), both men felt that they couldn't afford to pass up an opportunity to reclaim Kestrel, no matter how much they all distrusted Maya. Sloane hadn't even needed to order Sydney to cooperate with Maya; in her heart she knew she had no choice.

Sometimes being a spy just sucks, she thought.

Her face frozen behind a stony expression, she

pulled up a chair and sat down across from Maya. Sydney nodded at the two looming bodyguards, who discreetly stepped out of earshot, leaving Sydney alone with the former bandit queen. A loaded Beretta rested beneath the lapels of Sydney's dark suit, and an eight-inch carbon steel blade was strapped to her calf beneath her pressed black slacks. In theory the weapons gave her a distinct edge over the unarmed assassin, but Sydney kept her guard up anyway.

"Excellent!" Maya gushed. Although her plate was empty, the spicy aroma of curry lingered in the air. "I look forward to working with you, side by side for once."

"Never mind that," Sydney said, not at all flattered. She tucked her hair back behind her ear. "Spill."

Maya sighed, as though disappointed that Sydney was not as keen on their temporary partnership as she was. Assuming a lotus position atop the couch, she proceeded to brief Sydney on her role in the heist:

"As you surmised, I did not hack into Kestrel's navigational controls myself. I had an accomplice, a brilliant hacker by the name of Terry Fujiwara.

Perhaps you've heard of him? He's known online as VixNut1?"

The latter name sounded vaguely familiar to Sydney, perhaps from some long-ago briefing on computer espionage, but she couldn't immediately recall the details. *Marshall can fill me in on this guy later,* she thought, *assuming he's at all famous in computer circles.* "Go on," she prompted Maya, aware that Marshall and the others were all monitoring this interrogation back at the bunker. She visualized them all gathered in Sloane's office, watching the scene on their laptops. It gave her a degree of comfort to know that Vaughn and Dixon and even her father were keeping an eye on her—and Maya.

Let's hope the same applies in the field, she thought. The prospect of being on her own with only Maya Rao to watch her back did not exactly fill her with confidence. *I'd rather go skinny-dipping with an anaconda.*

"I fancy I know my way around a keyboard," Maya continued, extolling the talents of her previous partner, "but Terry operates at a whole other level. He can punch through firewalls like they're made out of tissue paper, and make entire banks of supercomputers roll over and play dead. I could never have seized control of Kestrel without him, which means that now the Baden Liga is out to kill him, too." To Sydney's surprise, an uncharacteristic note of concern entered Maya's voice. Her infuriating smugness evaporated. "We have to find Terry before they get to him first!"

"Why do you care?" Sydney asked, suspicious of the other woman's sudden show of emotion. Since when had Maya worried about anyone except herself?

Maya raised her left hand, flaunting the diamond solitaire upon her ring finger. "Because he's my fiancé."

Fiancé?

Taken aback, Sydney fought an urge to glance at her own left hand. She hadn't worn the engagement ring in years, but that didn't mean that she didn't remember how much it had meant to her. Even more than five years later, and after too many other intervening losses, Danny's death still haunted her. She vividly recalled the horror and despair she had felt upon finding her own fiancé's lifeless body in her bathtub.

Is Maya facing the same kind of anguish, Sydney wondered, *or is she deliberately messing with my head?* Sydney prayed it was the latter; the last thing she wanted to do was feel a shred of sympathy for the ruthless Indian assassin—or discover that she and Maya had something in common after all.

"I assume that ring has been thoroughly scanned for concealed weapons or transmitters," she said calmly, not letting Maya's unexpected revelation shake her professional demeanor. She eyed the diamond ring as though it was nothing but a potential breach in security.

"Naturally," Maya assured her. "Sloane's flunkies here were nothing if not thorough. Trust me, it took considerable wrangling to be allowed to keep the ring at all, even after it had been cleared by security." She held the ring up before her eyes, and her voice grew hoarse with emotion. Her dark eyes misted slightly. "It was worth it, though."

Am I buying this? Sydney asked herself. Maya was putting on an Oscar-worthy performance, but Sydney still had her doubts. This was, after all, Maya Rao, who had once posed as a nun in order to seduce and assassinate a prominent Italian politician. By all accounts, she had been *very* convincing, which was particularly impressive, since the politician had been a woman.

On the other hand, as much as Sydney hated to admit it, she knew for a fact that sometimes even the most despicable of felons were capable of forming a deep connection to at least one other human being. Arvin Sloane, as treacherous and cold blooded as he was, had sincerely loved his late wife, Emily, even if his insidious machinations had ultimately led to her death.

If even Sloane was capable of love, wasn't it conceivable that Maya truly cared for this alleged fiancé?

It's possible, Sydney conceded, deciding to reserve judgment for the time being. *But that doesn't mean I'm cutting her any slack.*

"So where is he now?" she asked.

"I wish I knew," Maya replied. "We were supposed to rendezvous in Honduras after we completed the transaction. The plan was for me to turn over the UCAV to the Baden Liga at the same time they transferred our payment to an offshore account. But then everything went to hell and I had to go into hiding. By the time I made it to our prearranged meeting place, I was days late and the place was crawling with hit men out for my scalp." She shook her head at the memory. "Obviously the site had been compromised. Terry must have realized that and gone deep underground. He's cautious that way, bordering on paranoid." What sounded like a genuine note of affection colored her voice, even as she regained her composure. "Just to complicate matters, he was monitoring the exchange via a concealed webcam, so he would have seen me get shot, but not necessarily get away. As far as I know, he thinks I'm already dead."

Just like Vaughn thought I was gone, Sydney thought, *after the Covenant faked my death.* She felt a pang at the thought of those two missing years—and how they had affected her fragile relationship with Michael Vaughn. *We're still trying to get over the scars left behind by that ordeal.*

"So you have no idea where he is now?" she asked. "No way to contact him?"

Maya shook her head. "He's shut down all lines of communication—e-mail addresses, unlisted phone numbers, you name it—so that nobody can trace them back to him. It's like he's dropped off the face of the earth." Sydney could hear the frustration in her voice. "That's why I need you—and Sloane's considerable resources. If anybody can help me find out where he's hiding, it's you and Sloane and whomever else you're working with these days." She smiled wryly. "If you can track down all those six-hundred-year-old Rambaldi artifacts, you should be able to locate one frightened computer genius."

Provided he's still alive, Sydney thought. Perhaps the Baden Liga had already eliminated him?

"Even assuming you're telling the truth, how does finding Fujiwara get us Kestrel?" It was a cruelly pragmatic question, but it had to be asked. "Sloane's not going to be interested in a simple rescue mission. What's in it for us?"

"I'm not sure," Maya confessed, "but if I know Terry, he's already trying to get Kestrel back from the Baden Liga. He doesn't like being outsmarted and double-crossed any more than I do. It's a point of pride with him." She spoke with confidence, as though she knew him better than anyone else on the planet. "Believe me, he knows how that bird thinks better than anyone else, including the Pentagon's own computer whizzes. He may already know where the Baden Liga are storing it prior to the auction."

Maybe, Sydney thought dubiously. It was a slim lead, but it was better than nothing. Plus, if the Baden Liga were after Fujiwara too, or were perhaps holding him hostage somewhere, then finding Fujiwara might lead them to the terrorists themselves. *It's worth a shot.*

"Tell me more about him."

APO BUNKER

"VixNut1? Sure, I've heard of him!" Marshall declared. He jumped up from his seat and started gesturing excitedly. "The guy's a legend in the hacker world. He's the dude who hacked into the Pentagon mainframe in search of top secret files from Area Fifty-one and caused every ATM in the country to display alien autopsy photos on their monitors. He also shut down every single U.S. government Web site for twenty-four hours on the fiftieth anniversary of the Roswell Incident." Marshall paced about the lounge, too full of nervous energy to sit still. "So we're going after VixNut1 . . . wow!"

Sydney was impressed by the fact that Marshall was such a fan of Fujiwara and his accomplishments. *I guess Maya wasn't exaggerating his abilities.*

She had returned to APO's underground headquarters to work out the next phase of their investigation, leaving Maya behind at the safe house. Under no circumstances did Sydney intend to let Maya learn anything more about APO than was strictly necessary, including the exact location of their hidden offices.

"Could this VixNut person have hacked into Kestrel's navigational systems?" Marcus Dixon asked. His dark, angular features bore a grave expression. Some twenty years older than either Sydney or Vaughn, he had been Sydney's partner in the field in the old SD-6 days.

"Sure," Marshall said. "Now that I think of it, he's one of the few people on the planet who could pull it off." He ducked his large head sheepishly. "I probably should have thought of him before, except that it's not exactly his style. He's never done anything this heavy duty before. UFOs are his big thing; he's convinced that the government has been hiding proof of extraterrestrial life for decades. In the past he's always been more into pranks and publicity stunts than, say, hijacking top secret military hardware."

Until now, Sydney thought. Had Maya led him astray, turning him from harmless stunts to major international espionage? If so, she had gotten her alleged fiancé into seriously hot water.

Just like I got Danny killed.

"What do we know about him?" Jack Bristow asked. His face and voice were icily composed, hiding his thoughts and feelings behind a smooth, all-but-inscrutable mask. He tapped the keys of his laptop, calling up the relevant files from APO's extensive database. He scowled at the results, disappointed with the scarcity of relevant intel.

"Not a whole heck of a lot," Marshall confirmed. "VixNut1 is notoriously secretive. Nobody has ever met him in person, except for Maya Rao, I guess, and there aren't even any known photos of him available. Rumor has it that, years ago, he devised a highly sophisticated worm that prowls the Internet in search of any and all personal data relating to VixNut1 . . . and devours it immediately, leaving absolutely no tracks behind. Granted, no one has ever actually proved that this worm exists, but people still think it's out there, like Bigfoot or the Loch Ness monster." Marshall refrained from disclosing whether he believed in the semimythical worm, quickly changing the subject. "Heck, until Sydney talked to Maya Rao, I had no idea that VixNut1's real name was Terry Fujiwara!"

"*If* that's his real name," Sydney pointed out. "I'm still taking everything Maya tells us with a grain of salt."

"As well you should," her father agreed, nodding sagely. Despite the recent tension between them, he clearly approved of her skeptical attitude.

Sydney wasn't sure how she felt about that. *Only in my family,* she thought wryly, *is never-ending suspicion considered a positive trait.* Then again, considering the twisted history her relatives shared, how could it not be?

"I'm not sure I buy this whole fiancé angle," Vaughn said. His handsome features had assumed a more serious expression now that they were back at work. "Maya Rao, as evil as she is, is still a beautiful and dynamic woman. Is it just me, or does it strike anyone else as odd that a woman like that would fall for some nerdy computer guy?" He glanced over at Marshall. "Er, no offense."

"None taken," Marshall said meekly. Slightly deflated, he dropped back into his seat, where Sydney saw him furtively sneak a peek at a wallet photo of his wife and baby, no doubt for reassurance.

"Perhaps she's just using him," she suggested. "I can definitely see Maya seducing Fujiwara just to get access to his computer skills." Never mind Maya's misty eyes and hoarse voice back at the safe house; Sydney found a Mata Hari scenario a lot more plausible. "It's the oldest trick in the book."

She instantly regretted that last remark. *Idiot!* she thought, mentally slapping herself. How could she have forgotten, even for a moment, that Vaughn's late wife, Lauren, had used Vaughn just the way that she was suggesting Maya had possibly used Fujiwara—and the way Irina Derevko had used Jack Bristow?

Good job, Syd. Way to pour salt in those wounds!

"A distinct possibility," her father acknowledged. If the similarity to his own situation disturbed him, his stoic demeanor betrayed no trace of it. "Which means that Rao's motives for locating Fujiwara might not be as sentimental as she would have us believe. We should be alert to the likelihood that she has another agenda."

Sloane leaned forward in his chair. "In any event, Fujiwara remains our best avenue toward recovering Kestrel." He smiled slyly. "If I had possession of the

UCAV, I would want to have the only person capable of hacking into its controls tightly under wraps. At large, Fujiwara is too big a variable to ignore."

Spoken like a true criminal mastermind, Sydney thought contemptuously. He had a point, though; the Baden Liga wouldn't rest until they had killed or captured Fujiwara, which, if nothing else, made Maya's so-called fiancé useful as bait, provided APO could get their hands on him.

Which is where Maya and I come in.

Sloane turned toward Sydney. "What else did Maya tell you about him?"

"He's thirty-five years old, Asian, a bit on the spindly side. If we send a sketch artist to the safe house, she should be able to provide a pretty good description of him. No major distinguishing marks or features." *That's not going to make my job any easier,* she thought. "Going beyond the physical, apparently he's just as paranoid and secretive as Marshall said. That's why Maya insists on accompanying me on the assignment; she claims that she's the only one Fujiwara will trust."

"I don't like that idea," Dixon said with a frown. "It puts you in too much danger. I'd rather keep Maya locked up tightly in the safe house while we look for Fujiwara."

Sydney appreciated her partner's concern. "Trust me, I'd much prefer to have you watching my back than Maya Rao, of all people, but that's not going to fly. According to Maya, Fujiwara will bolt if he's approached by anyone except her." She shrugged. "We could always try to take him by force, but that complicates matters, especially when we need Fujiwara's cooperation to track down Kestrel."

"It might still be worth it," Dixon argued. Sydney wondered if he was recalling that ambush in Rajasthan years ago. "She's come close to killing you before. We shouldn't give her another chance."

"An occupational hazard," Sloane said, dismissing Dixon's objections. "If we didn't sometimes work in concert with former adversaries, none of us would be sitting in this lounge right now."

No, Sydney thought. *You'd be sitting on death row, awaiting execution for numerous murders and acts of high treason.*

She could have done without the reminder.

"One more thing," she said. "Fujiwara supposedly suffers from severe migraines, brought on by stress. He keeps them under control by using a variety of medications. Perhaps we can try to trace his prescriptions?"

Vaughn shook his head. "That's not much to go on." He threw up his hands impatiently. "How are we supposed to find someone who is famous for being unfindable?"

"I think I have an idea," Marshall said.

CHAPTER 4

PACIFIC PARADISE HOTEL
SINGAPORE

Robots, aliens, and intergalactic warriors swarmed the hallway of the hotel's meeting facilities. A copper-plated cyborg flirted with a green-skinned amazon in an aluminum foil bikini as they stood in line for the snack bar. A band of growling Klingons marched in unison down the corridor, eliciting a round of applause from bystanders. The theme from *Star Wars* played over the Muzak system, while a hanging canvas banner welcomed Sydney to the Official Twenty-fifth Anniversary *Space Vixens* Convention.

To her slight embarrassment, she blended right in. A latex space suit clung tightly to her athletic figure, the electric blue rubber as smooth as polished glass. A crystalline tiara bearing the image of a swirling nebula rested atop her tangerine-colored wig, which was cut short in order to show off her delicately pointed ears. Makeup added a flattering purple tint to her skin, while the front of the wig came to a dramatic widow's peak just above her third eye.

I've worn a lot of outlandish disguises in my career, she thought, *but this one really takes the cake.* According to Marshall, she was the spitting image of Caludia, elf-queen of Galaxy Z.

I'll take his word for it.

Her forehead itched where the phony eye was glued on, and she resisted the urge to scratch at it. Meanwhile her actual orbs, disguised behind fluorescent green contact lenses, scoped out the scene.

Scores of science fiction fans, in all manner of costumes, wandered the hallway, chatting with one another in excited tones. Rows of tables were lined up along both sides of the corridor, heavily laden with various flyers and freebies. A variety of fan clubs and organizations, from Starship Bangkok to the Interstellar Alliance, manned the tables. Stacks of free posters and buttons hyping the latest Hollywood releases were snatched up eagerly by the roaming fans. Actors and actresses Sydney had never heard of autographed photos for fifteen bucks a pop. She didn't see any literature promoting the Baden Liga, but perhaps they weren't recruiting Trekkies this year.

"I don't know," she whispered almost subvocally. She shook her head in disbelief at the bizarre environment she was attempting to infiltrate. "Are you sure about this?"

"Positive," Marshall answered from their headquarters in Los Angeles via the receiver concealed within her pointed ears. "VixNut1 is the world's biggest *Space Vixens* fan. Heck, he practically invented *Vix* fandom back in the early eighties." Sydney could hear the enthusiasm in his voice. "Even with his life in danger, there's no way he's going to miss this special anniversary convention. The entire original cast is going to be there!"

"If you say so," Sydney said uncertainly. She was vaguely aware that *Space Vixens* was an old TV show with a rabid cult following, but that was pretty much the extent of her knowledge on the subject. Still, she assumed Marshall knew what he was talking about when it came to geek obsessions.

She couldn't help wishing that the convention were being held anywhere but Singapore. *This was where my dad arranged for Danny and me to escape to,* she recalled, *except that SD-6 got to Danny first. We never made it here.*

Would Maya and her fiancé have better luck? Despite herself, Sydney felt a twinge of sympathy for her old enemy, assuming that Maya was telling the truth about her and Fujiwara.

"Any sign of him?" she asked the woman beside her.

Plastic space armor hid Maya's distinctive features from any lurking assassins. The molded chrome-colored plates made her look like a cross between a stormtrooper and a hood ornament. Unlike the Z-ray pistol on Sydney's hip, which was actually a working Taser, Maya's laser rifle was just a cheap plastic fake. Temporary alliance or not, Sydney was not about to let Maya get her hands on a real weapon.

"Not yet," she told Sydney, her voice slightly muffled by her plastic helmet. She turned her head slowly as she searched the crowded hallway. "I don't see him anywhere."

Sydney was afraid of that. With most of the attendees dressed as mutants and androids, locating Fujiwara was no easy task. Never mind the difficulty of trying to find one individual computer geek in the middle of a science fiction convention!

"Let's keep looking," she said with a sigh of resignation. She scanned the name badges of the other guests as they prowled the convention, looking for some variation on *VixNut* or *Fujiwara*. It was a long shot; chances were, the missing hacker was using one of his many false identities, but she figured it was worth a try while they killed time waiting for the convention's big event: a live Q-and-A session with the original cast of the TV show.

If Fujiwara was going to be anywhere, Marshall had insisted, he would be at that event. Sydney intended to check out the audience *extremely* carefully.

With Maya's help, of course.

Lucky me.

"Excuse me." A Brooklyn accent interrupted her thoughts. Sydney peered through her contact lenses at a young man carrying a clipboard. Unlike many of his fellow fans, he had eschewed a costume in favor of shorts, sandals, and a baggy *Space Vixens* T-shirt bearing the image of none other than Caludia herself.

How about that, Sydney thought. *I really do look like her.*

The name badge pinned to his shirt identified the speaker as Brian Kershner, Convention Member #1703. His unruly blond hair and scruffy beard gave him a somewhat hippieish appearance.

"Would you mind signing my petition?" he asked, thrusting the clipboard at Sydney. "We're trying to get them to release all four seasons on DVD. The original, uncut Korean versions, of course, not the dubbed American episodes." He shook his head as though the idea of releasing the latter was too ridiculous to be believed. "I mean, can you imagine?"

"Tell me about it!" Sydney agreed, as if she knew what he was talking about. Accepting the clipboard, she signed the petition with her current alias. "Say, I've been looking for some friends of mine. You haven't seen VixNut1 around, have you?"

Brian laughed out loud. "Right, like I've actually laid eyes on the legendary VixNut1!" He eyed her skeptically, apparently convinced that she was pulling his leg. "Don't tell me you've met VixNut1 in the flesh."

She heard Marshall groan in her ear.

"No, no, of course not," she said, backing off. "He was just nice enough to send me some e-mails a while back, and I was hoping I could meet him here."

"Oh, he's here, all right. I'd bet my entire X-Men collection on it. But I wouldn't recognize him if he was standing right next to me." He took back his pen and clipboard. "The true identity of VixNut1 is one of the great fannish mysteries."

"I see," Sydney replied, not having to fake her disappointment. "Maybe you know another pen pal of mine, Terry Fujiwara?"

Brian shook his head. "Doesn't ring any bells." He offered the clipboard to Maya, who pointedly ignored him. Shrugging, he turned his attention back to Sydney. "I love your costume, by the way. Caludia's my favorite character, in case you can't tell. So, do you think she was really the long-lost avatar of Oblivitron?"

The what of what? He may as well have been speaking ancient Sumerian, as far as Sydney was concerned.

Marshall came to her rescue. His voice whispered helpfully into her ear.

"Actually," she parroted, "I think she was a *clone* of the avatar, like they hinted in the third season."

Brian nodded thoughtfully. "A valid argument, except that we were explicitly told in season four that cloning technology was not perfected until well after the Third Etheric War, which would make cloning the avatar impossible unless there was some sort of time warp involved. . . ."

"Which could have happened offscreen during the flashback in 'Dawn of the Bio-Lords,'" she countered, feeling rather like William Hurt in *Broadcast News*. She suspected Marshall was enjoying this opportunity to put his extensive knowledge of arcane sci-fi lore to use.

All very well and good, she thought, *but this isn't getting us any closer to finding Fujiwara.*

"Certainly there's a lot to think about," she ad-libbed, trying to wrap this up. She glanced conspicuously at the chronometer on her wrist and started to step away. "Always glad to meet another Caludia fan."

But Brian seemed in no hurry to conclude the

discussion. Oblivious to her body language, he tagged along after her. "Then again, that entire flashback could have been an illusion created by virtual reality, like in 'Masques of Deceit.' To trick the Vixens into going after the Lost Scrolls."

This guy's harder to shake than a K-Directorate tail, Sydney thought. She was still trying to think of a way to politely extricate herself from the conversation when Maya lost her patience.

"Get lost, geek!" she hissed through her helmet. She lifted her laser rifle menacingly. "Before I smash this over your media-addled skull."

"Hey, no need for the attitude!" Brian protested, backing away nonetheless. Even through the silly plastic armor Maya's threatening presence came through loud and clear. "I can take a hint!"

To Sydney's discomfort, the ugly encounter attracted curious looks from the other attendees. In order to escape the attention, she grabbed Maya by the arm and dragged her out of the hallway into the convention's dealer room. More *Space Vixens* fans milled around tables piled high with action figures, comic books, calendars, posters, fanzines, videos, and DVDs. Costumed figures haggled with hard-nosed dealers over homemade lightsabers and laser pistols. A barbarian in a fur loincloth held a model spaceship up to the light, inspecting it for flaws.

"Nice work," Sydney congratulated Maya sarcastically. "Way to keep a low profile."

"We were wasting time," Maya replied, sounding not at all apologetic. She elbowed her way roughly through the congested fans. "Excuse me if I didn't feel like debating TV trivia while my fiancé's life is in danger."

"Well, we might have better luck at finding him if you'd just take off your helmet like I suggested earlier." She made no effort to hide her irritation. "Why not give him a chance to recognize you?"

"Forget it," Maya snapped. "There's a price on my head, remember?" She nodded at the fans around them, any one of whom might be a hired killer. "I'll unmask when we find Terry, and not before."

Judging from her tone, there was no point in arguing with her, so Sydney let the matter drop. She pretended to examine a used Caludia action figure (SPECIAL COLLECTOR'S ITEM!) while furtively checking out both the dealers and their customers for some resemblance to the portrait of Fujiwara that APO's sketch artist had prepared from Maya's description.

An abundance of greasepaint, fake teeth, and prosthetic foreheads made the task near impossible. Her heart sank as she observed an albino ape-man rummaging through a box of old paperbacks. *He could be standing right next to me and I'd never know.*

Still, you'd think that Maya would have better luck spotting her own true love. Sydney liked to think that she would know Vaughn anywhere, even if he were dressed as the abominable snowman. *Then again, I didn't even know my own mother was plotting to kill me. . . .*

The crowd began to clear out of the dealer room, a sure sign that the big Q-and-A session was about to start. Sydney and Maya followed the procession into a large ballroom that had been filled with row after row of folding metal chairs. A dais had been erected at the far end of the spacious chamber, supporting a long table equipped with multiple microphones. Another microphone had been set up at the end of an aisle running beside the rows of seats, presumably to allow the fans to question their idols.

While the other attendees rushed to score the best seats, Sydney and Maya lingered by the entrance, paying extra attention to the fans in the last row. Sydney figured that if he was present, Fujiwara would want to sit near an escape route. "See him yet?" she whispered to Maya.

The armored figure shook her head.

A peppy emcee bounded onto the dais. Sydney tuned out his opening spiel in order to concentrate on the back row, which had rapidly filled up with a colorful assortment of attentive fans. She scrutinized the seated suspects, quickly eliminating several candidates for obvious reasons. The overweight woman with the nursing baby was out, as was the hyperactive eight-year-old who was practically bouncing in his chair. Unless Fujiwara was an incredible master of disguise, which his file did not indicate, the various black and Caucasian fans were unlikely to be him, and for Maya's sake, Sydney hoped that the cuddling couple in the matching *Space Vixens* uniforms did not include the assassin's missing fiancé. In any event, the very affectionate duo, who really needed to get a room, both looked too convincingly adolescent to be the thirty-five-year-old computer genius.

So much for the easy eliminations, Sydney thought. Unfortunately, that still left at least a dozen possible candidates seated at the rear of the ball-room, including an old man in a wheelchair, a woman wearing a tinted fishbowl helmet, a scale-covered lizard man, three Terminators, two Cylons, and the grim reaper himself, complete with hood and scythe.

In theory Fujiwara could be any one of them.

Thunderous applause and a standing ovation greeted the entrance of the six surviving stars of *Space Vixens,* some of whom looked a little the worse for wear. Sydney recognized a few of them from late-night movies and infomercials. *Isn't that the guy from the Viagra ads?* she thought, clapping enthusiastically in order to maintain her alias. Flashbulbs went off one after another, as if this were a Hollywood movie premiere and the starlet had just arrived on the red carpet.

"Say, Sydney," Marshall addressed her via the earpiece, "would you mind turning a little more toward the stage? I'd kind of like to hear some of this." She imagined Marshall back at headquarters, turning up the volume on his receiver so as not to miss a word from the dais. "I don't suppose you'd mind asking the cast a couple of questions? I'd love to find out what went on behind the scenes during the big hyperreincarnation episode. . . ."

Marshall wasn't the only one with questions. As the audience returned to their seats and the panel got under way, fans started lining up behind the floor microphone, waiting for their turn to interrogate the stars.

Suddenly Sydney had an idea.

"Hey, Marshall, help me out here."

Moments later Maya took her place in the line while Sydney remained behind to keep an eye on the crowd from her post by the exit. Leaning up against the ballroom wall, she tapped her foot impatiently as she watched Maya slowly make her way to the front of the line.

This had better work, Sydney thought.

She had learned way more than she ever wanted to know about the making of *Space Vixens* by the time Maya finally took her turn at the microphone. "I have a question for the entire cast," the disguised assassin began. "Do you feel that cyborg death cruisers of Gamma Epsilon VI inspired recent developments in unmanned military aircraft? Specifically, do you think that real-life UCAVs could be reprogrammed as easily as the death cruisers were?"

The TV stars on the dais looked at one another in confusion, as did many of the fans in the audience—

including *most* of the latecomers in the back row. Sydney's eyes widened, however, as the lizard man suddenly sat up as though electrified. A jaw covered with purple press-on scales dropped in stupefied amazement. Slitted yellow contact lenses nearly popped from the reptile's bulging eyes.

A second later the bogus alien grimaced in pain. His gloved hands fumbled inside his metallic green jumpsuit before extracting a translucent amber prescription bottle. He popped the cap off the vial and tossed a pair of tablets into his mouth, swallowing them down without even a gulp of water.

A sudden migraine perhaps?

Gotcha, Sydney thought.

She slowly closed in on the seated lizard man, drawing near enough to decipher the name on his badge: UNDERCOVER E.T.

Cute.

Not wanting to spook him, Sydney considered her approach. Should she drop Maya's name, or would that only freak him out? If she identified herself as CIA, would that blow APO's cover, or would Maya just assume that Sydney had lied about her true affiliation to gain Terry's confidence? God knows, the lizard man (Fujiwara?) already looked agitated enough. Glancing about fearfully, he spotted Sydney coming toward him. Their eyes met through their respective contact lenses. His face went pale beneath his scales.

Wait, she mouthed, giving him what she hoped was a friendly smile. She held up her hands to show she meant no harm.

His yellow eyes went straight to the ray-gun on her hip. He jumped to his feet, knocking over the folding metal chair, which hit the floor with a clatter. In a panic, he hopped over the fallen chair and dashed for the exit.

"Terry, stop!" Sydney shouted, taking off after him. A convention security guard got in her way, and she deftly flipped the sumo-size man over her shoulder. "I'm with Maya!"

If the fleeing hacker heard her, he gave no indication of it. After racing into the hallway outside, where a throng of fans who couldn't get into the packed Q-and-A session were watching the event via closed-circuit TV sets mounted to the walls, he ran madly down the crowded corridor with Sydney right behind him. Not for the first time that afternoon she wondered why the hell an extraterrestrial elf-queen had to explore the cosmos in six-inch heels.

"Outrigger here. Phoenix is pursuing target."

Disguised as something called a cyber-druid, Marcus Dixon watched Sydney chase the fleeing lizard man out of the ballroom. He was tempted to join her, just in case she required assistance, but that wasn't why he was there. Instead he remained in the standing-room-only section of the audience, keeping a close eye on Maya Rao.

Nobody at APO trusted Maya for one minute, which was why Dixon had been assigned to tail the notorious terrorist discreetly for the duration of her mission with Sydney. Caring for Sydney as he did, Dixon was more than happy to do so. *If and when Maya shows her true colors,* he thought, *I want to be there to keep her from stabbing Sydney in the back.*

Literally or *figuratively.*

A glossy black cloak and hood, emblazoned with foil comets and swirling nebulae, hid his true identity from Maya, as did the silver mask he wore, which was adorned with stylized circuit diagrams. He and Maya had only occasionally glimpsed each other over the years, never quite at close range, yet he had taken care to make sure that she would not recognize him. Sydney was aware that he was accompanying them on their travels; Maya, at least in theory, was not.

Granted, Maya was bound to expect something of the sort. She was too experienced and savvy not to. No doubt she was keeping a close eye out for any other APO operatives besides Sydney.

Dixon didn't intend to make it easy for her.

"Got that, Outrigger," Marshall replied via the headset concealed beneath Dixon's hood. "You think it's really him?"

"Let's hope so." Dixon's right hand held a gnarled wooden staff topped by a fist-size crystal bulb. The crystal was actually a combination antenna and amplifier, which helped boost the signals to and from his and Sydney's communicators. "I'm uncomfortable relying on Maya as our only lead."

If Sydney did manage to apprehend Fujiwara, a.k.a. VixNut1, it was possible that they would no longer need to cooperate with Maya Rao, which would be the ideal outcome. As Sydney's long-time partner, Dixon wanted her safely clear of the duplicitous assassin as soon as possible. As far as he was concerned, Sydney was in danger every minute she spent in Maya's company.

I haven't forgotten Pushkar—or all the other times Maya tried to kill us.

He cast a lingering look at the doorway through which Sydney had disappeared in her pursuit of Fujiwara. His concern for her well-being was trumped by his confidence in her abilities. *Sydney can take care of herself,* he thought, *especially against a computer whiz with no known combat experience.*

On the other hand, he'd been through too many close calls not to know that even the simplest operation could sometimes go awry. And that a panicky civilian could often be more unpredictable and dangerous than the most lethal professional.

Be careful, Sydney. Reluctantly he turned his eyes away from the exit. He sighed beneath his mask; this wasn't the first time he'd been forced to maintain his post while Sydney placed herself in harm's way.

He turned his attention back to Maya Rao. Having baffled the panel with her question, the disguised terrorist marched briskly away from the microphone and headed toward the rear of the ball-room. She hurried past the cloaked druid without a sideways glance, making a beeline for the exit. Dixon assumed that she was trying to catch up with Sydney and her quarry.

Right behind you, he thought.

He gave her a five-second head start, then fol-lowed her out into the hallway. He found her stand-ing in the middle of the corridor, obviously uncer-tain which way to go. He looked around but couldn't spot either Sydney or the purple lizard man. Clearly Fujiwara, if that was indeed him beneath the scaly makeup, had wasted no time putting the ballroom behind him. Dixon could only hope that Sydney was hot on his trail.

Maya clenched her armored fists. The chrome helmet hid her face, but Dixon could easily envi-sion her frustrated expression. It was a good thing her laser rifle was a worthless prop, or else she might well have been tempted to clear a path through the hall with the gun. Her head pivoted anxiously as she searched the scene for evidence of a chase.

For a moment her gaze seemed to settle on Dixon, much to his discomfort. Had she somehow seen through his disguise? He drew back his voluminous sleeve and made a show of inspecting his wristwatch, trying to convey the impression of an ordinary conventiongoer who just happened to be waiting in the corridor for some acquaintance or another. He leaned on his staff and pretended to admire all the exotic costumes on display, not just the gleaming space trooper a few yards away.

Don't mind me, he silently urged Maya. *I've nothing to do with you.*

He sweated beneath his robe until, at last, Maya looked away. She took off down the corridor, presumably in hopes of locating Sydney or Fujiwara. He gave her a much longer head start this time before cautiously resuming his surveillance. As he pursued the disguised assassin, he stayed alert for potential hiding places, ready to duck for cover in an instant should Maya glance back over her shoulder.

"Outrigger to Merlin," he addressed Marshall. "What is Phoenix's status?"

"No news yet," the op-tech specialist's voice informed him. "I think she's kind of busy at the moment. I can hear her breathing over the communicator, and it sounds like she's running a marathon . . .

which is kind of hot, if you know what I mean, but not very informative."

"Understood," Dixon said, gleaning the essential facts from Marshall's typically discursive assessment. It sounded as if Sydney was still attempting to apprehend Fujiwara. "Keep me informed."

Behind the futuristic silver mask, Dixon's somber face was troubled. He didn't like the way this was going.

Had Maya really recognized him, despite his outlandish disguise?

I hope not, he prayed. *For Sydney's sake.*

Sydney sprinted down the hall after Fujiwara.

A life-size cardboard cutout of a blond-haired, blue-skinned Space Vixen occupied a position of honor in front of a recruiting booth for the Singapore chapter of the international fan club. Fujiwara grabbed on to the 2-D figure as he ran by, and hurled it back at Sydney, who batted it out of the way without breaking her stride. The distraction barely slowed her down, and she found herself gaining on Fujiwara.

"Terry, listen to me!" she called out to him. "I don't want to hurt you! I'm here to help!"

Her hands went to the weapon on her hip. She didn't want to zap Fujiwara with the Taser, but she would if she had to. *Just in case,* she thought, *what's the best way to get his unconscious body out of the hotel before the local police arrive?*

He ran into a darkened video room, where thirty or forty fans sat watching a *Babylon 5* marathon. An outer-space dogfight was projected onto Fujiwara's face and torso as he leaped in front of the screen and shouted, "Look, in the hall! It's George Lucas!"

Screaming "Fire!" would have caused less of a mob scene. The entire audience surged out into the hallway, coming between Fujiwara and Sydney, who suddenly felt like a salmon fighting her way upstream. Taser in hand, she forced her way through the horde into the dimly lit function room, only to find a fire exit door swinging closed on the other side of the room. The exit led to an empty stairwell, with no indication as to whether the lizard man had fled up or down the stairs.

Damn! Sydney thought.

Figuring fifty-fifty odds were better than none, she took off down the concrete steps. An elderly Asian couple glanced at her in alarm as she sprinted

past them on the stairs, but she encountered no fleeing lizard men, purple or otherwise. Panting, she
emerged from the stairwell into a parking garage
located below the basement of the hotel.

Fujiwara was nowhere to be seen.

I've lost him, she realized. *And scared him out
of his wits in the process.* The elusive hacker was
going to be twice as hard to track down now. *As if
he weren't already paranoid enough.*

She paused to catch her breath, in no great
hurry to inform Maya that her fiancé had given her
the slip. Sydney wondered how Maya would react to
the news. Tears? Anger? Contempt for the American
agent's incompetence? Sydney wasn't sure which
reaction she would prefer.

However, they hadn't ended up completely
empty-handed. There was still the name Sydney
had spotted on Fujiwara's ID badge.

Undercover E.T., indeed.

"Marshall," she said to the empty air of the
parking garage, "I have another favor to ask."

Cracking the convention's database was pretty much
child's play for Marshall, who quickly determined
that Undercover E.T. was a fan name claimed by one

Patrick Okata. From there it was only a matter of seconds before Marshall tracked down the exact hotel room registered to Okata.

Number 4740.

"I can't believe you let him get away," Maya groused as they exited an elevator onto the fourth floor of the hotel. She had found Sydney in the stairwell not long after Fujiwara made his escape. Now the two women headed down the corridor toward the room in question. Empty pizza boxes and room service trays littered the carpet outside many of the rooms. A maid's cart was parked in front of the fire exit. An ice machine chugged loudly farther down the hall.

Sydney assumed Dixon was somewhere nearby, perhaps in one of the adjoining rooms.

"What did you expect me to do, drop a camel on him?" she shot back. She was disappointed that Fujiwara had escaped, but she wasn't about to let Maya Rao, of all people, make her feel guilty about it. "These things happen. You know that."

"Maybe to you," Maya said acidly.

Last I heard, Sydney thought, *Nasir Azad was alive and well and living under an assumed name in Parkesburg, Pennsylvania.* She gave Maya a defiant look. *Your track record's not so flawless either.*

Maya must have realized she was pushing Sydney too far. "Sorry to snap at you," she apologized. "I'm just so worried about Terry. We were so close to being together again!"

Her desperate yearning was apparent even through the featureless chrome helmet. *If she's faking it,* Sydney thought, *she's putting on a hell of an act.*

"I wouldn't give up on that reunion just yet," she said, offering an olive branch of sorts. "I'm a long way from quitting."

A DO NOT DISTURB sign hung on the doorknob of room 4740. Placing her ear to the door, Sydney didn't hear any movement or voices inside. Not even a TV set or running shower.

She suspected that Fujiwara was long gone, but perhaps his room still held a clue that might indicate his whereabouts.

A door opened a few rooms down the hall, and out walked a family of Australian tourists who didn't look like they were here for the convention. Sydney and Maya feigned small talk outside the door while they waited for the vacationers to exit the scene. The family eyed the costumed figures with amusement. Sydney caught the teenage son not-so-furtively checking out her butt.

Hormones and skintight latex, she thought. *A dangerous combination.*

As soon as the elevator doors closed on the curious civilians, Sydney produced an electronic key card from her sleeve and slipped it into the lock. The high-tech skeleton key did the trick; a green light flashed above the door handle.

Sydney drew her Taser, just in case a trigger-happy hacker was waiting inside. She nodded at the door.

"You first," she told Maya.

It was a reasonable call; Fujiwara was less likely to take a shot at his own fiancé.

Maya muttered a curse in Hindi, then reached up and removed her helmet. Perspiration gleamed upon her face. Her sable locks were plastered to her brow. She had a bad case of helmet hair.

Taking a deep breath, Maya turned the handle and kicked the door open. She lunged into the room in a lightning-fast attempt to surprise anyone who might be hiding inside.

Taser raised and ready, Sydney charged in after her.

As expected, however, the room was empty.

"Clear!" Sydney pronounced after confirming

that the bathroom and shower held no nasty surprises. The image of Danny's lifeless body bleeding out into her own tub flashed through her mind, but she quickly pushed it aside. She breathed a sigh of relief that she hadn't found Fujiwara lying in the same ghastly state.

Nobody, not even Maya, deserved a discovery like that.

An impressive stockpile of pill bottles was lined up on top of the bathroom counter. Sydney scanned the labels on the bottles. Imitrex. Fioricet. Relafen.

All migraine medications.

Bingo, she thought.

Emerging from the bathroom, she closed the door to the hall to ensure their privacy while they searched the room. Her adrenaline rush subsided as she flicked on the lights in order to get a better look.

The hotel maids had clearly heeded the DO NOT DISTURB sign. Room 4740 was in complete disarray. Dirty laundry lay crumpled on the floor and unmade bed. The leftover remains of a room service pizza sat on a table, and travel guides and notebooks were strewn atop a small desk area. The window drapes were drawn tightly shut. Air-conditioning hummed in the background. A dog-eared copy of *Beyond This Earth: UFO Secrets Revealed!* rested on an end table, next to a pad of hotel stationery.

From the look of things, Sydney guessed that Fujiwara had not returned to his room after losing her in the stairwell. He must have fled the hotel immediately, leaving his belongings behind. *He could be anywhere in Singapore by now,* she realized. *Or even Indonesia.*

The third eye on her forehead, which concealed a miniature camera, flashed repeatedly, capturing the details of the scene for future examination. Perhaps the analysts back at APO headquarters would spot something she had missed.

Maya rummaged through Fujiwara's discarded suitcase, which was lying on the seat of a plush easy chair. "Found anything good?" Sydney asked.

Maya shook her head. "No passport, no laptop," she reported. She lifted a silly-looking tie from the luggage. Glow-in-the-dark flying saucers hovered against a starry blue background. "I gave him this tie for our anniversary," she said, choking up. Her dark eyes blinked back tears. "We laughed so hard. . . ."

Once again Sydney had to wonder just how

genuine Maya's grief was. *My mom seemed to care about me, too, until she took out a contract on my life.*

She wandered over to the desk and began sorting through the scattered papers. Among the assorted convention schedules, UFO reports, and downloaded guides to Singapore, she found a print-out of what appeared to be the French Quarter of New Orleans. The street names—Bourbon Street, Esplanade Avenue—leaped out at her, seemingly out of place in the Far Eastern hotel room.

"Do you know any reason why Fujiwara would be interested in New Orleans?" she asked Maya.

The other woman looked away from the half-empty suitcase. "No, why?"

"Take a look at this," Sydney said.

She held the map out for Maya's inspection. There were no annotations or markings on the map, nothing to indicate what Fujiwara might have been looking for.

"Very strange," Maya commented. "As far as I know, Terry's never even been to New Orleans. He's certainly never expressed any interest in going there."

Is she telling the truth? Sydney wondered. She

had to remember that Maya was not exactly a reliable source. "What about the Baden Liga? Do they have any connections to New Orleans, or Louisiana in general?"

"Not that I know of," Maya answered. "But maybe Sloane knows something I don't. You should consult him."

Well, naturally, Sydney thought, but she wasn't through searching Fujiwara's room yet. Wandering over to the end table beside the bed, she glanced at the memo pad lying next to a complimentary hotel pen. The top sheet had been torn away, but she could still make out the indentations made by Fujiwara's pen. It appeared to be a single name: Theophile Benoit.

Who?

CHAPTER 5

BUDAPEST, HUNGARY

It was, Michael Vaughn thought, the first time he had ever seen Jack Bristow sweat.

Towels wrapped around their waists, the two agents sat in the steam room of one of Budapest's world-famous Turkish baths. This particular bath-house dated back to the sixteenth century, when the Ottoman Empire had ruled over the neighboring towns of Buda and Pest, long before they were unified into what is now known as the Paris of the East. Green marble columns supported the domed ceiling. Stained-glass hexagons embedded in the dome allowed tinted sunlight to enter the chapel-like chamber. A bribe to the attendant had ensured that they had the steam room to themselves.

The thick white vapor swirled around Vaughn, causing him to sweat profusely. The heat seeped into his bones, yet failed to dispel his growing impatience. Despite the luxurious steam bath, he couldn't help wishing he were in Singapore instead, keeping a close eye on Sydney's new partner, Maya Rao.

He had to remind himself that what they were doing here in Budapest was important too.

Without his wristwatch it was hard to keep track of the time. *What time is it in Singapore now? Has Sydney checked in with headquarters?*

"Do you think he's coming?" he asked Jack.

"Yes," Sydney's father said tersely. Beads of sweat dotted his brow, but Jack Bristow's icy expression remained as inscrutable as ever. "Zubatov knows better than to ignore a summons from Sloane—or myself."

Vaughn could believe it. He knew firsthand just how ruthless both men could be. Jack was no double-dealing scumbag like Sloane, but he could be just as brutal when it came to protecting his country—and his daughter. Vaughn was often grateful that he and the elder Bristow were on the same side.

At least most of the time.

Considering who her parents were, Vaughn often wondered where Sydney had gotten her warm and caring nature. Her dad was the coldest of cold fish, and her mother was a murdering sociopath, yet somehow Sydney had more heart than both of them put together, even after everything she'd been through over the past few years. Although recent events had put a strain on their romance, Vaughn remained in awe of Sydney's spirit and resilience; she was the most remarkable woman he had ever known.

If that treacherous Indian bitch hurts Sydney, he vowed, *I'll hunt her down and kill her myself— just like I killed Lauren. No matter what it takes.*

Jack Bristow wasn't the only one who would stop at nothing where Sydney was concerned.

Footsteps padded outside the steam room. Vaughn tensed in readiness, wishing he had a gun hidden beneath his towel. Their present environment made concealed weapons problematic, which was no doubt what their contact had had in mind when he insisted on meeting them here.

A lean, cadaverous figure approached through

ALIAS

the steam and sat down on the marble bench opposite Jack and Vaughn. Yevno Zubatov had once been
a high-ranking officer of Zero Defense—and Maya
Rao's handler. These days he was supposedly out of
the terrorism business, but he still had connections
to the global underground, which he was occasionally willing to share in exchange for being left alone
to enjoy his retirement, despite a criminal record
several kilometers long.

"Hello, Jack," Zubatov said with a thick Russian
accent. His silvery hair was slicked back above his
gaunt, pallid features. He looked like death warmed
over. His dry, papery skin was stretched so tightly over
his bones that he resembled a human skeleton. The
key to a rented locker dangled from a cord around his
bony wrist. "It's been a long time." He eyed Vaughn
through the swirling mist. "I don't believe I know you."

"An associate of mine," Jack declared without
further explanation. "We're here for information on
Maya Rao."

Their ultimate goal was to confirm—or disprove—
Maya's story regarding her involvement with Fujiwara
and the Kestrel heist. Even though it would make
recovering the UCAV more difficult, part of Vaughn
couldn't help but hope that Zubatov would prove

Maya a liar, since that might bring an immediate halt to Sydney's partnership with the former bandit queen. The sooner Sydney was rid of Maya, the better.

Zubatov nodded gravely at the mention of Maya's name. "An extraordinarily talented woman," he recalled. "You should have seen her in her youth, terrorizing half of India with nothing more than a handful of Dalit outcasts." He shook his head. "It was a great loss to the cause when she abandoned Zero Defense to freelance. I fear her more mercenary instincts won out over her commitment to global revolution."

"So she's been a free agent for some time now?" Jack pressed. Zubatov's information seemed to jibe with Maya's own account, at least so far.

"Since at least 1999," the Russian confirmed. "She's taken on a number of assignments for a variety of employers."

"Including the Baden Liga?"

A cryptic smile played on Zubatov's lips. "Perhaps."

Vaughn suspected that the supposedly retired terrorist knew more than he was letting on. Still, he continued to let Jack take the lead in questioning Zubatov.

"What more can you tell us about her current status?" the older agent asked.

Zubatov seemed to know what Jack was fishing for. "I can confirm that a sizable contract has been placed on my former protégé's life, by parties unknown to me. The Baden Liga are a distinct possibility, but I will leave that to you to discover." He threw up his hands. "As you know, I do not involve myself in such affairs any longer."

Anger overcame Vaughn's discretion. According to CIA files, Zubatov had been directly involved in the 1998 bombing of the U.S. embassy in Kenya, as well as numerous other atrocities. Under the circumstances Vaughn was not inclined to let the Russian jerk them around.

"Listen to me, you cold-blooded ghoul!" he snapped. His flushed face darkened an even deeper shade of red, and his hand slashed through the turbid fog between them. "I don't care how useful certain agencies consider you. If I find out that you've been holding out on us, I swear that you'll be spending the rest of your 'retirement' at the bottom of the Danube."

Zubatov arched a bushy gray eyebrow but did not appear intimidated by Vaughn's aggressive attitude. "I assure you, my intemperate young friend,

I have told you all that I am at liberty to reveal." Rheumy gray eyes peered at Vaughn from hollow, sunken sockets. "And spare me your melodramatic posturing. You cannot threaten a dying man."

Dying? Vaughn was momentarily taken aback.

The Russian nodded at Jack. "The cancer eats me alive as we speak. Pain, and the shadow of impending death, are my constant companions." His labored breathing lent support to his claims. "The one compensation is that it leaves me very little to lose, except perhaps the privilege of being allowed to die in peace."

Zubatov rose slowly from his bench, his dilapidated bones creaking audibly. "*Viszontlátásra,* Jack. It's been a pleasure doing business with you again. Please be sure to convey to Arvin Sloane that I cooperated fully." His bloodless skin had grown only slightly pinker in the sweltering atmosphere of the steam room. "He owes me one."

"Not as much as you owe the victims of your crimes," Jack said coldly. "But, for the time being, I'll defer collecting on that debt."

"That is as much as I can expect from you, I suppose." Zubatov slipped out the door of the steam room. The dense mist swiftly rushed in to fill the space he had vacated.

Jack turned toward Vaughn. "The next time you intend to threaten an informant, I would prefer that you let me know in advance. I'm not accustomed to playing the good cop in such scenarios."

Vaughn did not apologize for his outburst. "I felt that Zubatov was withholding information." He looked Jack squarely in the eye. "And I'm worried about Sydney."

"As am I," Jack stated. "Still, Zubatov's intel appears to confirm Maya's account of her current precarious situation. It's possible that she's telling the truth about Kestrel and Fujiwara."

Vaughn scowled. "I don't know. My gut tells me that there's something fishy going on here."

He expected Jack to lecture him on the unreliability of hunches. Instead a worried look appeared on the older man's face.

"For what it's worth, I feel much the same way."

ABOVE THE PACIFIC OCEAN

It was a twenty-seven-hour flight from Singapore to New Orleans. Sydney wished she were sharing it with anybody except Maya Rao.

The two women sat beside each other on the

chartered jet. Having shed her sci-fi costume and makeup, for good she hoped, Sydney was dressed casually in a turtleneck sweater, jeans, and sneakers. From her aisle seat she peered past Maya out the window. She couldn't see the separate jet that was transporting Dixon to New Orleans as well, but she knew it was out there, pacing them.

I'd rather be on that flight, she thought, wistfully imagining a relaxing chat with Dixon. Perhaps he had some new photos of his kids. *I wonder how Steven's soccer team is doing. Aren't they up for a championship or something?*

An electronic chime alerted her that more-serious matters awaited her.

Donning matching headsets, Sydney and Maya watched intently as a screen lowered itself from the cabin ceiling. Rather than an in-flight movie, however, the screen displayed a color photo of a solidly built black man wearing an expensive suit. With a shaved skull and cold brown eyes, the man looked to be approximately fifty-five years old and not someone to mess with. Identical scars, obviously carved out on purpose, adorned both his cheeks, the thin white lines forming distinct patterns whose meanings were unknown to Sydney. A silver amulet, fashioned in the shape of two intertwined pythons, rested upon his chest.

Doesn't look like a typical Space Vixens *fan to me,* she thought. *More like somebody who eats Trekkies for lunch.*

"Theophile Benoit," Sloane briefed her via the headset, "is a Haitian expatriate who fled to the U.S. following the collapse of the Duvalier regime in 1986. Although he denies it officially, reliable intel suggests that he was once a member of Papa Doc's notorious Tonton Macoutes."

Sydney repressed a shudder, and not just from the unsettling sensation of having Arvin Sloane whisper into her ear. The Tonton Macoutes, a Creole phrase that roughly translated to "bogeymen," had been François Duvalier's dreaded secret police, which he had used to murder and intimidate his political enemies. Voodoo trappings had added a supernatural flavor to the terror inflicted by the Tonton Macoutes upon the oppressed Haitian people.

In other words, Sydney thought, *this is not a nice person.*

But what was his connection to Fujiwara?

"Benoit now resides in New Orleans," Sloane continued, "where he runs a thriving voodoo temple catering mostly to the tourist trade. The CIA and FBI have long suspected Benoit of high-tech arms smuggling and other transgressions, but his considerable wealth and political connections have protected him so far."

"I see," Sydney acknowledged, speaking into the headset's mouthpiece. Could Benoit have Kestrel? His background in arms smuggling made him a likely suspect. Was that why Fujiwara had written down Benoit's name on the memo pad? "Does Benoit have any known connections to the Baden Liga?"

"Not that we know of," Sloane reported. As he spoke, a series of surveillance photos of Benoit flashed across the screen. One picture showed Benoit presiding over some sort of voodoo ritual in a long white robe. He held a machete in one hand and a dead chicken in the other. Other photos showed Benoit posing with prominent civic leaders. Sydney recognized a couple of past and present U.S. senators.

"This doesn't make sense," Maya protested. Like Sydney, she was dressed casually. Handcuffs kept her chained to her seat, a reasonable precaution that Sydney had insisted upon, despite Maya's objections. "It was definitely the Baden Liga who hired Terry and me to snatch the UCAV."

"You ever have any dealings with Benoit or his people?" Sydney asked her.

"Never," Maya said firmly. "I'd never heard of the man before."

"Well, your fiancé clearly knew something about him." A thought occurred to Sydney. "Perhaps the Baden Liga has already sold Kestrel to Benoit."

"Unlikely," Sloane informed both women. "My sources indicate that the auction for Kestrel has not yet taken place. I suspect that the Baden Liga still want to have Fujiwara under wraps before they attempt to market the UCAV." Wry amusement could be heard in his voice. "Who would want to buy an unmanned aircraft while the hacker who disabled it remains at large?"

Which suggests that the Baden Liga hasn't caught up with Fujiwara yet, Sydney thought. The elusive hacker was still alive—and up for grabs.

"Besides," Sloane continued, "Benoit is an arms dealer, not a potential terrorist. He'd have no use for Kestrel, unless he intended to resell it for an even higher amount."

Always a possibility, Sydney thought. Weapons

of mass destruction, and the means to deliver them, were big business these days.

"In any event, it sounds like New Orleans is calling our name," she observed. "There has to be *some* reason Fujiwara had that map in his room, and the fact that Benoit is based there can't be a coincidence. We just need to find out what the connection is."

"I agree," Sloane said. The surveillance photos on the screen were replaced by a real-time image of Sloane in his office. His gaunt, weathered features elicited a frown from Sydney. Her jaw tightened involuntarily. "And Sydney, be careful. I had a few run-ins with the Tonton Macoutes back in the old days. If Benoit used to run with that crowd, he's nobody you want to cross."

Like you, you mean?

Sloane signed off and the screen retracted into the ceiling. Sydney and Maya removed their headsets.

"He seems genuinely concerned about you," Maya commented, although she could hardly have missed Sydney's negative reaction to Sloane's image. "How sweet."

Did she know that Sloane's avuncular act made Sydney want to rip his eyes out? "There's nothing sweet about Arvin Sloane," she said through gritted teeth. "Believe me."

"And yet you've worked for him for, what, more than twelve years now?" Maya's dark eyes flashed impishly. "Methinks you protest too much."

What's that supposed to mean? Sydney thought angrily. "I have my reasons."

"I'm sure you do," Maya said in a condescending tone. "Would it surprise you to know that I've sometimes had to work with allies whom I held in absolute contempt? Present company excluded, of course."

"Thanks, I think," Sydney said harshly. "I wish I could return the compliment."

Maya sighed wearily. "Your holier-than-thou attitude is hardly warranted. Tell me, just off the top of your head, how many people have you killed?"

That's none of your business, Sydney thought. Her memory couldn't help racing back, though, over several years of firefights and hand-to-hand combat against various foes. Names and faces flashed through her mind:

Fintan Tate, whom she killed in Africa.

Kazu Tamazaki, whom she sliced to death with a samurai sword.

Oleg Madroczk, whom she gunned down in Frankfurt.

Giles Macor, who was sucked into the engine of his own 747 when she brought the jet down.

Anthony Geiger, whom she shot through the heart during that final raid on SD-6.

And, hardest of all, Noah Hicks, aka the Snowman. The first real love of her life.

Those are just the ones whose names I know, Sydney realized guiltily. In truth, there had been plenty of anonymous guards and foot soldiers too. Strangers who had met their end in one life-or-death battle or another. *Too many strangers.*

"Lost count, haven't you?" Maya asked her, as though she had read Sydney's mind. "No matter. So have I. That's just the kind of women we are."

"I told you before," Sydney insisted. "I'm nothing like you."

"Really? Let's narrow things down a bit. What about innocent lives? Ever killed anyone who didn't deserve it?"

Against her will Sydney recalled the panicked expression of Christopher Ryan, whom she had been forced to kill in order to convince the Covenant that they had successfully brainwashed her. *I had no choice,* she reminded herself in anguish. *The Covenant was going to kill him anyway. . . .*

"Forget it," she told Maya. "I'm not playing this game."

"Tough," Maya asserted. "I'm not done yet." She peppered Sydney with questions, like a prosecutor grilling a hostile witness. "Ever lied to a loved one? Ever pledged allegiance to one faction while secretly working for the opposition? Ever compromised your principles for the sake of a mission?"

Of course I have, Sydney admitted, but only to herself. At one point or another, she had deceived just about everyone she cared about, and been deceived by them in turn. Hell, there were still things she couldn't tell her own sister, and God only knew what secrets Nadia might be hiding. *That's just the way our lives are.*

But hopefully there was still room for love and compassion as well. *There has to be,* she thought despairingly, *or what's the point?*

Maya, on the other hand, seemed to be enjoying herself. "Just how clean are your hands, Sydney? How far are you willing to go?" She gave Sydney a knowing wink. "Tell me, just between us girls, have you ever slept with the enemy?"

"Like you did with Fujiwara?" Sydney shot back, tired of being put on the defensive. *Let's see how Maya likes the third degree.* "How far did *you* have to go to ensnare the poor guy in your greedy little scheme?"

The glee evaporated from Maya's taunting face. When she spoke again, her voice was hoarse with emotion. She thrust her engagement ring in Sydney's face. "I *love* Terry," she declared fervently. "And if you don't believe that, then maybe you're even more coldhearted than I am."

The hell with this! Sydney thought furiously. She unbuckled her seat belt, lurched out of her seat, and stalked up the cabin until she'd put four rows of seats between Maya Rao and herself. But her guilt and uncertainty followed her.

I'm not sure whom I'm angrier at, she thought in frustration. *Maya for getting under my skin, or me for letting her.*

Was she really all that different from Maya Rao? Sydney tried to convince herself that, on a fundamental level, she had one thing Maya didn't have: a conscience. Maya had worked for Zero Defense and the Baden Liga, for Pete's sake!

Then again, I worked for SD-6 for seven years

before I found out they were the bad guys. And now, even knowing what I do, here I am working for Arvin Sloane again.

Am I truly a better person than Maya—or am I just fooling myself?

Settling into her new seat, she stared unhappily out the window. Shapeless clouds, lacking any clearly defined borders, offered no easy answers.

It was going to be a long flight.

CHAPTER 6

NEW ORLEANS

Although it was barely past two in the afternoon, the party was already getting started in the city's famed French Quarter. Jazz music poured out of the open doorways of the bars and nightclubs, into sunlit streets packed with strolling tourists and street performers. The smoky clubs shared the bustling avenues with souvenir shops, strip joints, Cajun restaurants, and sidewalk cafés. Elegant wrought-iron balconies, overflowing with flowers and foliage, jutted from historic redbrick buildings in various stages of preservation. The muggy air smelled of gumbo, chicory, and lush tropical blossoms.

Posing as tourists, Sydney and Maya made their way down Bourbon Street. Wide-brimmed hats and tinted sunglasses offered them a degree of anonymity. A peroxide-blond wig also helped to conceal Maya's identity from potential assassins.

Or so they hoped.

August in New Orleans was hot and incredibly humid. Sweat blanketed Sydney from head to toe, causing her shorts and T-shirt to stick to her skin. Having chosen sneakers over sandals, she found herself having serious second thoughts about her footwear. Walking down the sidewalk was like wading through a thick, invisible soup. She sipped from a bottle of water, refraining from the Hurricanes and other alcoholic beverages readily available throughout the Vieux Carré; many of her fellow pedestrians were less abstemious, chugging down their beer-filled "go cups" openly in the streets. *No wonder they call this place the Big Easy,* she thought. *Where else can you find drive-through liquor stores?*

At least it wasn't Mardi Gras. Sydney didn't even want to think about trying to locate Fujiwara in the middle of that mob scene. Back in their college days she and her roommate Francie had impulsively flown to New Orleans to check out the festivities; she winced in memory of the truly epic hangovers they both had ended up with, along with a suitcase full of carnival beads that they had earned in ways they hadn't wanted to remember.

A sense of melancholy came over Sydney. The beads were gone now, destroyed in the fire that had consumed her home three years ago, and Francie was gone as well, killed by Allison Doren, a ruthless female assassin not unlike Maya Rao. *And here I am again, with Maya for company instead of Francie.*

Not exactly an improvement.

"Penny for your thoughts?" Maya asked.

"Trust me," Sydney answered curtly. "You don't want to know."

La Maison du Vodou was located at the corner of Bourbon and Melusine Streets, in a restored two-story town house sporting an intricate iron balcony with a serpentine motif that recalled the intertwined pythons on Benoit's amulet. It was one of numerous establishments in the Quarter offering visitors a taste of an "authentic" New Orleans voodoo experience, but the only one owned and operated by Theophile Benoit.

Not trying very hard to conceal his Tonton Macoute roots, Sydney observed. She wondered if his reputation as a voodoo practitioner still served to cow his enemies and followers. *At least Sloane has never claimed any sort of occult authority, unless you count his old obsession with Rambaldi's prophecies.*

Despite her own exposure to the mysteries of Rambaldi, Sydney remained skeptical where the supernatural was concerned. She wasn't about to let Benoit's voodoo shtick spook her. *I know what real evil is, and it has nothing to do with curses and zombies.*

"Here we are," she announced. "After you."

Maya shook her head. "I still think this is a waste of time. Why would Terry come to a place like this?"

"That's what I want to find out," Sydney said. She nudged Maya toward the entrance. "Come on."

Maya didn't budge. "You go. I'll stand watch out here." Next to La Maison du Vodou a tall painted fence advertised, HOT GIRLS! AMATEUR MUD WRESTLING EVERY NITE! Maya tilted her head at the garish sign. "Perhaps I'll catch the next bout?"

"Sorry. Not an option," Sydney insisted. Even with Dixon discreetly tailing them, she wasn't going to let Maya out of her sight unless she absolutely had to. A loaded Beretta, hidden in her purse, added a little extra persuasiveness to her argument. "You're coming with me."

"Ah, togetherness," Maya rhapsodized sarcastically. Taking Sydney's arm, she let the American agent escort her toward the door. "Who knew we'd end up so inseparable?"

Entering the temple, they discovered that the ground floor of the building was essentially a gift shop, hawking cheap souvenirs and voodoo paraphernalia. Skulls, candles, dolls, rattles, drums, pots, herbs, gourds, amulets, potions, crystals, and charms were crammed onto the shelves and counters, along with postcards and paintings of Marie Laveau, the legendary voodoo queen of old New Orleans. Chromolithographs of Catholic saints were mixed with sacred thunderstones consecrated to various voodoo spirits. A wooden barrel was filled to the top with the bleached skulls of unlucky alligators, their toothy jaws still impressively fierce looking. Incense scented the air. Rhythmic drumming played through speakers mounted in the ceiling.

"Charming," Maya murmured. "And I thought

my native village was a sinkhole of ignorant super-
stition."

Sydney ignored her.

"Can I help you girls?" a cashier asked them.

"No thanks, hon," Sydney answered with an
impeccable Southern accent. "We're just browsing."

In fact, she was checking out the security
setup. Closed-circuit cameras, she noted, were
tucked in amid the skulls and gris-gris. A single set
of stairs, located midway across the shop, led to
the second story of the temple, where Benoit was
reputed to run his operations. EMPLOYEES ONLY, read
a sign attached to a chain stretching across the
first few steps. A security guard, with his beefy
arms stretched across his chest, stood nearby, just
in case anyone didn't get the message.

I need to find a way to get up there, Sydney
realized. If Benoit had any information regarding
Fujiwara and Kestrel, that was where it was likely
to be found.

But not right now. There were plenty of customers and employees around, but not enough to
allow her to slip past the guard unnoticed.

Perhaps after dark?

Exploring further, the women ventured out an

exit at the rear of the store, which led to an enclosed courtyard behind the temple. Having read up on voodoo during the flight, Sydney guessed that this was the *peristil,* an outdoor space used for public rituals.

A vertical wooden post, painted in rainbow-colored bands, was set in a circular concrete base at the exact center of the courtyard. A whip hung from the post as a symbolic reminder of voodoo's roots in slavery. The post itself, which was called the *potomitan,* linked the earth to the sky, and the material world to the world of the spirits. Offerings of rum, cigarettes, and other delicacies rested upon the concrete base of the *potomitan.*

From her research, Sydney recognized the other ritual elements arrayed in the *peristil:* an iron bar set in the middle of an unlit bonfire, symbolizing Ogoun, the spirit of war and fire; and a model ship hanging from a tree, representing Ezili, the spirit of love. A large black cross loomed to one side of the courtyard, in honor of Baron Samedi, the lord of the dead. It was, Sydney had to admit, a bit spooky.

"I don't see any stolen warplanes, do you?" Maya asked in a low voice.

Ha, ha, Sydney thought, unamused. Obviously

there was no way the UCAV could fit anywhere in or around the temple. She wondered momentarily whether Kestrel was hidden in one of the warehouses down by the river. *I should find out whether Benoit owns any property down by the docks.*

A tour guide, wearing a white cotton dress and a bandanna, appeared to be delivering a lecture to a small group of attentive tourists. Sydney and Maya quietly joined the audience in time to catch the tail end of the talk.

"Brought to the United States by displaced Haitian slaves more than two hundred years ago, voodoo remains a thriving part of the culture of New Orleans." She pronounced the city's name as "N'Awlins," a sure sign that she was a native. "Here at La Maison du Vodou, the voodoo spirits—the loa—live on, bestowing their guidance and gifts upon humanity, in exchange for the reverence and offerings of believers. From the ancient tribal religions of West Africa to today's contemporary spiritual counselors and herbal therapists, voodoo continues to grow and evolve, even as it remains a vital link between the material world and the spirit realm.

"And don't forget," the guide concluded, "a

genuine voodoo ritual is held in this very courtyard every night at sunset. Tickets are available in the gift shop behind you, with special discounts for children and seniors. Don't let yourself be suckered in by some of the so-called rituals being offered by our competitors; we offer the real thing, one hundred percent authentic." She flashed a winning smile at the tourists. "Thank you and enjoy your visit to the Big Easy."

A round of applause brought the lecture to a close. As the crowd dispersed, seeking tickets and other treasures in the gift shop, Sydney lingered in the courtyard. Maya tapped her foot impatiently.

"Are we done here," she asked, "or do you plan to join this benighted cult?"

Why not? Sydney thought.

Suddenly she knew how to penetrate the upper reaches of the temple.

All she needed was some special equipment and apparel. . . .

Maya was less than thrilled by Sydney's notion.

"I said it before," she protested, pacing unhappily across the floor of their hotel room. Her hat, wig, and sunglasses lay discarded upon her bed.

"This is a waste of time. Why bother infiltrating Benoit's temple? If he is connected to the Baden Liga, then Terry's not going to come anywhere near the place. And if Benoit has captured Terry somehow, then he's probably already dead." She shuddered at the thought. "Either way you're not going to find Terry there."

"That's not the point," Sydney replied. Leaning back against the headboard of her queen-size bed, she stared at her laptop as she surfed the Internet in search of more information on voodoo rituals. After the muggy atmosphere outside, the air-conditioned hotel room came as a blessed relief. "I'm going to be looking for information, which may or may not help us track down Fujiwara."

Sloane, in fact, had already signed off on Sydney's plan—and vetoed Maya's objections. Now Sydney just had to wait for APO to set everything up and provide her with the necessary gear; fortunately, Marshall had sounded quite intrigued by the possibilities.

"Besides," she pointed out, "you keep forgetting something: I'm not just looking for your fiancé. Recovering Kestrel is my top priority."

"So much for your famous conscience," Maya taunted Sydney. "Nice to know that an expensive piece of military hardware is worth more than a man's life." She looked down at Sydney accusingly. "You're sounding more like Sloane every day."

Ouch, Sydney thought, feeling the sting of Maya's remarks. On one level she knew that there was a bigger picture here, that the stolen UCAV endangered America's security and therefore posed a deadly threat to millions of innocent lives, yet she still felt uncomfortable relegating Fujiwara's safety to a secondary concern. Maya was right about one thing: That was exactly the way Sloane thought.

Not to mention my mom and dad.

Unwilling to let Maya know that she'd hit a nerve, Sydney kept her face frozen in a neutral expression. Probably a wasted effort; the Indian assassin seemed to possess an uncanny talent for pushing Sydney's buttons. A natural gift, or one Maya had acquired through long and deliberate study of her rival?

Some roommate, Sydney thought bleakly. Naturally, APO had the budget to spring for separate rooms for her and Maya, but Sydney had wanted to keep a closer eye on Maya. The drawback, of course, was that she now had to share a room with her nemesis, just like she had in Singapore. *Let's hope it doesn't take Sloane and the others too long to set up my new alias.*

A wave of homesickness overcame her, and she suddenly wished that she were back in Los Angeles, hanging out in her house with Nadia or sharing a romantic evening with Vaughn. Heck, she even found herself missing APO's subterranean lair. At least there she had the gang to keep her company, as opposed to Maya Rao.

Where are my friends now? she wondered. *Are they safe?* Last she'd heard, Vaughn and her father were still in Europe investigating Maya's story—without any conclusive results so far—while Nadia and Eric Weiss were on their way back from Guatemala. Dixon, of course, was only one room away, checked into the very same hotel, but she had to pretend he wasn't there, which still left her feeling cut off from everyone important in her life. *I wonder what Will is doing tonight?*

"Well?" Maya demanded, her accusations still hanging in the air. She loomed at the foot of the bed, arms akimbo.

Sydney declined to respond to the other woman's barbs. "I need a shower," she announced brusquely. The stickiness brought on by New

Orleans's sultry climate clung to her skin. She hopped off the bed and retrieved two pairs of sturdy metal handcuffs from an attaché case. "Okay," she informed Maya. "You know the drill."

Maya eyed the cuffs with contempt. "You're serious?" she asked incredulously. "Again?"

"You bet," Sydney answered. She had no intention of letting Maya pull a Norman Bates number on her in the shower. She drew her Beretta, just like she always did when she and Maya played out this scene, which was getting old really fast. "Just be glad we're not talking a straitjacket and leg irons."

"Your restraint overwhelms me," Maya said drily.

Sydney pointed the gun at a well-padded easy chair. Glowering venomously, Maya took the hint and sat down.

So far, so good, Sydney thought.

As always, the possibility of violence hung over the scene as she approached Maya with the cuffs. Sydney held her breath, braced for combat, but Maya put up no resistance . . . this time. Keeping her gun aimed at Maya's head, Sydney cuffed the other woman's hands behind her back, then cautiously cuffed her ankles together.

Gun or no gun, she half expected Maya to kick her teeth out.

But Maya just sat there, fuming.

Sydney let out a sigh of relief as she completed the operation. Standing and stepping away from the shackled killer, she inspected Maya carefully, assuring herself that she hadn't overlooked anything.

"Don't go far," Sydney quipped as she gathered some clean clothes and headed toward the shower. She was looking forward to the relative privacy of the bathroom.

"Don't be long," Maya countered. "And save me some of the hot water."

Sydney took her gun with her into the bathroom.

Just in case.

CHAPTER 7

LA MAISON DU VODOU
BOURBON STREET

Drums pulsed in the moonlit courtyard. Flickering torches cast writhing shadows onto the high brick walls enclosing the sacred space. Despite the sweltering heat, a bonfire blazed brightly, turning Ogou's iron bar red hot. Smoke rose from the fire into the clear night sky. Musky incense permeated the air.

A gaggle of hushed tourists circled the *peristil*, gazing wide-eyed at the unfolding spectacle. The opening invocations had already been performed. The four corners of the compass had been saluted by the voodoo priest, also known as the *houngan*. Water had been ritually spilled, consecrating the space. Robed initiates had paraded before the audience, bearing brightly colored flags covered with sequined designs honoring the various loa. An apprentice priest held up a ceremonial sword, symbolizing Haiti's revolutionary past.

The *houngan*, a tall man wearing a gaudy crimson robe, kissed the sword and saluted the flags. The unnamed priest was most definitely *not* Theophile Benoit; apparently the powerful voodoo leader had better things to do than perform nightly for curious vacationers.

The flag bearers retreated to the rear of the courtyard, settling in behind the three drummers, who beat out an intricate rhythm upon drumheads made of stretched goatskin. A fourth musician kept time upon a flattened metal bell. A chorus of female initiates chanted in unison. The percussive music competed somewhat with the raucous din of the mud wrestling competition being held next door, but managed to win out in the end.

The *houngan* proceeded to invoke the loa. Walking deliberately around the wooden post in the center of the courtyard, he sprinkled rum upon the ground and let cornmeal trickle through his fingers, using the finely ground powder to trace out elaborate designs throughout the courtyard. Each design, or *vever*, represented a specific voodoo spirit and, in theory, invited the loa to take part in the ceremony. The priest worked from memory, tracing the complicated patterns while calling out to the spirits in Creole. Among the chanted invocations could be heard the names Papa Legba, Baron Samedi, and Damballah.

When the *vevers* were completed, the *houngan* extended his hand, and an apprentice hurried forward to offer the priest a rattle composed of a hollow gourd filled with snake vertebrae. Colored beads adorned the rattle. A silver bell was affixed to its handle.

The *houngan* sprinkled rum on the *vevers* and shook his rattle over them. More initiates came forward to lay offerings of smoked meats, peanut cakes, and rice upon the sacred symbols. The priest nodded in approval, then lit the candles placed upon the concrete base of the central post.

That's my cue, Sydney thought.

The drumming sped up as she emerged from the women's chorus, where she had been waiting, with just a touch of stage fright, for this very moment. A sleeveless white cotton dress, belted at the waist with a bright red sash, clothed her lithe figure. A necklace of cowrie shells dangled around her neck. False black hair tumbled down her back.

And a ten-foot python was draped over her shoulders.

To the throbbing rhythm of the bell and drums, Sydney whirled across the floor of the courtyard. Her bare feet glided across the warm stone tiles as she swayed back and forth to the music, her motions as sinuous as those of the serpent lying across her neck. She rolled her shoulders and wildly tossed her loose black hair. Her entire body undulated as she wove between the post and bonfire, dancing carefully around the scattered offerings. Light applause and murmured "ooh's" and "ah's" issued from the appreciative audience.

Guess I'm a hit, Sydney thought with relief. She had spent the last forty-eight hours learning the dance moves from downloaded video clips, while APO had hurriedly set up her cover story— and "persuaded" the temple's usual dancer to call in sick at the last moment. Nevertheless, she was grateful that she wasn't exactly dealing with an expert audience; even if she got the routine slightly wrong, it was unlikely that the tourists would know the difference. As long as there were snakes, drums, torches, and exotic local color, they would be happy.

Sydney rather suspected that this "authentic" ritual was more of a staged performance than an actual religious rite. No doubt the real ceremonies, if there were any, went on far away from the eager stares and flashbulbs of the paying customers. *Works for me,* she thought. Certainly the stressed-out manager of tonight's show had not seemed terribly worried about her spiritual credentials when she conveniently offered herself as a substitute for their absentee dancer. Never mind when and where she had been initiated into voodoo. She just had to look the part.

That was the thing about aliases. If there was one thing she had learned over all these years, it was that people were often surprisingly ready to accept things at face value, especially if that face was a pretty one. *Thank goodness most people seldom look deeper than that!*

The drumming grew even faster, assuming a more frenzied tempo. Sydney's gyrations grew quicker and more provocative. She raised the writhing python above her head and spun about as though possessed, thrusting her hips backward and forward. Her exertions soon left her drenched in sweat, the moist sheen upon her face and arms catching the glow of the bonfire and torches. The python hissed in her grasp, its forked tongue flicking out from between its scaly jaws.

Sydney searched the faces of the crowd as she danced. She didn't expect to spot Fujiwara among the audience, but who knew?

No luck, though. The elusive hacker was nowhere to be seen.

The only face she did recognize was Maya's. Sydney's unwanted partner waited in the audience, disguised as an elderly tourist with white hair and wrinkles. She winked at Sydney as they briefly made eye contact.

Glad you're enjoying the show, Sydney thought archly. *I hope you appreciate how far I'm willing to go to find your missing fiancé.*

Not to mention the stolen UCAV.

Sydney glanced toward the rear of the temple, where a security guard stood posted by a sealed back door marked EMPLOYEES ONLY. The bored-looking sentry watched her perform with only minimal interest. One eye tracked her progress; the other appeared to be made of glass. Despite the heat, the one-eyed guard wore a lightweight blue jacket and slacks. Was he armed? Sydney hoped she wouldn't have to find out.

The second-story windows of the temple were dark. Presumably Benoit himself had left for the evening. According to the newspapers, the noted civic leader was attending a charity function elsewhere in the city. She would never have a better opportunity to search his office. All she needed now was a timely distraction.

Which was what the python was for.

Despite its realistic appearance, the serpent was actually a mechanical replica fashioned by Marshall. No one at APO had wanted to risk tonight's operation on the unpredictable behavior of a live snake, and Sydney hadn't been in a hurry to dance with a genuine ten-foot wrapped around her. Plus, the artificial serpent came with a few vital bonus features. . . .

Raising the python before her face, she pressed a concealed tab at the back of the snake's aluminum skull. The coiled mechanism suddenly twisted in her hands, breaking free of her grasp. "Watch out!" she shrieked. The python dropped onto the floor of the courtyard and slithered into the crowd of startled spectators. "I can't control it!"

The audience members panicked as the python wriggled between their feet. To add to the confusion, Maya let out a hysterical scream and started thrashing wildly. "Help me!" she gasped, clutching her chest. "My heart!"

Bedlam ensued as the frightened tourists pushed and shoved one another in their haste to get away from the loose constrictor. The drums fell silent. The dumbfounded chorus members stared in bewilderment, while the *houngan* and his acolytes hesitated at the fringes of the scene, uncertain how to cope with the chaos.

Sydney repressed a smile. Everything was going as planned.

Keeping a close eye on the security guard, she quietly edged toward the back door. As she neared her goal, Maya let out an anguished cry and crumpled to the ground, nearly getting trampled by the other audience members, who were being chased by the hissing mechanical python. "Help me, please!" the apparently stricken old woman pleaded. "Somebody help me!"

Cursing under his breath, the guard abandoned his post. He ran to Maya's side, where she grabbed on to him with what must have been surprising strength. He tried to help her to her feet, only to be dragged down onto the ground as well. "Calm down, lady," he protested breathlessly. "I'm trying to help you!"

With all eyes on the snake and the frantic audience, Sydney darted over to the door. She yanked it open and ran inside, then pulled the door shut behind her. A mounted security camera greeted her entrance, but Sydney was unconcerned; the bogus python also doubled as a video scrambler that had effectively shut down the temple's security monitors.

Take it from Eve, she mused. *Some snakes just can't be trusted.*

She found herself in a storeroom packed with boxes of voodoo-themed merchandise. A set of stairs led to the upper floor, and she took the steps two at a time until she reached the landing. A row of unmarked wooden doors lined the corridor ahead, with no clear indication as to where Sydney should begin her search. Midway down the hall the main stairway led down to the gift shop below. Farther on, moonlight shone through a curtained glass door at the far end of the hall. She glimpsed the iron railing of the second-story balcony through the lacy drapes.

A possible escape route? she speculated, having been trained always to take note of such things. *Good to know.*

First, however, she had a mission to complete. The sweat on her body cooled as the temple's interior air-conditioning met her skin, making her shiver. Her bare feet stepped softly on the carpeted floor as she sneaked down the hall and tried the first door on her left.

Locked.

Despite the tumult below, Sydney knew it wouldn't be long before the situation was brought under control—and someone noticed that the mysterious dancer responsible for the mess had gone missing. With luck, the *houngan* and the others would just assume that she had beaten a hasty retreat after botching her debut performance so badly, but Sydney had learned the hard way never to depend on luck. She couldn't afford to waste any time.

She cracked open one of the seashells on her necklace, exposing a set of lightweight lock picks. The locked door soon succumbed, and she stepped inside the darkened room. As there appeared to be no windows in this particular chamber, she risked switching on the lights. A soft fluorescent glow immediately revealed that this was no office.

Ceremonial flags adorned the walls, along with brightly painted *vevers.* An altar consisting of a long wooden table covered by a pristine white cloth occupied the far end of the room. Candles, stones, bottles, and other objects rested atop the altar.

Sydney guessed that this was where the temple's more private rituals were conducted, as opposed to the theatrical ceremonies put on in the courtyard. She doubted that she would find any vital intel here but examined the artifacts on the altar anyway, looking for something she might be able to use as a weapon if necessary. Worried about being searched before her performance, she had left her guns and knives locked away in a safe back at the hotel.

Her gaze lighted upon a machete, which was nestled on the altar between a water-filled crystal vase and a stack of tarot cards. A bottle of white Haitian rum sat on the table next to an offering of yams and beans.

These will do, she decided, snatching up both

the machete and the rum. She thrust the machete into the sash around her waist and hefted the bottle by its neck. She hoped she wasn't offending any particularly touchy spirits, but she felt more comfortable with a weapon or two. *Sue me.*

Figuring there was nothing more to be accomplished in this room, Sydney crept back to the entrance and opened the door just enough to peek out into the corridor. The coast seemed to be clear, so she slipped out of the ritual chamber and tried the door across the hall. As she expertly picked the lock, she thought she heard an electronic hum on the other side of the door.

Promising, she thought.

She pushed the door open slowly, grateful that its hinges didn't squeak. The glow from a computer screen bathed the room beyond in a pale blue light. Sydney glimpsed an expensive walnut desk, flanked by polished wooden filing cabinets. Photos of Benoit posing with A-list celebrities and politicians decorated the walls.

Pay dirt.

As she stepped furtively into the office, it took Sydney a second to realize she was not alone. An executive desk chair rolled across the floor on the other side of the desk, and a startled face looked up from behind the glowing computer screen.

Fujiwara.

"Outrigger to Merlin. Phoenix is in play."

Pretending to be just as alarmed by the mechanical python as everyone else, Dixon backed up against the stone wall of the courtyard. A detailed latex mask, not unlike the one Sydney had employed when she impersonated Lauren Reed, concealed his angular features from Maya Rao. False teeth and a silver-gray toupee assisted his disguise, while a baseball cap, camera, and oversize Hawaiian shirt helped him blend in with the other members of the audience, including Maya.

Sydney had slipped into the temple only moments before, leaving Dixon to keep watch over Maya, who was presently thrashing with the hapless guard who had come to her assistance. Dixon had to admire the disguised assassin's performance; she was totally convincing as a hysterical older woman. It was a pity that she had wasted her talents in the service of international terrorism.

Let's hope Sloane doesn't try to recruit her when this is all over.

He glanced away from Maya and checked the back door of the temple. Had Sydney made it to Benoit's office yet? He couldn't help worrying about what Sydney might encounter upstairs. *This is Singapore all over again,* he lamented silently. Once again he was stuck shadowing Maya while Sydney put herself at risk. Having not begun his espionage career until the nineties, he had never dealt with the Tonton Macoutes himself, but he was well aware of their brutal reputation. If Benoit was anything like his fellow bogeymen, Dixon doubted that he had mellowed much over the years. He was likely to take a dim view of trespassers on his premises.

"Watch out! There it is!" a frightened tourist shrieked, pointing at the artificial python as it slithered randomly around the *peristil*. By coincidence it lunged at Dixon, who pretended to kick at it in fright. The technicians at APO had done an astounding job with the scaly mechanism; if he hadn't known better, he would have sworn it was the real thing.

Suddenly another guard came running out of the gift shop, holding a Smith & Wesson automatic pistol. The sight of the firearm caused nearly as much panic as the runaway snake had, but the determined gunman forced his way through the agitated tourists until he had a clean shot at the python as it thrashed and hissed before the bonfire. The muzzle of the pistol flared repeatedly, multiple gunshots hurt Dixon's ears, and the python jerked spasmodically beneath a hail of bullets that chipped apart the stone tiles beneath the bogus serpent. A cloud of dust and powdered stone arose from the floor. Maya screamed and clutched her hands to her ears, an act that Dixon found more than a little ironic.

Like Maya Rao would be afraid of a few gunshots!

Convinced that he had put an end to the source of the uproar, the second guard lowered his gun. To his surprise, however, no cold reptilian blood spilled from the creature's body; instead sparks erupted from the python's ruptured skin, along with the smell of burning circuitry. "What the devil?" he muttered.

"Look!" one of the tourists shouted to his companions. The relief in his voice quickly turned to hilarity. "Come back here! It was all a fake!"

"Oh, my God!" another visitor exclaimed. "I totally believed it!"

Apparently under the impression that the python's rampage had all been part of the show, Dixon's fellow audience members gathered around the sparking decoy. Puffs of noxious white smoke rose from the snake's computerized entrails. Applause and nervous laughter filled the courtyard.

The gun-toting guard wasn't laughing, though. He nudged the robot snake suspiciously with the toe of his shoe, his brows knit in concentration. "Claude!" he shouted to the other guard. "Forget that old lady! Get over here and look at this."

Perhaps realizing that the jig was up, Maya allowed the first guard to help her to her feet. She tottered back into the audience as Benoit's men contemplated the ersatz serpent. Awareness dawned upon Claude's sullen face, and he hastily looked around the courtyard, as if noticing for the first time that a certain dancer had gone missing. "The new girl!" he exclaimed. He cast an anxious glance at the doorway he had been guarding only a few minutes before.

"Upstairs!" he shouted, running for the door. He drew his own gun from beneath his jacket. "Hurry!"

Watch out, Sydney, Dixon thought. *You're getting company.*

Terry Fujiwara, in the flesh.

The last time Sydney had laid eyes on the

infamous hacker, plastic purple scales had hidden his true features from her; now, however, Sydney recognized him at once from Maya's description and the sketch artist's portrait. The lanky Asian American had unkempt black hair that looked like it hadn't seen a comb in days. Stubble peppered his jaw, and the purple shadows under his eyes testified to many sleepless nights on the run. He was dressed entirely in black. The better to break and enter into Benoit's office?

Certainly he looked as though he had just been caught with his hand in the cookie jar. His brown eyes bulged from their sockets at the sight of the bottle in Sydney's hand—and the machete on her hip. The blood drained from his face and his Adam's apple bobbed nervously. He backed away from the computer.

Sydney couldn't tell if he recognized her from Singapore. After all, she'd had tangerine hair and three eyes then. She lowered the rum bottle without letting go of it. "Listen to me, Terry!" she whispered urgently. She yanked off her wig to convince him that she wasn't just one of Benoit's voodoo disciples. "I'm with Maya. I'm here to help you."

Either he didn't care or he didn't believe her. He pulled a Colt automatic pistol from his lap and waved it in Sydney's face. His arm trembled, as though he was unaccustomed to handling firearms. "Shut up!" he snapped at her. "I'm tired of being lied to!"

He sounded just as paranoid as advertised. Sydney racked her brain for some way to get through to him. Admitting she was actually CIA struck her as the wrong way to go.

She stepped back from the desk. Placing the rum bottle on the floor, she raised her hands, showing him her open palms. "Terry, you have to believe me," she began in what she hoped was her most soothing tone. "We don't have a lot of time."

"Quiet!" he insisted, the muzzle of the Colt aimed right at her face. A swollen vein pulsated across his forehead. Evidence of a sudden migraine? Getting up from the chair, he retrieved a floppy from the computer's disk drive and tucked it securely into his pocket. "Back away." He circled around the desk and headed for the door. "I'm getting out of here. Don't try to stop me!"

Sydney considered trying to disarm him, but the last thing she wanted to do was create a commotion while Benoit's guards were still prowling around downstairs. She wanted to save Fujiwara, not get him killed.

Footsteps sounded on the front stairs. Guards coming to search the second floor? She didn't bother to conceal the alarm in her eyes. *Don't you see? We're on the same side,* she entreated him silently, acutely aware that their time was running out. *We have to get away, pronto!*

Their mutual anxiety did nothing to overcome Fujiwara's distrust. "Don't move!" he warned her, backing out into the hall. "Stay where you are!"

Yeah, right, she thought. Terry disappeared into the hall, and she gave him less than a two-second head start before cautiously peeking around the corner of the door. Mercifully, he was too busy running for the glass door at the end of the hall to fire back at her. He seemed to be heading straight for the balcony outside.

Snatching up the rum bottle again, she rushed into the hall after him, just in time to see two of Benoit's guards reach the top of the stairs, directly between Sydney and the fleeing hacker. The two men blinked in surprise to find intruders on both sides of them. Armed with automatic pistols, they hesitated, uncertain which trespasser to go after first.

"You!" one of the guards blurted out. Sydney recognized him as the glass-eyed sentry Maya had distracted earlier. "What the hell are you doing up here?"

"Looking for my snake?" she quipped. Taking advantage of the guards' confusion, she hurled the rum bottle straight at the first guard's head. It spun end over end through the air before crashing into the man's skull in an explosion of glass and alcohol. He collapsed to the ground, his gun slipping from his fingers. The pungent aroma of the rum suffused the air.

Remind me to get a stiff drink when this is all over, Sydney thought. *I suspect I'm going to need one.*

"Bitch!" the second guard snarled. Ignoring Fujiwara for the moment, he swung his gun toward Sydney and let loose a hail of gunfire. The sharp report of the weapon echoed through the hall.

She dived beneath the shots and toward the guard, tumbling nimbly across the carpet before springing back onto her feet within striking distance of the startled gunman. She wrenched the machete free, slicing right through the sash holding it to her hip, and swung it at the guard's arm.

Not wanting to maim the poor guy, whose culpability in Benoit's alleged crimes was unknown, she spun the machete in her grip and whacked his upper arm with the flat side of the blade. She delivered the blow with enough force to render the limb momentarily useless. His pistol went flying from his grip and bounced down the stairs beside them. Sydney spotted the first guard's gun lying on the carpet nearby and kicked it after the other one. It went off halfway down the steps, blowing a display of bottled love potions to smithereens.

Oops! Sydney thought.

Though disarmed, albeit not literally, the second guard remained a threat. He grabbed on to Sydney's throat with one hand and her right wrist with the other, holding the machete away from him. "Let go of the blade, *vèmin!*" he growled at her, practically spitting in her face. "Or I'll crush your pretty little neck!"

He was strong, Sydney noted uncomfortably, but not particularly adept when it came to hand-to-hand combat. After considering a number of possible countermoves, she went with a nonlethal option, kneeing him hard in the crotch. Given his efforts to throttle her, she didn't feel too bad about it. *Trust me,* she thought as her knee slammed upward into his private parts, *you're getting off easy.*

He grunted in pain, his agonized expression resembling that of a fish out of water. His grip on her throat loosened and she twisted free from his grasp, punching him in the stomach as she did so. He staggered backward, letting go of her wrist. A spinning side kick dropped him to his knees, the fight knocked out of him.

That took too long, Sydney thought unhappily. Fujiwara was getting away. Looking down the length of the hall, she watched him tug open the glass door, letting in a gust of hot air, and head out onto the balcony. Memories of Singapore flashed through her brain. *No way. You're not getting away from me this time.*

"Terry!" she shouted. "Wait for me!"

An alarm went off the minute the door swung open, a high-pitched siren that sounded like it could shatter glass. Agitated voices came from downstairs, and Sydney realized she could expect more company soon. Deftly avoiding the puddle of broken glass and rum, she chased after Fujiwara.

* * *

Gunshots rang out inside the temple, accompanied by the sound of shattered glass. Moments later a blaring siren sliced through the night, sending a chill down Dixon's spine.

Sydney!

"Show's over! Everybody out!" a flustered-looking salesclerk announced, and began herding the confused sightseers toward the front door of La Maison du Vodou. Dixon's concern and apprehension showed through his latex mask, but there was no need to conceal his anxiety. Unexplained alarms and gunfire would rattle anyone, not just a disguised intelligence operative.

What's happening upstairs? he agonized. Had Sydney been captured—or worse? Obviously she had not been able to slip in and out of the temple's upper reaches undetected, but how badly had the operation gone awry? One of the more serious disadvantages of APO's unofficial status was that Sydney could not flaunt a CIA badge to extricate herself from the situation; if contacted, the agency would disavow all knowledge of her activities.

Not that Benoit's men were likely to roll over in the presence of a badge anyway. They might well decide that it was easier to dispose of a federal agent than to tolerate any uninvited snooping, which put Sydney in a very hazardous situation, regardless of her government credentials—or lack thereof.

She's on her own, Dixon thought. *In more ways than one.*

Frustrated by his inability to come to Sydney's aid, he looked to see how Maya was reacting to the crisis. Would she attempt to go to Sydney's rescue?

Apparently not.

Still maintaining her guise as a tremulous old woman, Maya let herself be guided out of the gift shop and into the street outside. Dixon reluctantly followed her, resisting the temptation to run up the stairs to find Sydney instead. He spotted two guards lying sprawled upon the second-floor landing and drew comfort from the knowledge that Sydney was clearly putting up a fight. *Keep it up,* he urged her silently, wishing with all his heart that he were battling beside her at that very minute. *Don't let them get the better of you.*

"Thank you for visiting, sir!" the salesclerk chirped breathlessly, practically shoving him out the door. "Please come again!"

But not tonight obviously.

Outside, on Bourbon Street, the usual mob of celebrants crowded the French Quarter. Dixon kept a close eye on Maya, knowing how easy it would be to lose her in the rollicking festivities. He half expected her to wait outside the temple for Sydney, but instead she took off down the street, walking as quickly as her elderly disguise allowed. Unlike Dixon, she never even looked back.

He stayed about half a block behind her—no more, no less. He took frequent snapshots of the crowds and buildings in order to preserve his cover as an inconspicuous vacationer, while making sure Maya never wandered far from the viewfinder of his camera.

Turning off Bourbon, she headed down to the French Market, where she caught a cherry red streetcar on the new Canal Street Line. Dixon had to hustle to get onto the streetcar before it left with Maya, but he managed to climb aboard just in time. He remained standing at the rear of the car, waiting to see what stop Maya would get off at. Since the hotel she and Sydney were staying at was near the last stop on Canal Street, the streetcar was sort of a roundabout way to get there; it would have been easier just to walk back on Bourbon Street.

What's she up to? he wondered, highly curious to see what Maya would do now that she was temporarily free of Sydney's company. If she was going to slip her reins, and perhaps give herself away, now would be her perfect opportunity to do so.

Unless, of course, she suspected she was being followed.

Heat and humidity slapped across Sydney's face like a damp towel as she raced out onto the balcony. She heard a resounding splash and ran to the filigreed iron railing. Looking over the rail, she saw that the balcony overlooked the mud wrestling pit next door. Wooden bleachers flanked two sides of an enormous aluminum tub, which was filled knee-deep with thick brown mud. A noisy, mostly intoxicated audience packed the bleachers, laughing hysterically as a mud-covered Fujiwara climbed awkwardly out of the tub. A pair of mud-coated female wrestlers, their skimpy bikinis liberally splashed with ooze, glared at Fujiwara as he departed, apparently unhappy at having their thunder stolen by the unexpected drop-in.

A hanging cable clamped to the iron railing indicated exactly how Fujiwara had escaped La Maison du Vodou. Sydney guessed that he had lowered himself down the cable until he was only a few feet above the open tub. *Messy but effective*, she concluded. *Too bad I don't have time to do the same.*

Angry shouts and rapid footsteps erupted from the hallway behind her. A gunshot whizzed past her head, barely missing her skull. Sydney realized that she had overstayed her welcome.

And then some.

"Oh, hell," she muttered as she climbed up onto the railing and leaped from the balcony. She arced gracefully toward the waiting mud pit before landing with a splash in the muck below. The thick mud cushioned her fall to a degree, although her feet slid out from beneath her, causing her to land flat on her back in the mire. Flying mud sprayed the faces of the two female wrestlers.

Yuck! Sydney thought. After this mission Sloane was definitely going to owe her big-time. Wiping the mud from her face, she glanced up at the balcony, where Benoit's people, including the *houngan* himself, looked down on her with baffled

159

and outraged expressions. A temple guard drew his gun, only to be halted by the *houngan,* who apparently had serious reservations about the consequences of firing into the crowd below in front of dozens of witnesses.

The wiser head prevailed, and the trigger-happy guard put away his weapon. He gripped the iron rail in frustration, unable to do anything but glower menacingly at Sydney.

Good call, she thought as she scrambled clumsily to her feet, the cool mud oozing between her toes. She looked around for the exit, anxious to catch up with Fujiwara before he got too far ahead of her.

The upstaged wrestlers had other ideas, though. "What the hell?" one of the women bellowed. Sydney caught glimpses of blond hair, tattoos, and a pink bikini through the muck clinging to the wrestler's muscular figure. "You almost landed on top of me, you moron!" The woman turned to her equally splattered opponent. "C'mon, Darlene. Let's teach this hoodoo hoochie a lesson!"

"You said it, Bella!" the other woman said. This one appeared to be a redhead, although it was hard to tell with all the brown glop in her hair. She was taller, and more silicone enhanced, than her component. "Two against one is just the way I like it!"

The audience whooped enthusiastically at the prospect of yet more mucky mayhem. Bets were made on how long Sydney would last against the incensed wrestlers, with the odds not exactly running in her favor.

You have got to be kidding me! Sydney thought, appalled at this dismaying turn of events. She groped for the machete, only to realize that she had lost it somewhere beneath the sludge. So much for using the blade as a deterrent. . . .

"Look, I'm sorry about the intrusion," she began, backing slowly toward the rim of the tub. The slippery floor beneath her made a faster retreat problematic, and her light cotton dress was soaked through with mud, weighing her down. "I don't want trouble."

"Tough luck, sister!" Bella brayed. White teeth grinned at her from a mud-caked countenance. "We do!"

Great, Sydney thought. *I* so *do not have time for this.*

She stepped back and quickly assessed the situation. Chances were, Darlene and Bella lacked advanced martial-arts training, but she was outnumbered and on their turf. And a particularly gloppy turf at that.

This is a new one. In the past Sydney had engaged in hand-to-hand combat on everything from rooftops to glaciers, but never in a tub of gooey mud in front of a braying audience. She adopted a defensive stance, her weight on her forward leg, her open hands held up in front of her. *If only my profs at the university could see me now. . . .*

"How about that?" Darlene mocked her. "Looks like we've got some sort of Crouching Dragon on our hands!" She bent over and began circling Sydney in a clockwise direction, while Bella went the other way, trying to catch Sydney between them. "You're in the wrong place, karate girl! This here's New Orleans, not Jackie Chan land!"

Keep moving, Sydney reminded herself. It was important to keep both of her opponents in sight, preferably lined up and in each other's way. She bobbed and wove, being careful to maintain her footing on the mud-covered mat. *I have to hit them hard and fast,* she realized, *and get this fight over with ASAP.*

She couldn't let Fujiwara get away . . . again!

Out of the corner of her eye she saw Darlene nod at her partner, and she readied herself for Bella's attack. *No kicks,* she decided; on the slippery mat it would be too easy to lose her balance. *Stick to hand techniques.*

With a rebel yell the blond wrestler came charging at her from behind. Sydney adroitly side-stepped the lunge, so that the other woman grabbed only empty air. A back fist strike nailed Bella in the chin, and she toppled rearward into the muck.

She didn't get back up.

Startled gasps arose from the awestruck audience, followed by energetic whoops and hollers. Her newfound cheering section unnerved Sydney; she wasn't used to being applauded for trashing an opponent. *Usually whoever's watching is shooting at me.*

"Hey, voodoo babe!" Darlene yelled belligerently. "You think you're so slick? Get a load of this!"

Not wanting to lose track of her second adversary, Sydney turned quickly to see what Darlene was up to, only to spy a huge wad of mud flying at her face. The glop struck her head-on, hitting her mouth, nose, and eyes. Blinded, she sputtered in shock, spitting out a mouthful of thick brown sludge. She hurried to wipe the mud from her eyes, but Darlene had already moved in for the kill. The redhead's ridiculously huge breasts slammed into Sydney as the wrestler grabbed on to Sydney and threw her to the mat.

Takedown!

Shaking the last of the mud from her eyes, Sydney quickly rolled over onto her hands and knees in order to avoid being trapped on her back. Darlene was on top of her, though, trying to force Sydney's face down into the gunk. The redhead caught Sydney in a headlock, with one elbow crooked around Sydney's neck and her other hand pressing down hard on the back of the agent's head. "How'd you like the free facial, bitch?" Darlene trash-talked. Her hand kept sliding off Sydney's mud-slick hair, giving Sydney a little wiggle room. "Bet you didn't see that coming!"

Fine, Sydney thought, fed up. *I can play dirty too.*

She turned her head and sank her teeth into Darlene's fleshy upper arm. The redhead yowled in pain, loosening her grip. Sydney took advantage of the moment to jab her elbow into the other woman's artificially amplified cleavage.

It was like hitting medicine balls filled with Jell-O.

Darlene gasped loudly. She rolled off Sydney, clutching her chest. Sydney took the stunned wrestler out with a sideways kick to the stomach, then bounced back onto her feet. She felt something cold and metallic beneath her bare sole and realized it was her lost machete.

Of course. Now *I find it!*

Sydney found herself the last woman standing. A referee ran forward to offer her some sort of trophy. *There's a ref?* she thought in exasperation. *Where the heck have you been?*

Her murderous expression discouraged any potential well-wishers from detaining her as she raced through the front gate of the wrestling show into the street beyond. Startled tourists gaped in amazement as her mud-caked figure dashed onto the sidewalk looking like a zombie that had just crawled out of an unusually mucky grave. The wet sludge sluiced down her back and legs.

Bourbon Street at night was five times more crowded than it had been when she and Maya first visited it three days ago. Festive sightseers swarmed the sidewalks. Glowing old-time gaslights competed with garish neon signs advertising everything from hot jazz to nude girls. Laughter rose over the live music emanating from the open doorways of the nightclubs. Ice and alcohol sloshed in the ubiquitous go cups. The good times were definitely rolling, which didn't make Sydney's task any easier. "Hey, mud pie," a drunk frat boy hollered, one of many catcalls directed at the goo-drenched agent. "Want to get filthy with me?"

"You look like you need a hot shower, babe!" another jerk called out. "My place or yours?"

Ignoring the jeers and come-ons, Sydney scanned the busy street, trying frantically to spot Fujiwara. The dense pedestrian traffic blocked her view, while obliterating any trace of his muddy footprints. Which way had he gone? Had anyone seen him? *He couldn't have gotten far on foot,* she thought. *Not in the state he was in.*

A street performer wailed on a saxophone at the corner of Bourbon and Melusine, not far from the entrance of La Maison du Vodou. His instrument case lay open at his feet, collecting coins and bills from the strolling revelers. He looked as though he had been there for a while.

She ran up to him. "Excuse me," she said urgently, interrupting a bluesy rendition of "When the Saints Go Marching In." "Have you a seen a young Asian man covered in mud, like me?"

The musician gazed at her with amusement. "Lord, girl, you are a mess!" Sydney got the impression that she was the most entertaining sight he'd seen in a while. "Sure, I've seen your fella. I couldn't hardly miss him." He tilted his head toward Melusine Street, pointing northwest. "He went that way. If you hurry, you can still catch up with him."

That's the idea, Sydney thought. She made a mental note to drop a twenty-dollar bill into the saxophone player's case before she left New Orleans. "Thanks so much!"

She took off up the street as fast as she could. Her sodden dress felt like it had been dipped in concrete, but she didn't let it slow her. Her bare feet dodged broken glass and cigarette butts as she sprinted through clusters of ambling pedestrians. "Coming through!" she shouted, a filthy, mud-dripping apparition whom people gladly stepped to one side to avoid. Jeers and laughter followed her. "Out of the way!"

As she ran, she had to wonder what had become

of Maya. She hadn't seen her supposed partner in the street outside La Maison du Vodou, not that she'd had much time to look for her. A chill ran down her spine as she realized that she had no idea what Maya might be up to at this very minute. Granted, Dixon was presumably keeping an eye on her, but it still made her nervous to have Maya at large like this. *I'll have to search her carefully for any newly acquired weapons if and when I see her again. . . .*

Melusine was not quite as jam-packed as Bourbon Street, so Sydney found herself making slightly better time. A few muddy shoe prints had survived to mark the sidewalk ahead, suggesting that she was catching up with Fujiwara. The prints, which had been left behind by a pair of dirty sneakers, still looked fresh.

A gap opened up in the crowd, and Sydney spotted Fujiwara about a block ahead of her. The terrified hacker was running as though a blood-thirsty voodoo cult was after him, as he had every reason to imagine that it might be. Looking back over his shoulder, he spied Sydney chasing after him. She couldn't tell if he still had the Colt, but she hoped that he wouldn't risk firing into the mobbed streets. *He's a hacker, not a killer,* she reminded herself. Unlike his reputed fiancée.

Fear gave Fujiwara a fresh burst of speed, and he plowed through a knot of tipsy tourists, who hurled obscenities at him as he left them behind. A mime in Marcel Marceau makeup stepped in front of Sydney, apparently deeming her a prime target for satire, but she threw him into the open doorway of a Cajun restaurant. The smell of all-you-can-eat crawfish wafted into the street, tantalizing her taste buds.

She didn't waste her breath calling out to Fujiwara; that had never worked before. Without Maya to reassure him, Sydney figured she'd have to tackle Fujiwara to get him to listen to what she had to say. Given all he'd put her through this evening, she wasn't inclined to be gentle about it. Maya might have to get her fiancé back in slightly damaged condition!

Rue Melusine ended before the gates of one of the French Quarter's many downtown cemeteries. Looming stone vaults and mausoleums could be seen through the iron bars of the gates. A metal sign warned visitors not to enter the cemetery after dark, but this did not appear to deter Fujiwara. A gunshot rang out down the street, provoking frightened cries and gasps, as he used his Colt to blast apart the padlock sealing the gates. Rusty hinges screeched in protest as he hastily shoved open the gates and darted into the unlit cemetery.

Sydney charged in after him, ready to duck just in case he opened fire on her. She took shelter behind a crumbling marble tomb, then peered around the corner of the macabre edifice.

In the moonlight the cemetery looked like something out of an Anne Rice novel. Massive burial vaults, in various states of disrepair, rose from the weed-strewn ground, which was too far below sea level to permit underground burials. Spires and religious statuary crowned some of the larger mausoleums, which were massive enough to house entire families, while even the smaller tombs were the size of huts. The mazelike cemetery resembled a small town built expressly for the dead.

Had Fujiwara trapped himself by taking refuge here? Sydney methodically worked her way through the cemetery, using the various monuments for cover. Here and there *vevers* had been spray-painted on whitewashed granite walls. A dilapidated tomb had spilled a heap of loose bricks onto the ground. Sydney helped herself to a brick, intending to use it for self-defense if necessary. She heard Fujiwara's muddy sneakers squish near the back of the cemetery and headed in that direction.

I need to get to him fast, she thought, *before the local cops show up to arrest us for trespassing.*

By the time she reached the far end of the cemetery, however, the squishing noises had ceased. A high, spiked fence, which even Sydney would have had difficulty climbing, blocked any further exploration, but Fujiwara was nowhere to be seen. He appeared to have vanished into thin air, leaving Sydney alone in the gloomy atmosphere of the cemetery.

Fine, she thought. Despite having lost her quarry once again, Sydney wasn't too unhappy with the outcome of tonight's chase.

I know where to look for him now.

CHAPTER 8

LOS ANGELES

"No, seriously, that was a great move!" Eric Weiss enthused. "That guy never saw what hit him!"

"Thank you," Nadia Santos replied, "but it was nothing. Just a standard savate kick, that's all."

"Yeah, but the way you spun in the air and caught that vial of nerve gas at the same time . . ." A somewhat chunky young man with a pleasant disposition, Weiss held open the door at the end of the secret corridor. At thirty-eight, he was roughly fourteen years older than his exotically beautiful companion. "I'd never seen anything like it!"

The constant buzz of the APO bull pen greeted them as they returned to headquarters upon the completion of their mission in Guatemala. Their business clothes were rumpled from the long flight home, but their spirits were high, and with good reason; a well-known pharmaceutical company, which had been boosting its bottom line by covertly manufacturing sarin instead of vaccines, had just been put out of business . . . permanently. *A good day's work,* Nadia thought.

She was glad to be home, though, and was looking forward to a full night's sleep in her own bed. *Is Sydney still in town, or is she off on assignment somewhere?* The dark-haired young woman was eager to tell her sister about the success of her mission.

"I thought we made a pretty good team," Weiss continued. Nadia suspected that his fulsome praise of her performance was largely motivated by his ongoing infatuation with her. "What do you say we celebrate by going out for dinner later? I know this great Vietnamese place on Sunset."

"Maybe some other time," she said politely. "Nothing personal, I just want to go home and crash as soon as our debriefing is over." Noting the disappointed look on Weiss's face, she gave him an encouraging smile. "Another night for sure. I *love* Vietnamese."

In truth she hadn't entirely decided how she wanted to deal with her coworker's crush. Weiss was a nice guy and fun to flirt with, but she wasn't sure she was ready for a serious relationship these days. Her life had changed so much in the last year or so. . . .

She had lost a mother she never knew, but gained both a father and a sister. Well, a half sister, to be exact. She had left her old life in Argentina to forge a new existence in America. She had tried to put espionage behind her, only to find herself employed by a covert black-ops unit masterminded by Arvin Sloane, a pardoned international criminal—who just happened to be her long-lost father!

That was a lot to cope with in just a few months. Was it any wonder that she wanted to go slow before making any other major changes in her life?

Especially after what had happened to Pablo . . .

Her soulful ruminations were interrupted by the sight of Marshall Flinkman, who came rushing across the bull pen toward them. "You're back, thank goodness!" he exclaimed with more fervor than Nadia thought their return warranted. He was practically hopping in his frantic need to communicate with them. "Sloane needs to see you right away!"

The excitement in his eyes and voice alerted her that something was up. Her blood went cold, and all thoughts of calling it a day vanished from her mind.

Sydney, she thought. *What's happened to Sydney?*

Her father welcomed her back with a hug before updating her and Weiss on the crisis regarding Kestrel. "Sydney believes she has a lead on Fujiwara's whereabouts," he informed them from behind the monolithic desk in his private office. "And Dixon is keeping a discreet eye on Maya. I would feel more comfortable, though, with two more field agents on the scene."

"Of course," Nadia agreed readily. She was exhausted, but if Sydney needed backup, how could she say no? Even if she had wanted to, Nadia knew she wouldn't be able to relax knowing that her sister was in danger hundreds of miles away.

And working with Maya Rao definitely constituted danger; Nadia had never met the infamous assassin, but Maya's reputation was enough to make Nadia fear for Sydney's safety.

"When do we leave?" Weiss asked, not at all annoyed that Nadia had spoken for both of them. As she glanced over at him warmly, she noticed, as she always did, the faded scar on his neck. The telltale mark had both fascinated and disturbed her ever since she first learned its origin: Weiss had once been shot in the neck—and nearly killed—by none other than Irina Derevko.

Her mother.

And he still wants to date me? She shook her head slightly at the thought. Sometimes she was still amazed at just how complicated her life had become. *If nothing else, though, getting to know Sydney has made it all worthwhile.*

"Your plane leaves in two hours," her father said. He slid a pair of folders across the top of his desk. "These are your new aliases. I'll notify Dixon that he should expect you shortly."

Tired and jet-lagged, Nadia struggled to keep up. Everything was happening so fast.

New Orleans, here we come.

CHAPTER 9

EDINBURGH, SCOTLAND

Meg McQueen's Close was a narrow lane leading downhill from the Royal Mile to Market Street, some sixty feet below. A post office had been built over the top part of the close, so that Jack and Vaughn had to enter the medieval alley by means of a dimly lit tunnel leading under the newer building. Vaughn ducked his head to avoid the hissing steam pipes running along the ceiling.

It was a cool, drizzly night. Droplets of cold water ran down the back of his neck and underneath the collar of his brown turtleneck sweater. An umbrella tucked beneath his arm, he followed Jack through the claustrophobia-inducing passageway until they emerged at the top of a steep stairway leading down to the street below. Sooty stone buildings, which dated back to the Middle Ages, rose up on both sides of the steps, so that the close resembled a mountain chasm, no more than seven feet across. The ancient stones were cold and clammy to the touch.

As it was well past one in the morning, no lights shone in the curtained windows of the buildings flanking the stairs. Heavy clouds obscured what Vaughn could see of the sky, while a chilly wind blew up the steps, keening like a banshee. Given a choice, Vaughn decided, he would have preferred the Turkish steam room.

What time is it in New Orleans now? he wondered. According to Sloane, Sydney and Maya had moved on to the Crescent City in their pursuit of Terry Fujiwara, with Dixon discreetly shadowing their every move. He and Jack, on the other hand, had followed leads from Budapest to Scotland in their continuing efforts to verify Maya's story. So far the results had been maddeningly inconclusive. He hoped tonight's meeting would clear things up, one way or another.

Has Maya told us the truth? We need to find out, for Sydney's sake. He still didn't like the idea of Sydney's working hand in hand with the likes of Maya Rao. *She might as well be teaming up with Sark or Anna Espinosa.*

The drizzling rain was letting up, so Vaughn kept his umbrella closed as the two men carefully descended the rain-slick steps. His senses were alert, his muscles poised for action. A loaded Glock automatic pistol was holstered beneath his gray tweed jacket.

Like many of the back alleys of the city's Old Town, Meg McQueen's Close was reputed to be haunted. Legend had it that back in the 1600s the Black Death had forced the town council to wall up entire neighborhoods, trapping innocent residents inside their plague-ridden homes, in a desperate attempt to contain the pestilence. Some said the spirits of those condemned souls still haunted Edinburgh's narrow wynds and closes, even after all these centuries.

But it was not ghosts that Michael Vaughn was on guard against tonight. Certain men, he knew, were far more dangerous than any intangible wraith.

Ramsey Yaw was waiting for them on a cobble-stoned landing about halfway down the stairs. A hulking bodyguard, wearing a cheap suit one size too small, accompanied the portly Englishman, who was warmly (and stylishly) attired in a tailored Burberry trench coat. A silk fedora protected his receding hairline from the inclement weather.

"Ah, right on time!" he greeted the two American agents. He leaned forward, using his own umbrella as a cane. Fawn-colored calfskin gloves gripped the polished ivory handle. "What a dismal night! I certainly hope you two gentlemen intend to make it worth my while to have ventured outdoors in such blustery conditions."

Unlike Yevno Zubatov, Yaw was not overtly sinister in appearance. Ruddy faced and genial looking, he came across as an amiable sort, like a favorite uncle or the family doctor. You'd never guess that he was actually one of Europe's leading assassination brokers, responsible for arranging dozens of contract killings a year—for a substantial commission, of course.

Yaw's bodyguard inspected them both warily as his employer spoke. The meager dimensions of the landing meant that the four men were only a few paces apart. The burly guard made eye contact with Vaughn, who coolly returned his gaze.

"Thank you for agreeing to meet with us," Jack said. The senior Bristow wore a dark overcoat over his customary business suit. "You come highly recommended."

"I assure you my reputation is entirely justified," Yaw said with a laugh. "If you'll indulge me, Liam here"—he indicated the looming bodyguard—"needs to guarantee that our business remains strictly between us."

"Naturally," Jack agreed. He raised his arms so that Liam could roughly frisk him for any concealed wires or recording devices. Finding the older agent free of bugs, the bodyguard subjected Vaughn to a similar inspection. He grunted when he felt the Glock beneath Vaughn's jacket, as he had when he'd encountered Jack's gun, but once again raised no objection. It was to be expected that Jack and Vaughn would bring weapons to a meeting like this; Vaughn assumed that Liam was also armed, and possibly Yaw as well.

His task complete, the bodyguard stepped back and nodded at Yaw. "They're clean," he pronounced gruffly.

"Excellent!" his employer stated. Handing off his umbrella to Liam, he rubbed his gloved hands together greedily. "Now then, how can I assist you? I assume you have . . . a problem . . . that you would like taken care of? If so, I can think of any number of qualified professionals who are currently available."

Jack got right to the point. "Actually, we're interested in another contract you recently issued. The one concerning Maya Rao."

"I don't understand," Yaw said, his cheery bonhomie cooling down a notch or two, not unlike the weather. A flicker of suspicion crossed his broad face. "I understood that you were interested in acquiring my services."

"You were misinformed," Jack said brusquely. "We're looking for information, not to outsource a murder." He did not act at all apologetic for having approached Yaw under false pretenses. "Who hired you to put out the contract on Maya Rao's life?"

Yaw scowled, clearly irked that no new business was in the offing. "I have no idea what you're talking about," he stated firmly, in case someone was listening in via a parabolic microphone. "And even if I did, you must know that all such matters are absolutely confidential. Discretion is a fundamental aspect of my services, for which I am generously compensated."

Picking up on his employer's increasingly hostile attitude, Liam stiffened and assumed a more combative expression. Vaughn shrugged, as if the tiff between Jack and Yaw was of little personal concern to him. *Hey, I'm just along to ride shotgun,* his attitude suggested.

"Nevertheless," Jack insisted, "I'm afraid you need to make an exception in this instance. We're not leaving without the information we came for."

"Stay as long you want," Yaw said sourly, "but I no longer see any point in staying out here in the cold. I should have stayed home, where I was dry and warm." He held out his hand to his bodyguard. "My umbrella, Liam—"

"Here. Take mine," Vaughn interrupted. He abruptly jabbed the point of his umbrella into Liam's gut.

"Oomph!" the Scottish bruiser grunted, staggering backward toward the edge of the landing. Before either he or Yaw could strike back, Vaughn flipped the folded umbrella around and swung it like a baseball bat at Liam's head. The wooden handle cracked against the bodyguard's jaw. Stunned, he was unable to defend himself from the coup de grâce: Vaughn thrust the umbrella between the man's ankles and gave it a deliberate twist.

"Watch your step," he warned the bodyguard, even as Liam somersaulted backward down thirty feet of stairs. Cries of pain came from his tumbling body as he bounced off the slippery steps before landing in a heap at the bottom of the close. The agonized grunts and groans subsided, his crumpled body lying motionlessly in a muddy puddle. Blood slowly colored the water red.

Was he alive? Dead?

Vaughn couldn't bring himself to care.

"Effective," Jack Bristow observed. "You're not as restrained as you used to be."

Vaughn assumed that was meant as a compliment.

Taken aback by the sudden change in his fortunes, Yaw edged toward the steps behind him, but Vaughn moved swiftly to block his path. Yaw found himself trapped on the cramped landing, pinched between Jack and Vaughn. The younger agent drew his Glock to discourage any further attempts at escape. He reached into Yaw's coat and extracted a Walther PPK pistol, which Vaughn relocated to the pocket of his own jacket.

"Now then," Jack addressed Yaw calmly, as though nothing untoward had just occurred, "I believe you were about to tell me who put the price on Maya Rao's head."

Yaw's fleshy face quivered like gelatin. "I can't!" he pleaded. "He'd come after me for certain. My life wouldn't be worth a pence!"

He?

Vaughn wondered whom Yaw was referring to.

"That should not be your immediate concern," Jack informed the agitated assassination broker. Without warning, he smacked Yaw hard across the face. The back of his hand left a stinging impression on the other man's profile. Yaw's hat splashed down onto the wet cobblestones. "You need to worry about surviving the next five minutes."

"Bugger off, you American bastard!" Yaw snarled, asserting himself. "I'll have every hit man in the Northern Hemisphere after your hide!"

"Not before you tell me what I need to know." His face betraying not the slightest trace of pity or regret, Jack methodically went to work on Yaw. He kneed Yaw savagely in the stomach, then punched him in the jaw hard enough to dislodge a couple of teeth. Yaw spit blood and broken enamel onto

187

Jack's shoes, but Sydney's father was only warming up. He took hold of Yaw's right arm and smashed it against an iron handrail. Bone snapped audibly, sounding like a rifle shot.

Yaw opened his mouth to scream, but Jack clamped his hand over the man's bleeding lips. "One more time," he said. "Who put the contract out on Maya Rao?"

Vaughn watched the brutal interrogation without flinching. Once, Jack's methods would have bothered him, but that was before the Covenant stole Sydney away from him—and gave him Lauren in her place. His heart had grown a lot colder since then.

The mission is all that matters, he thought. *That and protecting Sydney.*

Yaw whimpered pitifully beneath Jack's hand. Tears flowed down his flushed red face, so that he resembled a bawling newborn. Jack released his grip.

"It was Benoit!" Yaw blubbered frantically. "Theophile Benoit!"

The voodoo guy? Vaughn thought. Sloane had briefed him and Jack on Benoit earlier that day. *The one whose name Sydney found in Fujiwara's hotel room?*

"Not the Baden Liga?" Jack pressed.

Yaw shook his head. Shaking like a leaf, he cradled his shattered arm. "No, no . . . it was Benoit. But he wanted me to put the word out that the Baden Liga were involved. Nothing definite, just hints and rumors." Bruises and broken teeth marred his features. "He paid extra for that."

And plenty, Vaughn guessed. Yaw had been playing a dangerous game; the Baden Liga might not like having their name taken in vain.

Vaughn exchanged a worried glance with Jack. Clearly Maya had not been telling them the full truth. Why would Benoit be out to kill her if she had been double-crossed by the Baden Liga?

Jack seemed determined to get to the bottom of the mystery. "Why does Benoit want Maya dead?" he demanded, placing his hand on Yaw's unbroken left arm. The other man cowered at the implied threat. "What's the connection between them?"

"I'm not entirely certain," Yaw admitted. He looked too frightened not to be telling them the truth. "But I've made some inquiries of my own, which lead me to suspect that—"

Before he could complete the sentence, a shot rang out from the top of the stairs. A bullet hole blossomed in Yaw's forehead and he toppled backward toward Vaughn, who instinctively reached out to catch him. The man's limp, dead weight made it instantly obvious that Ramsey Yaw was not going to be answering any more questions; the notorious assassination broker had just been assassinated.

But there was no time to reflect on the irony of the man's demise. Muzzles flared from the tunnel above, and more bullets plowed into Yaw's lifeless corpse. Sparks flew where stray shots ricocheted against the stone steps and walls.

They were under attack. . . .

German accents shouted to one another in the tunnel. *"Töten Sie sie! Lassen Sie sie entkommen nicht!"* Gunshots punctuated every guttural syllable.

The Baden Liga? Vaughn surmised. Apparently the infamous German terrorists had indeed identified the source of the rumors linking them to the death threat against Maya Rao. *God forbid,* he thought sarcastically, *that the Baden Liga should be accused of financing a ruthless murder.*

He dropped Yaw's body onto the wet cobblestones and fired back at the snipers with his Glock.

Beside him, Jack drew his own gun and added his fire to Vaughn's.

"Our position is untenable," the veteran agent noted, unrattled by Yaw's sudden execution. The smell of cordite filled the air as they exchanged fire with the faceless killers.

"Tell me about it," Vaughn said. The terrorists had the higher ground and possibly superior numbers. He and Jack were definitely in the wrong place at the wrong time—assuming, that is, that the snipers' primary target had indeed been Yaw.

An uncharacteristic gasp escaped Jack's lips. Vaughn looked down to see blood streaming from the other man's leg.

Jack had been hit!

Grimacing in pain, the elder agent looked like he was about to join Yaw on the ground. Vaughn hurriedly threw his arm under Jack's shoulder to hold him up, while simultaneously unleashing a salvo of covering fire from his Glock.

We're too exposed here, he realized. *We need to retreat, pronto!*

To his right a recessed alcove held a boarded-up doorway. A weathered sign above the niche indicated that the door had once led to a butcher's shop. *Appropriate,* Vaughn thought; he and Jack were in serious danger of becoming dead meat.

The shallow doorway offered a modicum of shelter from enemy fire, so he clumsily helped Jack into the alcove. They backed up against the nailed wooden planks as the snipers' bullets whizzed past them. Panting, Vaughn supported Jack's weight while firing around the corner at the shooters in the tunnel.

He spared a second to glance down at Jack's perforated leg. In the nocturnal gloom it was hard to judge the blood's color, but it appeared to be dark and venous, not brightly arterial. The fact that it was flowing and not spurting was also a good sign, suggesting that the bullet had not nicked a major artery. *A lucky break,* he acknowledged; still, he knew Jack required medical assistance as soon as possible.

But Jack seemed unconcerned about his injuries. "This is accomplishing nothing," he asserted through gritted teeth, his arm draped over the younger man's shoulders. Although pale from shock, Jack Bristow's face betrayed no emotion. "We need to update Sloane on the Benoit connection. Get word to Sydney that Maya is lying."

He's right, Vaughn thought, straining to keep Jack on his feet. *We don't have time for this, not while Sydney is partnered with that treacherous snake of an assassin.* He knew all about women like that. Lauren had been good at shedding crocodile tears too.

Gunfire continued to blaze from the top of the stairs, ricocheting off the steps and handrail. Vaughn had hoped that the faceless snipers would depart now that they had successfully murdered Yaw, but they didn't seem to be abandoning the gunfight. Had they identified him and Jack as American agents, or were they simply intent on eliminating two inconvenient witnesses?

Either way Vaughn didn't intend to cooperate. He quickly scoped out the available escape routes. From where he stood, it was quickly apparent that there were only three ways to go: up, down, or across.

Up was not an option; that's where the bad guys were. A suicidal charge into hostile fire was not going to do him—or Sydney—any good.

Down wasn't much better. There were at least thirty feet of narrow steps between him and the street below. Even if he didn't have to transport a wounded man, there was no way he could reach the bottom of the close before taking an avalanche of bullets in the back. Chances were, they'd both end up dead at the foot of the stairs, alongside Yaw's lifeless bodyguard.

That left across, where Vaughn spotted another doorway on the other side of the landing, beyond Yaw's bleeding corpse. Unlike the entrance behind him, the opposing door was merely locked, not boarded up with plywood planks. If he could make it across the landing, he might be able to force the door open.

Sounds like our best bet, he decided.

But how was he supposed to traverse the no-man's-land the narrow landing had become? He and Jack would be in clear sight of the snipers above.

Resting Jack against his shoulder, he peered around the corner and up at the murky tunnel running beneath the post office. He could barely make out the snipers, who remained hidden in the shadowy depths of the tunnel, with only the intermittent flashing of their gun muzzles revealing their presence. There seemed to be three of them, but Vaughn couldn't be sure.

His gaze fell on another set of steam pipes, running along the upper lip of the tunnel, above the flaring guns. *There's an idea,* he thought.

Leaning out farther, he aimed his Glock at the pipes and squeezed the trigger. A barrage of bullets blasted the rusty pipes apart. Billowing clouds of hot steam spewed from the punctured conduits like the angry breath of a newly roused dragon. *"Verdammen sie!"* shouted an angry voice as the scalding vapor filled the mouth of the tunnel, hiding it from view.

Vaughn nodded in satisfaction. *It's now or never,* he realized. Moving briskly, he carted Jack across the bloodstained landing, taking care not to trip over Yaw's crumpled body. The crucial doorway loomed before him, a FOR RENT sign posted behind a glass window in the pine door. Vaughn shot apart the lock, then kicked the door in with as much force as he could muster. Under the circumstances, the darkened premises beyond looked more inviting than a five-star hotel.

He half dragged, half carried Jack into the abandoned space, which had apparently once belonged to a clothing shop. Naked mannequins, clothed only in dust, kept silent watch over the barren establishment. Torn and faded posters advertised cashmere sweaters and scarves.

Vaughn searched the deserted store for a back exit of some sort. He could still hear the released steam hissing outside, but it was already dying away. He listened avidly for the sound of footsteps on the stairs. Had the terrorists given up at last, satisfied with having taken out Yaw?

Assume the worst, he advised himself. *No doubt Jack would agree.*

He aimed his Glock at the breached front door, only to discover that he was out of ammo. Rather than take the time to reload, he retrieved the confiscated Walther from his pocket and fired out the open doorway to discourage pursuit. The shots echoed loudly against the walls of the shop.

"If necessary," Jack told him, "you have to leave me behind." He pulled away from Vaughn, trying to stand up on his own, but his injured leg betrayed him; grunting in pain, he sagged against the younger agent. "It's vital that you escape and warn Sydney."

"We haven't reached that point yet," Vaughn said. He was worried about Sydney too, but he didn't think she would want him to abandon her father, no matter how strained their relationship

was. He knew what it was like to lose a father. . . .
"We're both getting out of here right now."

A curtained doorway divided the front of the shop from the storeroom beyond. Vaughn helped Jack through the curtain and between the aisles of barren shelves until they found a back door leading to an interior elevator.

Merci, Vaughn thought, momentarily reverting to his French roots. Assuming the elevator was still running, it provided them with an alternative route out of Meg McQueen's Close. Once they made it to a major thoroughfare, like High or Market Street, they should be safe; he couldn't imagine that the terrorists were going to pursue them in such public venues.

Part of him regretted that the snipers were going to get away scot-free, but that couldn't be avoided. The Baden Liga could be dealt with on another day. Right now his priorities were clear: He had to get Jack the medical assistance he needed, then update APO on what they had just learned about Maya.

Despite his own pressing circumstances, he couldn't help worrying about Sydney. If Maya had lied to them about who was really after her, what else might she be concealing? And did the Baden Liga have anything to do with Kestrel after all?

Be careful, Sydney, he mentally beseeched her. In his mind's eye he saw Maya Rao sneaking up on Sydney from behind, a gleaming knife in her hand.

Don't turn your back to her!

CHAPTER 10

SAINT LOUIS CEMETERY NO. 4
NEW ORLEANS

By day the antique cemetery was only slightly less creepy than it had been the night before. The crumbling vaults continued to hold their air of mystery and the macabre, despite the glaring sunlight. Depending on their age and state of repair, the tombs ranged in color from sooty gray to pristine white. In places, red brick showed through crumbling whitewashed plaster. Weeds sprouted from the gabled roof of a neglected stone mausoleum. Rubble littered the crisscrossing walkways between the tombs. Palm trees swayed along the iron fence enclosing the cemetery.

Candles, flowers, playing cards, and other offerings rested in front of many of the tombs, some of which bore chalk marks in the shape of *X*s. The chalked crosses meant that such tombs held the bones of a deceased voodoo leader whom cultists still appealed to for supernatural assistance; each chalked *X* represented a boon requested by a hopeful supplicant.

I could use a little help locating Kestrel, Sydney thought, adjusting her sunglasses. *Too bad I didn't bring any chalk or sacrificial gifts.*

"Nearly eighty percent of New Orleans lies below sea level," a tour guide explained, "which made underground burials pretty much impossible back in the old days. One heavy rain and, voilà, the coffins came floating up to the surface!"

A small throng of tourists chuckled at the grotesque image. Although the Quarter's cemeteries were open to the public during the day, it was considered unsafe to wander them alone. Sydney wasn't particularly worried about getting mugged—she figured she and Maya could take care of themselves—but why attract unwanted attention? It was just easier to tour the cemetery as part of a group.

At least until they found what they were looking for.

In tourist garb, complete with sunglasses, wigs, and cowboy boots, they covered the same ground Sydney had explored the night before. This time Sydney was better equipped, however. Her Beretta rested snugly in her purse, while her green thermal sunglasses allowed her inquisitive gaze to penetrate the brick and stone walls of the tombs.

"Any luck yet?" Maya asked.

To her relief, Sydney had found the other woman waiting for her back at their hotel room when she returned from the cemetery the night before. According to Dixon, who had kept Maya under surveillance all the way back to the hotel, the Indian assassin had done nothing more suspicious than take a streetcar ride after she and Sydney had parted company at La Maison du Vodou, aside from ordering room service at APO's expense. Marshall, who was carefully monitoring all calls to and from the hotel, had not reported any irregularities either; Maya had not attempted to contact anyone in Sydney's absence.

"Not yet," Sydney whispered. "He's here, though. You can count on it."

Tuning out the guide's spiel, she continued to scan the tombs via her X-ray glasses. As expected, most of the vaults contained nothing but decomposing bones, along with the occasional lizard or rat, but Sydney was patient; the tour was just reaching the rear of the cemetery, where she had lost Fujiwara several hours earlier.

Her gaze fell on a moderate-size tomb, slightly larger than the average toolshed, with whitewashed stone walls and a peaked roof. A marble slab sealed the entrance to the vault, while an inscription above the doorway identified the tomb as belonging to the Toussaint family. Often, Sydney knew, the same tomb was used to inter multiple relatives; the hot, humid environment meant it took only about a year or so for a corpse to decompose entirely, freeing up the space for a newer occupant.

Kind of an icky notion, but practical.

From the outside the Toussaint tomb looked indistinguishable from the others surrounding it, except for something that only Sydney was in a position to notice. Unlike the other tombs, this one resisted her thermal sunglasses; its walls read as completely opaque. Clearly, it had been deliberately insulated to foil any sort of invasive scan.

But who would be paranoid enough to do something like that?

Sydney smiled and nudged Maya, nodding at the tomb in question. *Good try, Terry*, she thought, *but you outsmarted yourself this time.*

She and Maya ducked behind the nearest mausoleum, letting the tour group move on without them. She eyed the shielded stone vault triumphantly.

Got you now.

Across the street from the front gates of the cemetery a wizened harmonica player performed on the sidewalk. A battered tan raincoat hung loosely on his slender frame. Braided dreadlocks tumbled onto his shoulders. Passersby tossed change into the battered felt hat at the street performer's feet, rewarding a merely adequate rendition of "Blue Bayou."

The trick, Dixon thought, *is to play well enough to be credible, but not so impressively that you risk drawing a crowd that might interfere with your surveillance operation.* As it happened, he had no idea how to play the harmonica, but Marshall had obligingly supplied him with one that played itself. Adjusting the quality of the music had been the biggest challenge.

"I've always liked that song," Marshall commented in his ear. "What's really weird, though, is that there's a parallel universe out there where Linda Ronstadt became first lady of the United States. Because she was dating Jerry Brown, you know?"

Dixon let Marshall ramble while he concentrated on "playing" the harmonica. His face itched beneath his new latex mask. In order to avoid raising Maya's suspicions, last night's disguise had been replaced by a whole new alias. So far it appeared to be working; Maya had paid no attention to the seemingly innocuous harmonica player when she and Sydney arrived at the cemetery hours before. Now he watched the entrance intently, waiting for them to emerge. His right foot tapped along with the melody emanating from his instrument.

He couldn't help wondering what his children would think if they saw him in his current disguise. Would they be mortified to see their father performing for small change? He made a mental note to check on them after he went off duty tonight; the worst part of being a field agent again was being separated from his kids so often. He wished that he could spend more time with them, especially now that their mother was gone.

I'm doing my part to keep them safe, he

reminded himself, *so that they can grow up in a country secure from terrorism and hostile powers.* This wasn't just a rationalization for his frequent absences; it was the truth. *My kids—and the country—will be safer once Kestrel has been recovered.*

"You stink, man!" a harsh voice interrupted his reverie. "What kind of dirge is that? Play something more lively."

Intent on the cemetery gates across the street, Dixon hadn't noticed the stranger approach until the man was practically on top of him. *Sloppy,* he reproached himself. Looking around, Dixon discovered that an entire pack of husky-looking men were closing in on him.

There were five of them, all young and muscular, with cold eyes and cruel smiles. Before Dixon even had a chance to react, they surrounded him on the sidewalk, hemming him in with their shoulders, blocking off his escape routes. He didn't see any weapons, but that didn't mean the men weren't armed.

"Everybody's a critic," he said lightly, lowering his harmonica. His breezy tone concealed a growing sense of apprehension. *Have I been made?* he worried. Were these Benoit's men—or just a bunch of young toughs looking for trouble? Either way he doubted they were all that interested in his music. "Any requests?"

"Yeah," a second man spoke up. His distinct Haitian accent was a bad omen. "How about 'The Staying Out of People's Business Blues'?"

"Don't think I know that one, mister." Dixon kept playing his part, hoping to undermine whatever suspicions the men might be harboring. He had his service pistol hidden beneath the wrinkled raincoat, but he was unsure whether he could draw it before the men piled on him. His martial-arts training might give him a chance, but again the odds were against him, especially if any of these men proved to be experienced fighters. For the moment his best strategy was to stay in character and try to brazen the encounter out, while hoping that Marshall would realize that he was in trouble. "How 'bout a little Dixieland jazz?"

"Whatever," a third man said mockingly. "Time for a little donation first." He reached into his pocket and threw a handful of something into the hat on the ground. The objects clattered instead of jingled; they obviously weren't coins.

"I figure this is just what you deserve. Isn't that right, old man?"

Dixon glanced down at the hat. Bleached white chicken bones lay scattered atop his meager collection of coins and dollar bills. Straight from La Maison du Vodou?

Typical bogeyman tactics, he appraised. This had Benoit written all over it. Dixon heard one of the men come up behind him and braced himself for action. The harmonica dropped from his fingers into the waiting hat. *So much for talking my way out of this.*

"Outrigger?" Marshall sputtered via the earpiece. "What's happening? I don't like what I'm hearing!"

Neither do I, Dixon thought. "Condition red!"

That was all he had time to say to headquarters. His attacker tried to throw an arm around his neck, but Dixon grabbed on to the man's wrist and expertly flicked him over his shoulder into the man in front of him; there was a reason Dixon was ranked as a black belt in kung fu. The two men crashed to the pavement before him, even as their companions charged Dixon from both sides.

A forceful kick to the abdomen sent the man on

his left staggering backward, but that still left two more opponents to contend with. Dixon reached for his gun, only to have another man seize his arm and yank it behind his back before he could reach the grip of the pistol. Breaking the hold almost instantly, Dixon jabbed his elbow into the man's jaw, but by now his earlier foes had scrambled to their feet again.

Four against one, they attacked Dixon in unison. A fist slammed into his face, knocking loose his false teeth, while a vicious blow to his kidneys caused him to gasp in pain. The largest of the men, who looked big enough to be a linebacker, grabbed on to him from behind, pinning Dixon's arms to his sides. Another man punched him in the groin, and he would have doubled over if not for the massive arms wrapped around his torso. Someone reached beneath his raincoat and relieved Dixon of his gun. An upraised hand slapped him hard across the face.

Dazed, Dixon was unable to free himself from the big man's bear hug. He could only stand there, trapped, as the original speaker stepped in front of him and held up a closed fist before the prisoner's face. Dixon readied himself for another blow, but instead the gang member opened his fist, exposing a handful of gray powder on his palm.

"Have a little grave dust on me."

He blew the powder into Dixon's face. The captured agent tried to hold his breath, but it was too late. The finely ground particles invaded his nose and lungs.

The powder took effect almost instantly. His vision blurred and a sudden dizziness came over him. His legs turned to rubber and he sagged helplessly in the grip of his foes. He felt a tingling in his extremities, followed by a pronounced numbness. *Some sort of neurotoxin,* he guessed. Perhaps a variant of the infamous "zombie powder" used by voodoo sorcerers?

He struggled to keep his eyes open, but his lids felt like they were weighted down with lead. The voices of his assailants seemed to come from miles away. Someone produced a bottle of rum and doused his clothing with its contents, so that he reeked of booze. "No problem, folks," he heard one of the men address some concerned tourists. "Our uncle here has just had a little too much to drink, you know? We're going to help him home now."

No! Dixon appealed to the onlookers. *Don't listen to them!* His tongue refused to cooperate, however, and his desperate pleas never made it beyond the groggy interior of his skull. He was being abducted and he couldn't even call for help, let alone communicate with APO. He just hoped Marshall was getting this all on tape.

His head swam in the encroaching darkness. He barely heard a pair of heavy footsteps approach the men, followed by a deep bass voice with a rich Haitian accent:

"Good work. You three, take him back to the mansion. The rest of you, follow me. I have a sudden urge to pay my respects to the dead."

Powerful arms hoisted Dixon beneath his shoulders. Hanging limply between two of Benoit's men, he felt himself being dragged away from his post outside the cemetery. As concerned as he was about his own fate, he was just as worried about what might happen to Sydney in his absence. She was on her own, with no one to watch her back, and she didn't even know it.

Forgive me, Sydney . . . and watch out!

Hours after all the sightseers and civilians had gone home, Sydney and Maya kept watch over the suspiciously impervious tomb. They hid behind a neighboring monument, while peering around the corner at the Toussaint family vault. The sun was sinking toward the horizon, but the extreme heat gave no sign of abating. It was going to be another steamy night in New Orleans.

"What are we waiting for?" Maya asked irritably. Patience, Sydney had gathered, was not the other woman's strong suit. She fanned herself beneath the marginal shade of a gnarled dogwood. "If you really think Terry is holed up in that bone shed, let's open it up."

"Forget it," Sydney stated. "Who knows what kind of booby traps or hidden escape tunnels he might have in there?" To be honest, she was tempted to check out the fortified tomb as well, but after due consideration she didn't want to give Fujiwara another chance to get away from them. "Better to play stakeout instead."

If her suspicions were correct, the hacker would have to emerge from his sanctuary eventually.

"It's your call," Maya agreed grudgingly. "I'm just eager to see Terry again."

Sydney stretched her limbs while munching on a protein bar to keep up her strength. Frankly, she still had her doubts regarding the other woman's supposed relationship with Fujiwara. Using Maya's name had not helped Sydney win the man over so far; was that because he simply didn't believe her when she claimed to be allied with Maya, or was Maya lying about having won the nervous hacker's trust?

We'll find out soon enough, I guess.

Dusk was setting in when a jarring noise disturbed the sepulchral stillness of the deserted cemetery. Sydney exchanged a meaningful look with Maya, then raised a finger to her lips. Her heart racing, she stealthily peeked around the corner of their funereal hiding place. She drew her Beretta from her purse.

Sure enough, the marble slab covering the entrance to the Toussaint tomb slid open before Sydney's eyes. The eerie sight sent a chill down her spine, even though she knew there was nothing at all supernatural about this seeming resurrection. A flashlight beam issued from the open cavity, searching the area in front of the tomb. Moments later a shadowy figure crept out of the vault.

"Freeze!" Sydney shouted, stepping out from behind the corner of the other tomb. She aimed her Beretta squarely at the refugee emerging from the vault. Her high-tech sunglasses compensated for the murky light, revealing that the figure was indeed Fujiwara, clad entirely in black once more, his Colt automatic pistol thrust into his belt. A black backpack hung from his scrawny shoulders.

Instinctively he swung his flashlight beam toward Sydney. His frightened eyes widened in recognition.

"Who are you?" he blurted out. "How did you find me?"

There would be time enough for introductions later. "The gun," she directed him firmly, gesturing at the Colt. "Take it out . . . slowly."

"Sure. Fine. W-whatever you say," he stammered, swallowing hard. Complying with Sydney's instructions, he removed the gun from his belt. His right eye twitched and he winced in pain. "Just don't shoot."

Sydney didn't intend to. "Eject the clip," she ordered, "then toss the gun over there." She pointed at a scraggly patch of grass several feet to her left, between two imposing monuments. "Now toss the clip back that way," she added, indicating the opposite direction. "And chuck the backpack back into the tomb while you're at it."

Fujiwara did as he was told.

"That's better," she announced. "Now stay where you are."

She circled around Fujiwara in order to approach the open doorway to the tomb. Curiosity, as well as the need to make sure that no one else was lurking there, compelled her to peek inside the vault.

Oh, my God, she thought.

The interior of the tomb had been converted into a state-of-the-art panic room. Ceramic tiles insulated the walls and ceiling, shielding the vault from exterior scans while also soundproofing the chamber to prevent anyone from hearing Fujiwara moving inside. A plastic tarp hid the dirt floor underneath, and a futon rested on the tarp, along with one-gallon bottles of distilled water, a six-pack of generic cola, empty pizza boxes, and multiple laptops, cell phones, and computer disks. A UFO calendar hung on one wall, next to a *Space Vixens* poster. Sci-fi paperbacks littered the floor. Dirty laundry was piled in one corner, a few paces away from a small portable commode.

All the comforts of home, she thought. *More or less.*

She quickly determined that no one else, living or otherwise, was hiding amid the clutter. "Very impressive," she commented, wondering what Fujiwara would think of APO's secret headquarters beneath the Los Angeles subway system. "No wonder you were so hard to find."

"Who are you?" he repeated anxiously. He massaged his temple with his free hand, obviously fighting a migraine. "What do you want from me?"

Sydney wondered why Maya had not yet emerged from their hiding place. "I'm here to help you," she informed him, "just like I keep telling you." She gave him a friendly smile, but the petrified hacker could not look past the pistol in her grip.

I was afraid of this, she thought.

A modest horizontal tomb, topped by a flat marble slab, was laid out behind her. About the size of a picnic table, the granite sepulchre came to her waist. A terra-cotta vase filled with wilting roses rested at the foot of the tomb.

Sydney laid her gun on top of the slab. "Look, you've got to trust me," she said, showing him her empty hands. She stepped away from the Beretta. "I'm just after Kestrel . . . and you're my best lead."

Fujiwara looked uncertain. Hope warred with suspicion in his wary expression. "You still haven't told me who you are," he pointed out.

"Call me Eleanor," she told him, using the alias she'd adopted for this mission. "Eleanor Singer." She hated lying to Fujiwara at the same time she was trying to win his trust, but she wasn't about to reveal her real name to a relative stranger, especially one of dubious affiliation. "I'm with the authorities," she said vaguely, figuring that Maya would just assume she was lying. The fewer people who knew about APO's link to the CIA, the better.

"I don't trust the authorities!" he exclaimed. "They've been trying to silence me for years."

About the whole UFO thing? she thought. She couldn't believe Fujiwara was still worried about something so silly. *Says the girl whose face is on a six-hundred-year-old prophecy,* her memory reminded her sarcastically. *Who knows what Kendall has tucked away at Project Black Hole? . . .*

But that wasn't her problem today.

"Seems to me you don't have any choice." She looked him squarely in the eye, trying to convey both concern and sincerity. "I could be wrong, but my impression is that you're in way over your head this time. Trust me, there are worse people than the Feds looking for you now."

"You can say that again," Maya broke in, stepping out from the shadows at last. She smirked at Sydney and Fujiwara, like a cat that had just cornered a mouse. "Hello, Terry. You've been playing very hard to get."

The look on his face was not that of a man reunited with his long-lost love. Both bitterness and despair could be heard in his voice. "Maya!"

I knew it! Sydney thought. Maya had been lying all along!

With the speed of a striking cobra, the Indian woman dashed forward and snatched Sydney's gun off the marble slab. She aimed the Beretta at them. "Very sloppy, Sydney," she clucked at her American partner. "You're making this far too easy for me."

Fujiwara glared accusingly at Sydney. "And you said I could trust you . . . *Eleanor*?" He spit out the alias like a curse word. "But no, you're just like her, aren't you, *Sydney*?"

"I'm not with her, Terry," she replied grimly. "Not really." She eyed Maya with contempt. "So, I take it the wedding plans are off? And here I was so looking forward to being a bridesmaid."

Maya flaunted her engagement ring while keeping Sydney and Fujiwara at bay with the Beretta.

"A nice touch, don't you think? You should know by now that the secret to a good cover story lies in the details."

"I don't need a lecture from you on deceit," Sydney declared. She turned away from Fujiwara to confront the other woman directly. "Now what, Maya? Were you out to kill or capture Terry this whole time?"

Maya shrugged. "The latter if possible, the former if necessary. Terry's computer know-how is a valuable commodity, provided he's kept under control, but he's also too big of a loose end to leave dangling. One way or another he needed to be dealt with." She sighed theatrically. "None of which would have been necessary, of course, if he hadn't gotten away from me after we hijacked Kestrel together." She sneered at her so-called fiancé. "That was very uncooperative of you, Terry."

"You lying bitch!" he yelled at her, anger overcoming trepidation. "You used me!"

"Finally figured that out, did you? I must admit you did a good job of going underground. You had my associates and me stumped." She gave Sydney a mocking bow. "Thanks for tracking him down for me. I knew I could count on you."

"And I knew you'd take the bait," Sydney declared.

Heedless of the Beretta in Maya's hand, she charged at her rival. Maya squeezed the trigger repeatedly, but nothing happened. She stared in frustration at the unresponsive gun. "What the . . . ?"

You really think I'd be so careless as to leave a weapon just lying around for you? Sydney thought, closing the distance between her and Maya. The modified Beretta was the latest thing in personal firearms: a "smart gun" that responded only to her individual grip—and no one else's. *I figured you'd go for it if I gave you the chance.*

Now she knew for certain what Maya was really after.

Hoping to reclaim the gun, Sydney tried to kick it out of Maya's hand, but Maya nimbly ducked beneath the kick. She leaped to one side, facing off against Sydney across a swath of grass. "After this?" she taunted, holding up the Beretta. Before Sydney could stop her, she drew back her arm and hurled the gun over the iron fence surrounding the cemetery. "So much for that!"

"Fine with me," Sydney said, assuming a fighting stance, her arms raised defensively, her right leg forward. Maya matched her pose, so that they appeared like mirror images of each other. "Let's do this the hard way."

Going on the offensive, Sydney lunged forward and threw a karate chop at Maya's head. Maya parried the blow with her left arm, wincing as she did so. Sydney followed up with a left jab that slammed into Maya's face, knocking it to one side. Maya's faux blond tresses whipped about as she spun with the blow and twirled around to smack Sydney across the face. The green thermal sunglasses flew from Sydney's nose, shattering against the corner of a nearby mausoleum.

She counterattacked, throwing a punch at Maya, who blocked it easily. Out of the corner of her eye Sydney saw Fujiwara hesitating on the sidelines. His gaze darted between his panic tomb and the distant gates of the cemetery, as if uncertain which way to flee. He looked dazed, unable to keep up with the rush of events.

"Get out of here, Terry!" Sydney shouted. She didn't want to lose him again, but it was more important that he get away from Maya. "Run for it!"

"Don't you dare!" Maya threatened him in turn. She spun first one way, then another, chopping at

Sydney with the edge of her palm, while the American agent dodged and parried rapidly. Maya used her diamond engagement ring as a weapon, slashing at her enemy's skin. Bloody scratches streaked Sydney's forearm. "I'm warning you!"

Her menacing tone had the opposite of the desired effect. Scared out of his shell-shocked state, Fujiwara bolted for freedom, vanishing into the maze of closely packed tombs. He took his flashlight with him, leaving only the rising moon to illuminate the pitched battle between the two women.

Maya scowled angrily as she watched Fujiwara escape. *"Gote!"* she cursed in Hindi.

Sydney deflected another furious blow, pushing Maya's arm down with her own and opening the other woman up for a backhanded strike from the right. Flesh and bone connected with Maya's exotic features, causing the assassin's head to snap backward. A pained grimace replaced the scowl.

That'll teach her to play the grieving fiancé, Sydney thought vindictively. Obviously all of Maya's tearful displays had been an act put on for Sydney's benefit; knowing that Maya had deliberately been playing with her emotions made Sydney all the more determined to kick Maya's butt. *And to think I was starting to feel sorry for her!*

With Fujiwara out of the picture, Sydney was able to concentrate fully on her heated struggle with Maya. The cramped confines of the cemetery restricted her moves, but Sydney was up for the fight. Her Krav Maga training, developed by the Israeli special forces, had prepared her for hand-to-hand combat in a wide variety of environments.

Maya's own technique, she knew from past experience, was based on Gatka, a distinctive martial-arts style practiced by the Sikhs of northern India. Like Sydney, however, Maya blended in moves from other disciplines as well, to keep from being too predictable.

It's been a decade since we last dueled, Sydney reminded herself. *She's sure to have picked up some new tricks.*

Then again, so have I.

Recovering from Sydney's backhand, Maya grabbed on to her opponent's arm with both hands and swung Sydney into the bricked-up doorway of a run-down tomb. The jarring impact knocked the breath from Sydney, while causing the neglected masonry to partially collapse, leaving a gaping hole in the brickwork. Sydney caught a glimpse of the stygian blackness inside the vault.

"Sydney, meet bricks," Maya mocked her. She spit a mouthful of blood onto the ground. "Bricks, meet Sydney!"

With no time to catch her breath, Sydney pushed off from the battered tomb and whacked Maya in the side of the head with her fist, throwing the other woman off-balance. Stumbling, Maya almost hit the earth, but instead she sprang up at Sydney, kicking out at her legs.

Not so fast, Sydney thought. She jumped above Maya's kick, so that the assassin's leg passed harmlessly beneath her. Maya tried again as Sydney came back down, but this time Sydney ducked beneath the kick. She kicked back at Maya, who seized hold of her leg and shoved it aside. Sydney twirled, attempting to catch Maya on the second go-round, but the other woman's reflexes were too fast; she seized Sydney's leg and used it to flip the American agent onto her back.

"Nice move," Sydney commented. She rolled away from Maya and got back onto her feet.

"Thanks," Maya replied. A flying kick missed Sydney by inches. "I thought you'd like it."

Both women were breathing heavily now. Grunts punctuated every punch and kick, along with the smacking of limb against limb. Sydney had fought against Maya before, of course, with mixed results. In Calcutta she had decked Maya with a running wall kick, only to be chased off by her Zero Defense buddies. In Zurich they had dueled atop a speeding bullet train, only to have the fight interrupted when the train derailed. In Rio, Maya had come out on top, dislocating Sydney's arm, although Sydney had managed to escape (barely!) by hitching a ride on a Carnival float. In Nepal, Sydney had thrown Maya off a ledge onto a glacier, but apparently that hadn't been enough to kill her.

And then there was that damn camel in Pushkar. . . .

Her back against the side of a stucco-covered tomb, Sydney had no choice but to charge at her enemy. They grappled together, their straining faces only inches apart, shifting their holds with blinding speed as each strove to gain an advantage over the other. Sydney's ankle banged into a heap of rubble, and she fought not to lose her footing. They spun each other around, like two kids playing ring-around-the-rosy, until the centrifugal force tore them apart. Sydney stumbled back a few steps, then hurled herself feetfirst at Maya.

Contact!

The sole of her cowboy boot slammed into Maya's chest, sending her flying backward onto the grass before the horizontal tomb. Sydney charged forward to deliver another kick, even as Maya frantically scrambled to her feet, right behind the vase of roses.

Thinking fast, Maya kicked the vase at Sydney, who threw up her arms barely in time to keep the terra-cotta missile from crashing into her face. The vase exploded against Sydney's forearm, producing a burst of jagged fragments that drove Sydney backward, halting her momentum. She jerked her head to the side to protect her eyes from the debris.

But Maya wasn't done yet. A plate of grilled peanuts had been left as an offering before a chalk-marked tomb. Maya snatched up the china plate and threw it like a Frisbee at her foe.

The flying plate clipped Sydney in the forehead, opening up a cut above her right eye. Blood streamed down her face as Sydney teetered unsteadily on her heels.

Maya pressed her attack. Circling around to the

end of the horizontal tomb, she jumped up and ran diagonally across the length of the marble slab before leaping through the air at Sydney. Maya's weight barreled into Sydney like an animated battering ram.

"Ufgh!" Sydney gasped as she hit the ground hard. Her teeth slammed shut on her tongue. She tasted blood.

Maya landed on top of Sydney. She sat up quickly, straddling Sydney's waist, and drew back her right fist, ready to deliver a killing blow.

"Hah!" Maya laughed heartlessly. Her dark eyes gleamed in the moonlight. "I always knew I'd end up on top!"

Sydney grabbed Maya's left arm and rolled abruptly to the side, throwing the assassin off her. Maya yelped in pain as her bandaged left shoulder slammed down onto a concrete plinth.

That's right, Sydney remembered. *The bullet wound. I need to remember that.* Against an opponent like Maya the slightest advantage could mean the difference between life and death.

Panting and covered in sweat, the two women climbed to their feet, less than a yard apart. Hissing like a snake, Maya clutched on to Sydney's collar and swung her into the same timeworn brick doorway that Sydney had collided with earlier. This time the disintegrating mortar gave way entirely. . . .

Sydney crashed through the bricks into the pitch-black recesses of the vault. She felt a moment of primal terror as she found herself sprawled upon the dirt floor of the tomb, surrounded by fragments of human bone. Mice scurried away from her and spiders scuttled over her bare legs. The stagnant air smelled of decay and neglect.

For a second she felt as though she had been buried alive.

Then Maya appeared in the doorway, framed by the murky night sky. "Don't bother getting up," she informed Sydney, brandishing a jagged piece of pottery. "You're right where you belong."

Flat on her back in the dirt, Sydney realized she was at a distinct disadvantage. Every inch of her body ached, and she felt like she had been turned into a human wrecking ball. Blood trickled down the side of her face. Her leg throbbed in memory of the last time Maya had clobbered her.

Still, she refused to show weakness. Not to Maya Rao. Her fingers groped through the grave dirt, looking for a weapon among the moldering human remains. "Come and get me!" she dared Maya.

Before the Indian assassin could take Sydney up on her challenge, however, an unexpected figure assaulted Maya from behind.

"Leave her alone, you witch!" Terry Fujiwara called out. He wrapped his flashlight around Maya's throat and tried to drag her away from the demolished entrance to the tomb. "I'm not going to let you destroy another life!"

How 'bout that? Sydney thought, shaking her head in amazement. She took advantage of Fujiwara's timely arrival to rise to her feet. *I finally convinced him that I'm one of the good guys. Guess I should have tried attacking Maya earlier.*

Against the expert assassin, however, the well-meaning hacker was hopelessly outclassed. "You must be joking!" Maya snarled irritably before ramming the back of her skull into his face. "I don't care how smart you are. I'm having serious second thoughts about keeping you alive!"

Cartilage crunched and he reeled backward, clutching a broken nose. Blood spewed from his nostrils as Maya effortlessly whirled and caught him with a roundhouse kick to the head. Sydney's would-be rescuer crashed like a defective hard drive.

But he had given her the opening she needed.

Sydney's fingers sank into the eye sockets of a jawless human skull. She flung the dusty relic straight at Maya, nailing her in the back of the head. A resounding crunch echoed through the cemetery as Maya dropped to her knees, momentarily stunned by the blow. She lost her grip on the jagged shard, which clattered against the cement paving in front of the tomb.

That's more like it, Sydney thought.

Not wasting a second, she pounced from the tomb at the dazed assassin. Seizing Maya from behind, she yanked the blond wig from Maya's head and shoved the other woman's face into a marble plaque embedded in the pavement. Maya gasped as Sydney used the assassin's real hair to pull her head up again. With one hand on Maya's scalp and her knee in Maya's back, Sydney locked her fist around her adversary's left arm and wrenched it savagely. Maya let out an agonized cry as Sydney mercilessly exploited the bullet wound in Maya's shoulder.

It will be pretty damn ironic, Sydney thought, *if it turns out that Maya inflicted the injury on herself just to make her story more convincing.*

"Don't move," she warned Maya, "unless you want me to dislocate your arm." She twisted the captured limb for emphasis, eliciting another gasp from the kneeling woman. "Got it?"

Maya nodded.

"Good," Sydney said. Unsurprisingly, she found she preferred Maya as a prisoner rather than a partner. It was worth the bruises and sore bones to achieve this outcome.

Now what? she wondered, pondering her next move. Glancing at Fujiwara's prostrate form, she was relieved to see the battered hacker stirring once more. A groan escaped his lips as he slowly sat up where Maya had dropped him. His uncombed hair was even more of a mess than usual. A busted lip complemented his broken nose.

"Are you all right?" Sydney called out to him, while maintaining a tight grip on Maya's scalp and arm.

"Kinda sorta," he answered, his voice distorted by his facial injuries. He shook his head to clear the cobwebs from his brain, then looked as though he immediately regretted it. He massaged his forehead while gingerly probing his nose. He wiped the blood from his face with the bottom of his black T-shirt, which was already soaked through with perspiration. His complexion had a greenish cast, like he might vomit at any second. "Just a little sore . . . and queasy."

Sydney sympathized. She was bloody and bruised herself. "Do you think you can walk?" she asked. In theory Dixon was not far away; presumably he had shadowed them to the cemetery. *I'm surprised he didn't come running when he heard the fight break out,* she thought, slightly puzzled by his absence.

Maybe the noise hadn't carried that far?

"I have a friend waiting outside the cemetery," she informed Fujiwara, hoping that was indeed the case. "If we can make it there, he can help us hold on to Maya." She needed to rest a few moments, though, before she attempted to escort Maya across the cemetery. That had been quite a brawl.

She smiled at Fujiwara. "Thanks for the save, by the way."

"No problem," he said sheepishly, too nauseous to blush. "To be honest, I was halfway to the front gates before I realized that I couldn't just leave you alone to fight my battle. Caludia would not have approved."

Sydney couldn't tell if he was joking or not.

Clearly, though, defending Fujiwara against

Maya had delivered a valuable bonus; not only had she exposed and apprehended Maya at last, but she had also finally won the suspicious hacker's trust.

Now all she needed to do was recover Kestrel as well. *Let's hope Terry can help me there.*

Or perhaps Maya knew more than she was telling. Sydney didn't always approve of Sloane's interrogation techniques, but in Maya's case she was willing to look the other way while Sloane and her dad extracted whatever intel they could from the duplicitous assassin.

"Ready to go?" she asked Fujiwara. Her strength was returning, and she looked forward to turning Maya over to Dixon and APO, followed perhaps by a long, soothing bath. Grave dirt still clung to her sweaty clothes and skin.

Gross!

"Er, give me second," the hacker said. He climbed awkwardly to his feet and stumbled back into his tomb sanctuary. Sydney held her breath as he disappeared from sight, half afraid that he was going to pull another vanishing act. She sighed in relief when he emerged moments later, having retrieved his discarded backpack.

"I just needed to get a couple things," he explained. Squatting on the cement pavement in front of the tomb, he opened the pack and dug around in its contents, eventually producing a plastic pill bottle and a can of cola.

His head must be killing him, Sydney guessed. She was anxious to get Maya off her hands but allowed that it couldn't hurt to give the migraine-ridden fugitive a chance to self-medicate. She was tempted to ask if he could spare a painkiller or two.

To her surprise, Fujiwara downed a couple of tablets dry, leaving the cola can unopened. *What's that all about?* she thought as the hacker worked the pack back onto his shoulders. Sydney remembered the floppy disk Fujiwara had extracted from Benoit's computer the night before, and wondered if he still had the disk on him. *What sort of data is on that disk, anyway?*

The sound of approaching footsteps distracted her. Looking up, she glimpsed a trio of dark silhouettes coming their way. *Dixon?* she thought hopefully. *With backup?*

As the murky figures grew nearer, however, a feeling of apprehension came over her. The cold blue steel of automatic pistols caught the moonlight.

Sydney's muscles tensed in anticipation of trouble.

"Looks like we've got company," Maya announced, sounding altogether too pleased by this turn of events. Sydney tightened her grip on her captive, wondering how she was supposed to hold on to Maya and defend herself at the same time.

This isn't good.

None too gently, she dragged Maya to her feet, just in case she needed to use her as a human shield. "Get behind me," she instructed Fujiwara urgently.

Her caution proved all too warranted as the leader of the newcomers stepped out of the darkness, exposing the shaved pate and ritually scarred features of Theophile Benoit. Two armed henchmen accompanied him; Sydney recognized one of them as the security guard she had assaulted with the rum bottle the night before. A sizable bandage was taped to the guard's head. Judging from his baleful glare, he recognized her, too.

"Ms. Bristow, I presume," Benoit addressed her. He had a distinct Haitian accent and one of the deepest voices she had ever heard. From her research Sydney now knew that the intricate scars upon his cheeks were protective charms known as *gardes;* created by rubbing a singular blend of dried herbs into shallow cuts made by a voodoo priest during a special ritual, the scars were supposed to shield the bearer from harm. "Maya has told me all about you."

"Hello, lover," Maya said warmly. "I was starting to wonder what was keeping you."

Sydney's expression hardened. Obviously Maya had been in cahoots with Benoit all along, despite her protestations that she had never even heard of the notorious arms smuggler. Sydney wondered whether the Baden Liga had anything to do with stealing Kestrel at all, or if that all had been a fabrication on Maya's part to divert suspicion from her real ally.

Probably, Sydney thought. *I wouldn't put it past her.*

"Keep back!" she warned Benoit and his thugs. She shifted her grip from Maya's scalp to her throat. "Don't come any nearer or I'll break her neck!"

Was Maya bluffing? Probably not.

Here's hoping that Maya and Benoit are just as cozy as they sound, she thought, *and that Benoit values Maya a whole lot more than Maya cared about Fujiwara.*

"Now, why would you want to do a thing like that," Benoit teased her, "especially after you and Maya have worked so well together?" His silver amulet glinted in the moonlight; the intertwined pythons, Sydney had learned, were the sign of Damballah, the Great Serpent. Not a bad symbol for him and Maya, either. . . .

"Just like you planned?" Sydney prompted him. For the moment Benoit seemed content to keep his distance, yet Sydney wasn't sure how long she could maintain the standoff, given that she was both outnumbered and outgunned.

Where are you, Dixon?

"Of course!" Benoit laughed jovially. "After Maya and I failed to locate our elusive hacker friend on our own, we found ourselves forced to turn to you and Arvin Sloane for assistance." He flashed her a camera-ready smile. "You should know, Ms. Bristow, that Maya speaks quite highly of you."

Peachy, Sydney thought. "Imagine how flattered I'm not." A question occurred to her. "How did you find us here, anyway? Maya was searched for tracking devices, and she hasn't been in touch with anyone since we arrived in New Orleans."

Benoit wagged his finger at her. "That's not

entirely true." He gestured toward the bandaged guard. "Maya quietly identified herself to Claude here while she was grappling with him in the courtyard last night. During her bogus heart attack, remember?"

Sydney recalled how Maya, disguised as the hysterical old woman, had dragged the hapless guard down onto the floor with her. Apparently, distracting Claude was not all she had been up to.

"We've had Maya, and those around her, under surveillance ever since," Benoit explained. "When we heard the fight break out, I knew that, one way or another, your and Maya's temporary alliance had reached the breaking point." He gestured expansively toward Sydney and her charge. "And lo and behold, here is Mr. Fujiwara, ripe for the taking!"

Sydney heard Terry gulp loudly behind her. He fumbled nervously with his can of soda.

"But I've still got Maya," she reminded Benoit, giving Maya's arm an extra twist for good measure. The former bandit queen grunted through gritted teeth. She bit down on her lip to keep from whimpering.

Maya's obvious discomfort brought a frown to Benoit's face. "Your bargaining position is not as strong as you seem to think," he said, his deep voice now carrying undertones of menace. He signaled his gunmen, who took aim at both Sydney and Terry. "Are you willing to sacrifice Mr. Fujiwara's life as well as your own?"

"Are you willing to risk Maya?" Sydney challenged him, but despite her bravado, she knew she was running out of options. It was hard to imagine a scenario in which she and Terry came out of this standoff intact.

"Let Maya go," Benoit insisted, "and I assure you that neither you nor Mr. Fujiwara will come to any immediate harm."

Maya squirmed within Sydney's grasp. "I'd take him up on that," she advised her captor. "As much as I'd like to put a bullet through your brain right now, I'll concede that you're more valuable to us alive." Sydney heard, rather than saw, Maya's malicious sneer. "I wonder what Arvin Sloane would be willing to trade for your return?"

If you think Sloane cares about my safety, Sydney thought, *then you don't know him very well at all.* Admitting as much to Benoit and Maya, however, did not seem like a very strategic move. "I'd be more worried about pissing Sloane off."

Benoit shrugged. "I'll take my chances. I'm sure that even if Mr. Sloane is unwilling to deal with me, you have plenty of secrets that will be worth my time." He glanced at an expensive wristwatch. "Time's up, Ms. Bristow. Release Maya, or my men will start using you and Mr. Fujiwara for target practice."

"Hold on!" Sydney stalled. "Let me think!"

Fujiwara ran up behind her. Sydney expected him to plead for his life, but instead he whispered into her ear: "Close your eyes."

He popped the lid on his cola, then rolled it onto the ground between Sydney and their attackers. *What in the world?* Sydney thought. She squeezed her eyes shut, hoping that Fujiwara knew what he was doing.

The soda can exploded in a dazzling (and disorienting) burst of bright lights. Even through her closed lids the blinding flashes overwhelmed her retinas, causing her to see brightly colored spots and streaks. Tears gushed down her cheeks.

A strobe grenade, she realized, *disguised as a can of soda! Marshall will be so jealous.*

Benoit and his men shouted and swore, obviously blinded by the brilliant flashes as well. Shots rang out, but Sydney had already let go of Maya and rolled to one side. She heard bullets chip off pieces of the defenseless tombs. Bits of stone and plaster pelted her shoulders. Benoit's men were shooting wildly, but Sydney was equally bewildered, unsure which way to go.

"Stop it!" Maya shrieked frantically at the gunmen. "You're going to hit me by mistake!"

"She's right!" Benoit ordered his goons. "Hold your fire!" He called out to Maya. "Here I am, baby! Come to me!"

Sydney heard Maya's footsteps racing toward Benoit, then started as a sweaty hand grabbed on to her arm. "This way!" Fujiwara whispered. He tugged at her urgently. "We've got to get out of here!"

Sounds like a plan to me! Sydney thought. She knew that the strobe effect was bound to wear off momentarily. She jumped up from the ground and let Fujiwara guide her through the cemetery, occasionally stumbling over piles of collapsed masonry. She rammed her knee into a funerary urn and stubbed a toe on an unexpected step, but she kept on running, desperate to get away from their enemies. She prayed that she and Fujiwara were heading for the front gates.

"How can you tell where you're going?" she asked him anxiously. She opened her watery eyes, but all she could see were dancing blue splotches. She wiped the tears from her face with her free hand. "I'm completely lost!"

"Special contact lenses!" he said, panting like someone who wasn't used to doing so much running, let alone through a cemetery in the dark. His sweaty palm slid down to her wrist. "They filter out the strobe effect!"

Sydney's vision began to clear and she glimpsed the front gates of the cemetery. Gunshots chased after them, taking out chunks of masonry. She was grateful that the aboveground tombs made getting a direct shot at them problematic, especially since the shooters' eyesight was surely improving too.

"Where the hell did you get that thing?" Sydney asked, referring to the camouflaged strobe grenade. Since when did hackers have access to concealed explosives?

"On the Internet," he gasped. "Where else?"

Rue Melusine, with its gaslights and revelry, beckoned them. Sydney heard laughter and trumpet music ahead. They sprinted the last few yards until they passed through the cemetery gates, which had been left unlocked by Benoit and his men, and ran onto the cracked cobblestone street beyond. Within seconds they found themselves immersed in the Quarter's thriving nightlife. A mule-drawn carriage rolled past them, overflowing with rambunctious tourists.

Would Benoit and the others pursue them, guns blazing, into the crowded street? Sydney hoped not, but she wasn't willing to take that chance. She and Fujiwara hurried down the congested sidewalk as fast as the dense pedestrian traffic would permit. Their disheveled and blood-spattered appearance attracted plenty of wide-eyed glances, but thankfully, nobody seemed to be in a hurry to question them. *They probably figure we got thrown out of a bar for fighting,* she guessed. *No wonder they're keeping their distance!*

Not until they reached Bourbon Street, turning left to avoid passing La Maison du Vodou, did they slow their pace. Tourists surrounded them on all sides, offering them a degree of anonymity. Gaping vacationers gathered around a "living statue," admiring the gilded figure's astounding immobility. Farther on down the block a group of tumblers performed acrobatic feats on the sidewalk to the amusement of the crowd. A boom box provided a raucous hip-hop accompaniment.

Breathing heavily, Fujiwara rested his weight against an antique lamppost. "I think we lost them," he panted, his skinny frame shaking.

"Maybe," Sydney answered. She tried to remember the location of the nearest APO safe house. Returning to her hotel room was not an option; that was the first place Benoit and Maya would look for her. "We need to find some place to clean up!"

"No!" Fujiwara blurted out. "We don't have time. We have to hurry."

He stared at her with wide, febrile eyes. His entire body trembled with excitement.

"I think I know where Kestrel is!"

CHAPTER 11

APO SAFE HOUSE
NEW ORLEANS

Despite the anxious hacker's protestations, Sydney had realized they wouldn't get far looking like accident victims. And unarmed, to boot.

Hence, they'd made a detour to the nearby docks, where Sloane maintained a safe house overlooking the Mississippi. As far as Sydney knew, Maya had no knowledge of this hideaway's existence, which meant that they were probably safe for the time being. It concerned her, however, that Dixon was nowhere to be seen.

She had hoped to find Dixon waiting for her

here but could see no sign of his presence. Nor had she been able to contact him on any of the standard frequencies.

Was Dixon still tailing Maya without her knowledge? If so, why hadn't he intervened when Benoit and his goons ambushed them at the cemetery? Sydney knew that Dixon was perfectly capable of taking care of himself, but as she had learned through personal experience, even the best of agents could sometimes find themselves up a creek at the worst possible moment. She remembered all the times that Dixon had come to her rescue in the past, and vice versa.

If something happened to him while I was partnered with Maya Rao, she thought, *I'll never forgive myself.* Dixon was quite possibly the most decent man she had ever known, and a devoted father to his children as well. *He deserves better than to wind up a casualty in the war against terror.*

Such gloomy reflections followed her as she emerged from a much needed shower wearing a clean terry cloth bathrobe. With the blood, dirt, and sweat washed down the drain, she felt distinctly more human and better able to follow her new companion's hunch regarding Kestrel's location.

She found Terry, whom she no longer thought of as Fujiwara, hunched over a keyboard in the suite adjoining the bathroom. Fresh clothes, gear, and ammo were spread out on a twin bed in anticipation of their imminent excursion. Terry sat at a fully equipped computer station, printing out maps of the sprawling bayous outside the city. Gauze was taped over his broken nose, which Sydney had set as best she could. A microwaved TV dinner rested on his lap, while a battery of migraine medications were arrayed about the room.

He jumped slightly as he heard her exit the bathroom, apparently still hearing assassins behind every squeaky door and unexpected footstep. He lifted his gaze from the computer monitor and regarded her nervously. His jaw was black and blue where Maya had kicked him, and he looked faintly embarrassed by the sight of Sydney in her bathrobe, staring everywhere except at her bare legs.

"So, is your name really Sydney Bristow?" he asked.

"That's me," she admitted. "Sorry about that Eleanor business before. Nothing personal. Just standard procedure."

"I understand, believe me. You can't be too

careful these days." He sounded like he wanted to believe her. "I've got more fake identities than the FBI's ten most wanted."

"Like VixNut1 and Patrick Okata?" she suggested.

"To name a few." He took a bite of lasagna. "So I guess I'm really in no position to bust your chops about Eleanor, and all."

Fidgety and shy, Terry didn't strike Sydney as a dangerous criminal mastermind. "How did you get involved in this mess, anyway?" she asked him. "Why hijack a potentially lethal military aircraft?" She recalled what Marshall had told her of the hacker's earlier pranks and escapades. "From what I hear, that's not exactly your style."

"I know," he admitted guiltily. "What can I say, Maya zeroed in on my two greatest weaknesses: UFOs and sex." He shook his head at his own stupidity. "I mean, have you seen Maya? Wow, talk about elegant design. At first I couldn't believe that a woman like her could possibly be interested in me, let alone share my enthusiasm regarding extraterrestrial encounters. She was, like, the perfect woman—or so I thought."

"And Kestrel?" Sydney prompted him.

Terry sighed. "Maya claimed to have contacts

deep within the military-industrial complex, sympathetic insiders who wanted to lift the veil of silence over the whole UFO cover-up. According to Maya, the prototype for the UCAV incorporated alien alloys reverse-engineered at Area Fifty-one. The idea was that if we could get Kestrel into the hands of the international UFO underground, we could go public and force the government to reveal what they were hiding about the crash at Roswell and all the other close encounters they've hushed up over the years." He blushed at his own gullibility. "Hey, I know it sounds stupid in retrospect, but in my defense, the White Sands Missile Range, where Kestrel was being tested, is only about seven hundred miles from Area Fifty-one."

Doing her best to maintain a straight face, Sydney refrained from commenting on Terry's UFO obsession. In her years with the CIA she had never seen any evidence that the U.S. government was hiding any secrets regarding little green men. Then again, there was Project Black Hole, where the Rambaldi artifacts were being analyzed, not to mention an entire Department of Special Research, devoted to investigating paranormal threats to national security, so maybe Terry's theories weren't as wacky as they sounded. She made a mental note to ask Marshall what he thought, assuming she made it back to Los Angeles in one piece.

"I'm not a total idiot, however," Terry continued. "Eventually I figured out that Maya was just using me and that the reason she wanted Kestrel had nothing to do with UFO research. She had given me a false name, 'Tamara Singh,' but I managed to track down her real name online, not to mention her absolutely terrifying track record. I nearly had a heart attack when I read how many people she's killed!" He gulped at the thought. "I had to pretend that I was still with the program, though, or she would have killed or tortured me for sure. It wasn't until after we snatched Kestrel that I finally had a chance to get away from her, while she was preoccupied with her big score. It was close, but I managed to shoot her in the shoulder and make a break for it."

So, Sydney noted, *Maya's wound wasn't self-inflicted after all.* She tried to imagine how much nerve it must have taken for the fearful hacker to turn on Maya; it was a minor miracle that he was still alive. And to think that the infamous Maya Rao had actually been bested by a lowly computer geek. She must have been utterly humiliated!

Couldn't have happened to a nicer gal.

"And Benoit?" she asked.

Terry looked soberly into her eyes. "Look, I may be an outlaw hacker and all, but I'm no traitor. Terrorists scare me silly too. I knew I couldn't live with myself if I let Kestrel remain in the hands of America's enemies, so I went online to find out who Maya was really working with. It wasn't easy—there were a lot of false trails and bogus identities to sort through—but eventually I figured out that Benoit was my man." The very name sent a shudder through Terry's spindly frame. "Do you know what he used to do in Haiti, by the way? Yikes!"

"I know all about Duvalier and the Tonton Macoutes," she assured him. "Go on."

"Anyway, I guess I thought that if I could find Kestrel myself, I could make up for helping Maya steal the plane in the first place." He gestured at a nearby couch, where the contents of his backpack were spilled out onto the leather cushions—computer disks and electronic hardware mixed with ammo clips and phony soda cans. "I even whipped up an override device that I could use to reprogram Kestrel's navigational system if I could actually get my hands on the UCAV itself. All I needed to do was find out where Benoit and Maya were hiding the plane, then try to sneak in there when no one was looking."

A pretty ambitious operation for an amateur, Sydney thought. She sat down on the edge of the bed, across from Terry's work station. Despite her soothing shower, she was still sore from her brawl with Maya. "Why didn't you just go straight to the authorities?"

"With my record?" he asked her incredulously. "Are you kidding? They'd lock me up and throw away the key." He looked as though she had just suggested that he take a stroll through the core of a nuclear reactor. "To be honest, that option never even crossed my mind."

Figures, Sydney thought. She'd momentarily forgotten just how paranoid Terry was; apparently, being exploited by the bad guys hadn't been enough to overcome his lifelong distrust of the government. *Once a conspiracy nut, always a conspiracy nut, I guess.*

"So that was why you were breaking into Benoit's office last night." As she glanced over at the couch, the innocuous-looking soda cans caught her eye. "I have to ask, why didn't you use those strobe grenades when I confronted you at the temple?"

"I had one on me," he admitted, "just in case. To tell you the truth, though, those things scare me. I was hoping I could get away without having to use one, which it turns out I was able to do. Plus, I was afraid that the flares would attract as many guards as they repelled." He contemplated the grenades on the couch. "Tonight in the cemetery, on the other hand . . . well, obviously I didn't have any choice but to risk firing one off. It was sort of an emergency, you know?"

No argument there, Sydney thought. The camouflaged grenade had come in handy. Without it they both would probably be prisoners of Benoit right now.

Or worse.

Terry still looked pretty wiped out from their run-in with Maya and her confederates. His eyes were bloodshot and he kept massaging his forehead and temples. Dried blood and dirt caked his dark shirt and slacks. His hair was even more of a mess than usual.

"Your turn," she told him, gesturing toward the shower. "I'll hold down the fort here while you clean up."

She was anxious to contact APO while Terry was otherwise occupied; it had been too long since she last checked in with Sloane and the others. *I need to update headquarters—and find out what's up with Dixon.*

"Okay," he consented, getting up from the computer. He moved slowly and carefully, as though his sensitive head prevented him from making any sudden moves. Sydney had procured Terry fresh clothing from the safe house's stock, and he scooped up his new duds before disappearing into the bathroom.

She waited until she heard the water running before dialing Sloane on a secure line. As she waited for him to pick up, she braced herself, as she always did, for the sound of his voice, the same voice that had ordered the death of Danny, Francie, and so many others. . . .

"Hello, Sydney," he said pleasantly. "What is your situation?"

Overcoming her revulsion, she informed him of Maya's betrayal and of the assassin's apparent alliance with Benoit. "She's been playing us all along," she concluded, "in order to get to Fujiwara."

"Interesting," Sloane commented. "According

to your father and Vaughn, it was Benoit who arranged for the contract on Maya's life. I can only assume that this was done in order to conceal the true nature of their relationship—and to support her claim that the Baden Liga were out to get her."

Kind of like the way the CIA, in the person of Hayden Chase, made a big show of firing me, Sydney reflected, *in order to set up my new "independent" status within APO.*

Nothing in the spy game could ever be taken at face value, it seemed, not even a death threat.

"How are Vaughn and my dad?" she had to ask.

"Well enough," Sloane answered. "Your father received a minor injury in the field, but he's received medical attention and is expected to fully recover. He and Agent Vaughn are flying back from Europe as we speak."

Her mouth went dry at the news about her dad. Even though things were still tense between them, after what had happened with her mother, she wasn't prepared to lose him to an enemy knife or bullet. There were too many things they hadn't worked out yet, too many words left unsaid. *What kind of injury?* she worried. *How serious is it?*

She wanted to grill Sloane for more details, but

there were more-urgent issues that needed to be addressed first. "What about Dixon?" she asked. "I haven't been able to contact him."

"Neither have we," Sloane divulged. He stated this alarming development calmly, as though reporting a misdirected piece of mail. "We lost radio contact with him a couple hours ago. I think we have to assume that he's been compromised."

A couple hours ago? Sydney thought. That would have been while she and Maya were staked out in the cemetery, waiting for Terry to show himself. Benoit had mentioned that his people had been watching over Maya ever since she revealed herself to the guard at the voodoo temple. Had they also spotted Dixon trailing Maya—and done something about it?

"Maya and Benoit must have him," she said, leaving unspoken the ghastly possibility that Dixon might already be dead. *Benoit wanted to take me and Terry alive,* she reminded herself. *He might consider Dixon just as valuable.* "I need to go after him, see if they're holding him at La Maison du Vodou."

"No, Sydney," Sloane contradicted her. "Your mission is to recover Kestrel, not rescue a fellow colleague. I've been monitoring Benoit's activities since you first detected his involvement in this affair, and I have reason to believe that he's planning to auction off Kestrel sometime in the next twelve hours. We're racing against the clock here. You need to locate the UCAV before it switches hands again."

Sydney couldn't believe what she was hearing. "But what about Dixon?"

"Nadia and Agent Weiss are on their way to New Orleans. They can look into recovering Dixon. In the meantime I need you to stay focused on our top priority: finding Kestrel." His voice took on the gentle, fatherly tone she had come to despise. "I know this is hard for you, Sydney. Believe me, I'm just as concerned about Marcus as you are."

Like hell you are! Sydney thought angrily. It was Dixon, after all, who had accidentally killed Sloane's wife, Emily, during that botched raid on Sloane's hideout in Tuscany. Sloane had killed Dixon's own wife in retaliation, before they all ended up on the same side again. Supposedly that was all water under the bridge now, but how concerned could Sloane really be with the safety of the man who, however inadvertently, had killed Emily?

How do I know that Sloane hasn't been waiting for an opportunity like this, a chance to write off Dixon once and for all?

The worst part was that, on a strictly pragmatic level, she knew Sloane was right. Kestrel came first; the safety of America depended on it. *But what kind of person am I that I can actually see Sloane's point of view?*

"I understand," she acknowledged. She heard the water turn off in the shower and realized that Terry would be rejoining her shortly. The computer continued to spit out maps of the neighboring bayous. "I'm going after Kestrel now."

She put down the phone, feeling like she needed another shower to wash away the dirty realities of her profession. Maya's constant insinuations that she and Sydney were more alike than Sydney admitted crept back into her thoughts. Maya may have joined forces with a murderous crook like Benoit, but as far as Sydney knew, Benoit had never personally ordered the death of anyone Maya cared for.

Unlike Dixon and me, who both somehow man-

age to place our duty to our country above the fact that Sloane murdered the people we loved most. . . . We do it all for the greater good.

So does that make us better than Maya?

Or even less human?

CHAPTER 12

THE BAYOUS
OUTSIDE NEW ORLEANS

The lonely bayous were the last place one would ever expect to find a multimillion-dollar experimental aircraft. Brackish green water coursed sluggishly through a meandering maze of shallow ponds and tributaries. Moonlight filtered through thick canopies of lush vegetation. Spanish moss hung like curtains from the gnarled branches of ancient cypresses and myrtles. Hungry alligators lazed on the banks of muddy canals, barely causing a ripple as they slid in and out of the stagnant backwaters in search of a late-night snack. Willows and lily pads clotted the shores, while blinking fire-flies flashed on and off like warning lights.

The thick, humid air smelled of both growth and decay. Frogs croaked in the shadows, over the buzzing of nocturnal insects. Splashing noises broke the stillness of the water. An owl hooted in the treetops before flapping off into the night sky.

On second thought, Sydney reflected, *where else would you look for a bird of prey except in the wilderness?*

She and Terry piloted a rented aluminum skiff through the eerie bayous. Sydney sat at the back of the boat, manning the rudder, while the nervous hacker occupied a seat near the front, charting their course via a handheld GPS unit. A battery-powered lantern, perched on the prow of the skiff, provided barely enough light to navigate by. "This way," he informed her. "We're almost there."

These particular marshes were located on the outskirts of the city, not far from Benoit's private estate. According to the data Terry had retrieved from the voodoo priest's computer, Benoit had recently purchased a large chunk of worthless swampland, perhaps to hide Kestrel in. This part of the secluded bayou was also suspiciously close to the coordinates

that Terry, at Maya's request, had originally programmed into the prototype's navigational system.

Sneaky, Sydney thought, admiring their adversaries' ingenuity despite herself. Local folklore had
it that the pirate Jean Lafitte had hidden vast sums
of treasure in these very swamps, treasure that
remained undiscovered to this day. *I can believe it,*
she decided. The overgrown marshes looked like
they could swallow up anything, even an unmanned
aircraft. You could search the bayous for days without finding anything, unless you knew where to
look. . . .

As she steered the skiff through the murky
sloughs and inlets, she kept an eye out for unwanted
company. The verdant shores offered way too many
hiding places for her peace of mind. An entire army
of snipers could lurk behind the clustered willows
and cypresses, assuming they were willing to brave
the alligators prowling the banks of the swamp.

An ambush was a very real possibility.

"How are we doing?" she asked anxiously, keeping one hand on the grip of the Colt automatic that
she had picked up at the safe house. The sooner they
got out of the swamp, the better she would feel. Plus,
it was hard to concentrate on finding the UCAV when

Benoit and Maya were probably doing God-knew-what to Dixon at this very minute. She remembered a movie she saw once where the Haitian secret police torture the hero by driving a rusty nail through his scrotum. *Hang on, Marcus,* she mentally urged her longtime partner. *As soon as Kestrel is safe, I'm coming after you—and Sloane had better not try to stop me!*

"You can slow the engine," Terry said. He looked around the marsh intently. "By my calculations, we should be pretty much on top of it."

Sydney eased the motor down to its lowest gear, so that they were practically drifting along with the current. "Are you sure?" she asked him. This particular waterway, which wound its way between the western shore and a grassy barrier island, looked too narrow and shallow to be hiding the Cessna-size warplane.

"I think so," Terry answered, more hesitantly than Sydney would have preferred. What if they were just wasting time here while Dixon remained in jeopardy? Terry leaned forward in the boat, trying to peer past the glow of their lantern. "Try up ahead, just a little bit farther."

Why not? Sydney thought. As long as there was

a chance of finding Kestrel here, she was willing to explore the swamp for as long as it took, despite the risk involved. According to Sloane, time was running out.

A veil of clinging Spanish moss shrouded the passageway ahead. They drifted through the moss, the damp fibers brushing against their faces and shoulders, before the skiff emerged into the mouth of a sizable lagoon. The canopy of branches opened up above their heads, exposing the starry night sky. Moonlight shimmered on the dark, opaque surface of the lagoon.

"This must be it!" Terry exclaimed, almost capsizing the boat in his excitement. He hurriedly compared the readout on the GPS unit with the coordinates he'd marked on his maps. "It's probably right beneath us!"

Sydney had to admit that the site seemed promising. The isolated lagoon was wide enough to hold the UCAV and then some. It looked fairly deep as well, although it was difficult to tell from where she was sitting. "Okay," she said. "Let's go for it."

Diving equipment rested on the floor of the skiff. Sydney stripped off her T-shirt and cutoffs to reveal a stark black bikini underneath. She lifted a plastic bottle from beside her feet and dubiously inspected the label on the so-called gator repellent the Cajun proprietor of the boathouse had sold her. She glanced apprehensively at the scaly reptiles populating the banks of the lagoon several yards away. Was it just her imagination, or were the gators' slit yellow eyes looking back at her?

What the heck? she decided, uncapping the bottle. She smeared the greasy brown unguent onto her skin. It smelled suspiciously like tanning lotion, with perhaps a dollop of turpentine thrown in.

As long as it's not steak sauce . . .

A speargun also lay at her feet, just in case the repellent wasn't all it was cracked up to be, along with a high-powered searchlight and a titanium steel diving knife. She checked the light to make sure it was fully charged, then strapped the sheathed knife to her left thigh. Plastic cords were attached to both the searchlight and the speargun. She'd loop them around her wrists before she got in the water, in order to avoid losing either piece of equipment by accident.

A scuba mask, a Nitrox rebreather, and flippers completed her diving ensemble. Moving carefully, she switched places with Terry, turning over control of the skiff to her new acquaintance and giving him the Colt automatic.

"Don't go anywhere," she told him. Casting one last glance at the lounging gators, she loaded the speargun and swung her legs over the side of the boat. A buzzing dragonfly skated too close to the surface of the lagoon and was immediately gobbled up by a rising fish. "Wish me luck."

"Er, happy hunting," Terry answered. He looked relieved that he wasn't the one venturing beneath the water. "Watch out for the Creature from the Black Lagoon."

Sydney could never tell when he was joking.

Here goes nothing, she thought.

A muted splash accompanied Sydney's transition from boat to water. After the sweltering humidity the coolness of the water came as both a shock and a relief. She switched on her searchlight and scanned the water around her. To her relief the gators did not seem to be coming her way.

Yet.

Bubbles came from the mouthpiece of her rebreathing unit as she dived for the bottom of the lagoon. Powerful kicks propelled her downward while the moonlight above her grew fainter and fainter. The beam of her searchlight cut through the darkness below her, scouring the umbrageous depths for any sign of the plane.

C'mon, she thought tensely. *Where are you?*

At first she didn't see anything, just watery shadows and the occasional flash of a startled fish. As she descended, however, she spotted a vague shape resting in the silt at the bottom of the lagoon, perhaps fifteen feet below the surface. The object was roughly thirty feet long, with its matching delta wings projecting from the rear.

Her eyes widened behind her transparent mask. She held her breath, despite the mouthpiece gripped between her jaws. *Is this it?* she wondered. *Was Terry right after all?*

She kicked faster, anxious to discover the truth. Her searchlight beam reached ahead of her, revealing a streamlined metallic object that looked like a cross between a missile and a fighter jet. No windows were present or required. Blue-gray wings and the wide black band on the aircraft's tail aided Sydney in identifying the exact species of this bird.

Kestrel, she thought joyously. *At last.*

CHAPTER 13

OUTSIDE NEW ORLEANS

Cottonsilk was the name of Benoit's sprawling plantation outside of the city. Located along the fabled Great River Road and bordered by acres of uncultivated bayous, the elegant antebellum estate had belonged to generations of planters and slave-holders before falling into the hands of the wealthy Haitian expatriate. Cottonwood trees lined the winding drive leading up to the main house, a large white mansion in the Greek Revival style. Towering Ionic columns, more than forty feet tall, supported an imposing gabled portico.

"At least he'll always have Tara," Weiss quipped as the limousine deposited him and Nadia before the wide granite steps in front of the mansion. They were hardly alone; their limo was just one of a string of vehicles delivering groups of well-dressed men and women to Benoit's doorstep. Liveried doormen waited to greet them. Nadia glanced at her designer wristwatch. It was 9 P.M.

People were showing up right on time.

The reputed arms smuggler had clearly done well for himself, she reflected, contemplating the stately exterior of the great house. Heads turned as she climbed the steps beside Weiss; she was dressed to kill in a slinky black lace sheath with pearl and crystal accents. Weiss himself was wearing a tailored Armani suit, which looked, she noted, surprisingly good on him.

Thugs in servant uniforms guarded the open double doors ahead. "Names?" one of them demanded as Weiss and Nadia approached the entrance.

"Jacob Raab and Constance Rivera," Weiss volunteered, "of the Nth Wave." The latter was a supposed terrorist organization that Sloane had invented purely as a front; it existed mostly on paper and in the computerized databases of various law-enforcement agencies. "We're invited."

The doorman checked their names against a list. Nadia did her best to look bored and impatient while they waited to see if their hastily constructed cover story was going to hold up. When the doorman finally gave them the nod, she showed no sign of the relief she felt, acting instead as though their acceptance had been the only possible outcome.

"Please step over here to be searched," the doorman instructed. Nadia rolled her eyes but, along with Weiss, consented to the procedure. A scan with a metal-detecting wand was followed by a thorough frisking, which in Nadia's case seemed to go on longer than was strictly necessary. She memorized the frisker's leering face for future reference; if she was lucky, maybe she would have an opportunity to clobber him later. Another security guard carefully examined the contents of her metallic silver purse. He held up an inhaler and eyed her quizzically.

"Asthma," she explained, treating the security guards to her most dazzling smile. Her husky voice dipped an octave. "Sometimes I get breathless in the presence of so many handsome men."

Her seductive wiles worked like a charm. The grinning inspector dropped the inhaler back into her purse and handed the bag back to her. "This way, madam," he said, gesturing toward the front door. "And you, too, sir."

Nadia glanced around as yet another minion escorted them to the door. Although she and Weiss had cleared the gauntlet of security goons without incident, some of the other guests were not so fortunate. She watched out of the corner of her eye as various would-be attendees were required to surrender everything from throwing stars and switchblades to automatic weapons. She was glad that she and Weiss had not even tried to smuggle any obvious weapons into Benoit's exclusive soiree.

That certain invitees had come armed to the teeth was not surprising. The guest list appeared to be a veritable rogue's galley of representatives from assorted hostile nations, global crime rings, and radical organizations. Before she had even made it through the front door, she had already recognized at least a dozen faces from the FBI's "Most Wanted" list. Wasn't that Ivan Gorinsky of the Russian mob, and Aimee Darbeau of the Radiant Dawn?

A sudden raid on Cottonsilk—if such a thing were

possible, given Benoit's potent political connections—
might well yield a bounty of major arrests. *But that
wouldn't help us find Kestrel or Dixon,* she thought,
not necessarily in order of importance.

Was Marcus Dixon even still alive? There had
been no word from him ever since Marshall overheard a voice (Benoit's?) instructing that Dixon be
taken to "the mansion." The lack of further trans-
missions suggested that the agent's captors had
disposed of his personal communications gear.
Nadia could only hope that they had not already
disposed of Dixon as well.

She had known Dixon for less than a year, but
she had already come to regard him as a man of
profound integrity and devotion to duty. *Besides,
Sydney admires him, which is good enough for me.*

Although there was no way to be sure that
Cottonsilk was the mansion referred to in Dixon's last
transmission, Benoit's palatial estate was the obvious place to begin searching for the missing agent.
Fortunately, tonight's event provided them with the
perfect opportunity to do a little timely snooping.

"After all that," Weiss commented regarding
the tight security measures, "I feel like I should be
boarding a plane." He leaned toward Nadia and

whispered in her ear, "At least they didn't strip-search us."

"Don't give them any ideas," she said under her breath.

Their escort led them through a wood-paneled foyer into the mansion's breathtaking first-floor parlor. Hand-carved Corinthian columns supported the high ceiling, some eleven feet above the polished hardwood floor. Crystal chandeliers sparkled overhead. The tall casement windows were closed and shuttered, the better to protect the privacy of the guests. A lavish buffet table, draped in white linen, was piled high with samples of the local cuisine: barbecued shrimp, oysters on the half shell, boiled crawfish, crème brûlée, and more. A glistening ice sculpture, displayed as a centerpiece, had been cheekily carved in the image of the stolen Kestrel airplane.

Pretty nervy, Nadia thought, *although pretty easy to dispose of, I suppose.* In a few hours the incriminating sculpture would be nothing more than a puddle of water. *A blow-dryer or hammer would also do the trick, if necessary.*

"Don't say I never take you anyplace nice," Weiss joked, surveying the luxurious decor. Servers circulated among the guests, offering drinks and hors d'oeuvres. He snagged a mint julep for each of them. "Think Sloane would be interested in acquiring Benoit's caterer?"

Despite the festive trappings, the mood in the parlor was anything but social. The various bands of guests kept to themselves, huddling together in tight little clusters, while regarding the other attendees with open suspicion and sometimes even outright enmity. In particular Nadia noticed that the emissaries from the People's Liberation Brigade were staying as far away as possible from their counterparts in the Proletarian Revolutionary Front; there had been bad blood, and frequent hostilities, between the two terrorist groups ever since they'd schismatized into rival factions back during the late eighties.

There are a lot of conflicting political agendas here, she realized. The only thing Benoit's guests had in common was that they all wanted the UCAV—and they didn't want any of their adversaries to get it. *Just like us.*

So far she had not spotted Maya Rao at the mansion. Considering Sydney's discovery that Maya had been allied with Benoit all along, Nadia had half expected to find the treacherous bandit queen playing hostess at this event; apparently, however, she and Benoit were not yet ready to make their alliance—romantic or otherwise—public.

Also conspicuously missing were the Baden Liga. *After using them as a red herring to divert suspicion from himself,* Nadia surmised, *I guess Benoit would have been pushing his luck to invite them as well. Especially after they executed Ramsey Yaw for his part in the deception.*

A dais had been erected at the far end of the parlor, in front of a pair of closed satin curtains. A hush fell over the assemblage as Benoit ascended the dais. Nadia recognized him from the intelligence photos she had studied, as well as by the ritual scars upon his cheeks. He held up a hand to secure the room's attention.

"Friends, honored guests," he addressed them in a deep, resonant voice. "Welcome to my humble home, and thank you for journeying all this way for this very special event. I assure you that your travels have been well worth the effort. We have a singular item up for sale this evening, one that is truly state-of-the-art."

The curtains drew back to reveal a wall-size

movie screen. Photos and schematics of Kestrel flashed behind him as he spoke, provoking excited murmurs from the audience. The UCAV was clearly a hot ticket; Nadia guessed that the bidding was going to be just as fierce as the invitees' dispositions.

"The very latest in uninhabited combat air vehicles," Benoit declared, "Kestrel will almost surely give the United States an unfair advantage in the inevitable conflicts of the twenty-first century, unless you take advantage of this opportunity to avail yourself of the one-and-only prototype of this spectacular advance in military technology. As agreed, the auction will take place precisely at midnight, allowing you plenty of time to confer with your respective organizations. I urge you not to be overly cautious in your bidding; chances to gain a decisive strategic advantage over your enemies come along very rarely."

A hand shot up from the midst of the guests. Nadia recognized Ibn Rashid, a high-ranking officer of Immortal Jihad. "What about security?" he asked aggressively. "I have heard that Kestrel's remote programming has been compromised . . . by a defector from your organization."

The skeptical Arab was surely referring to Fujiwara, but Benoit betrayed no sign of discomfort at the query. "A minor matter," he dissembled smoothly, "which is being remedied even as we speak. I would not let such trivial details prevent you from seeing the bigger picture. Kestrel is unequivocally the future of air warfare. You do not want to be left behind."

No wonder Benoit moved up the auction, Nadia realized. With Sydney closing in, and rumors of the Fujiwara problem spreading, Benoit obviously wanted to make his killing and unload the purloined UCAV before things got too hot. *Sydney's got him worried, particularly now that she has Fujiwara and he doesn't.*

But Nadia had her own concerns at the moment—namely, how to find Dixon on an estate the size of Cottonsilk. The main house itself had more than twenty-five rooms, not counting the various outbuildings elsewhere on the plantation. That was a lot of territory to search, especially under the watchful gaze of Benoit's hired muscle. Even now uniformed security guards were posted at each of the parlor's exits, to discourage guests from wandering freely around the house. It was going to take some effort to slip out of here unnoticed, and even then she had no idea where to start exploring.

Hold on, Dixon, she thought. *We're coming for you . . . somehow.*

The old smokehouse had once been used for drying and preserving the plantation's meat supply. Smoke had blackened the shack's timber ceiling, while the lower portions of the walls had been bleached white by the large quantities of salt employed there in days gone by. A packed dirt floor had cut down on the risk of fire, not doubt contributing to the smokehouse's survival to the present day. The interior of the shack still smelled of smoked meat and drippings.

Dixon was barely aware of his surroundings. Drugged into a stupor, he hung against an exposed brick wall, suspended by a pair of modern steel handcuffs looped over an old meat hook. His arms were stretched above his head, nearly tugged from their sockets by the weight of his drooping body. His feet dangled a few inches above the floor.

His mind was lost in a fog of confusion. Visions of snakes, bones, and bonfires swirled through his disordered dreams. A harmonica tune played over and over inside his skull, accompanied by the frenzied pounding of voodoo drums. His glazed eyes stared blankly at the walls of the smokehouse. His mouth tasted of grave dust.

"Drink this!" a feminine voice instructed him curtly. He felt the lip of a hollowed-out gourd placed against his lips. A bitter odor assaulted his nose. Someone tilted his head back and clamped his nose shut before pouring a thick, viscous concoction down his throat. He almost gagged on the vile-tasting liquid, but he ended up swallowing a good portion of the brew. "That's right, drink up," the voice encouraged him. "This is just what you need."

Gradually the fog in his head began to lift. The drumming and phantom images receded, leaving his mind awake and alert once more. His vision cleared and he found himself a prisoner in what he realized was an abandoned smokehouse. His arms ached numbly, and he wondered how long he had been hanging like this. The edges of the handcuffs dug painfully into his wrists, while dozens of other sore spots reminded him of the beating he had received at the hands of Benoit's men. He instinctively tried to probe the bruises on his face, only to be held back by the merciless cuffs.

"Welcome back to the land of the living," said the voice, which he now recognized as belonging to Maya Rao. His eyes focused on the ruthless woman, who stood only a few feet away, wearing a short indigo sari with knee-high suede boots. The hollowed gourd remained in her hands. "Hope the antidote wasn't too revolting. I understand the main ingredient is jimsonweed, or the zombie's cucumber, as it's known to the so-called sorcerers of the West Indies."

Dixon remembered the powder the men had blown into his face outside the cemetery. He was less interested in the exact nature of the drug and its antidote than with bringing himself up to speed on his present circumstances. *How long have I been out?* he wondered. He shook his head to clear the cobwebs from his mind. *And what's happened in the meantime?*

That Maya was here at all, presiding over his captivity, was a very bad sign. *If she's here, where is Sydney?* Dixon experienced a stab of guilt at the realization that his capture had left Sydney with no one to watch her back. *Did Maya turn on her, just as we feared?* He prayed that his failure had not cost Sydney her life.

On a more immediate front, he noted at once that both his gun and his communicator were gone. Indeed, his rumpled raincoat, with all its concealed spyware, had been stripped from him at some point, so that he was wearing only a flannel shirt and a pair of faded overalls. He couldn't reach his ear, of course, but he could feel that the fitted earpiece was missing.

Unarmed, out of touch, in enemy hands, at an unknown location, he concluded, taking stock of his situation. *Not exactly an ideal scenario . . .*

Maya put the gourd down on a nearby bench. She stepped forward and reached up for his face, digging her nails beneath the seam of his latex disguise. "Now then," she said, "let's unwrap our present."

With one savage motion she ripped the mask from his face. Dixon gasped in pain as the glued-on latex was torn away from his skin; it felt like an entire layer of flesh had been peeled from his skull. Bits of glue and rubber clung to his raw, stinging features.

"Ah, Agent Dixon," Maya crowed triumphantly, "I rather suspected it was you." The flayed visage of the old harmonica player dangled from her fingertips. "Not quite as satisfying as having your esteemed partner in my clutches, but quite a coup nonetheless. I haven't forgotten that time you ran me off the road in Zurich. Spoiled my shot at the Greek ambassador, too."

Dixon was in no mood to go strolling down memory lane. "How did you see through my disguise?" he asked, curious to know what mistake might have led to his present dilemma. The jolt of the mask's removal had banished whatever lingering grogginess the zombie powder had left behind. "What tipped you off?"

"Don't take it too hard," she consoled him, smirking. "To be honest, I was never able to spot you for sure. Was that you in the wizard's gown in Singapore?" She shrugged carelessly, as though it hardly mattered. "In any event, I knew there had to be *somebody* keeping watch over me; that was only common sense. So when I faked the heart attack at the temple during the Great Snake Incident, I conferred with that guard I pulled down, and I made sure that some of Benoit's men were watching to see if anyone followed me back to the hotel. In fact, I deliberately took something of a roundabout route just to make it easier for my spies to single out any lurking shadows."

Dixon remembered their leisurely, and somewhat unnecessary, ride along the riverfront and Canal Street. Had Benoit's people seen him hurry onto the streetcar after Maya?

"After that it was a simple matter of keeping you under observation at all times, no matter what alias you assumed, and taking the appropriate action once it came time to, shall we say, sever my alliance with your erstwhile partner."

Maya's smug demeanor enraged Dixon. "Where is Sydney?" he demanded angrily. "What have you done with her?"

"I sincerely wish I knew," Maya answered. Her expression darkened. "The last time I saw your infuriating colleague, she was hightailing it out of the cemetery with Terry Fujiwara." Her eyes narrowed and her voice took on a more menacing tone. "Where would she take him? Where are they likely to be hiding now?"

Dixon smiled, relieved to hear that both Sydney and Fujiwara had managed to escape Maya's treachery, and that Sydney now had the elusive hacker in her custody. *Good for you, Syd,* he thought proudly. She had probably taken Fujiwara to Sloane's safe house down by the wharfs, but he had no intention of sharing that supposition with Maya Rao.

"Beats me," he lied. "If what you say is true, Sloane could have hidden Fujiwara anywhere in the world by now."

Which, come to think of it, was not entirely untrue. *Unless Sydney is still looking for Kestrel,* he thought. Had APO managed to recover the UCAV yet, or was the stolen warplane still unaccounted for?

Anger flashed in Maya's kohl-rimmed eyes. She tore the latex mask to shreds, then hurled it down into the dirt. "Do not lie to me!" she spit at him. "I will not let Sydney Bristow get the better of me, nor Arvin Sloane, for that matter. You will tell me everything you know about Sloane's new organization, and where he might be holding Terry, or I will introduce you to the torments of the damned!"

"I have nothing to say to you," Dixon said firmly. He had been subjected to torture before, and though he feared it, he resolved that he would resist Maya's efforts for as long as he was able, if only to buy time for Sydney to complete her mission, if she had not done so already.

He also knew that a rescue attempt was not beyond the realm of possibility. *Forget Sloane,* he thought. *Jack and Sydney and the others will surely do their best to extract me. I would be dead now if Syd had not rescued me on Mount Aconcagua after Anna Espinosa ambushed me and left me for dead. My fellow agents will come for me again. I just have to hold out long enough.*

"You think so?" Maya challenged him. She scooped up the gourd and dashed the remaining antidote in his face. "Listen to me, Agent Dixon. You think you have sampled the power of the zombie powder? Think again. Thus far you have tasted only an extremely mild version of the poison. Properly prepared, the powder is capable of inflicting permanent brain damage. A sort of herbal lobotomy, if you will. The victim is forever reduced to a mindless automaton with no will of his own . . . one of the living dead."

Dixon maintained his composure. "I'm not afraid of primitive superstitions."

"There's nothing supernatural about it," Maya insisted. "I'm talking about a unique combination of psychoactive herbs and natural toxins, developed over the course of generations by the bocors, or black magicians, of Haiti. I won't bore you with the entire recipe, but I believe that tarantula venom is involved, as well as the glandular secretions of a certain species of tree frog." She looked Dixon in the eyes, without a trace of humor in her voice. "Trust me when I tell you that the zombie powder rivals many of the mind-controlling drugs your own CIA experimented with in the previous century."

She walked across the smokehouse to where a leather pouch hung on another meat hook. Removing the bag from its resting place, she opened it and took out a handful of finely ground gray powder. Smiling maliciously, she strolled back toward Dixon. Her fist was held up before his face. Grains of powder sifted through her fingers.

"Think carefully, Dixon," she warned him, "while you still have the capacity. Tell me what I want to know, or I swear you will spend the rest of your life as a mindless zombie."

The picture she painted appalled Dixon to the core of his being. Even physical torture paled in comparison with the prospect of losing his mind, his very self. But the fearsomeness of Maya's threat had no effect on his decision. *I would rather be a zombie,* he thought, *than betray my country's trust.*

"Do what you want," he told Maya. He tried to think of some way to stall for time. Perhaps if he tried feeding Maya false or outdated information? Easier said than done; Maya was too experienced an operative not to see through any obvious lies. "I can't tell you what I don't know."

"Don't waste my time," she fumed. "Where is Sloane's new headquarters?"

Dixon held his tongue. His greatest regret was that he might forget the faces of his children.

Good-bye, Robin, Steven.

Maya scowled but kept her fist tightly shut instead of blowing the powder in his face. Had she been bluffing all along, or was she simply reluctant to zombify him before she had emptied his brain of its secrets? Dixon suspected the latter.

A knock at the door of the smokehouse intruded on the moment. "What is it?" Maya called impatiently.

The door swung open and one of Benoit's men rushed into the room. Dixon recognized him as the thug who had slapped him across the face outside the cemetery. "I'm sorry to disturb you, madam, but you need to hear this. Our sensors have picked up intruders in the swamp. They seem to be heading for the lagoon!"

Maya's face took on a demonic cast. "Sydney," she hissed venomously.

Dixon's interrogation was suddenly not a priority. "Alert Benoit . . . discreetly," Maya ordered the flunky. "Then get together some men and meet me at the pier. We need to deal with this immediately."

Maya thrust her handful of powder back into the pouch. For a minute Dixon thought that she had forgotten him entirely, but then she paused long enough to give him a parting glare on her way out the door.

"You've won a momentary reprieve," she informed him icily. "Use that time to reconsider your decision." She stood silhouetted in the doorway, moonlight pouring into the windowless shack. "I'll be back for you later . . . after I've killed Sydney Bristow."

"The bidding will start at fifty million dollars," Benoit explained to the guests, "with successive bids to occur in ten-million-dollar increments. Following the auction the merchandise will be delivered to the winner as soon as the appropriate funds have been electronically transferred to a specific offshore account, at which point—"

The host's recitation of the rules for the upcoming auction was interrupted by the arrival of a servant who joined Benoit upon the dais and whispered something into his employer's ear. Benoit's face gave no clue as to the nature of the communication, but he immediately appeared to shift gears.

"If you'll excuse me," he said smoothly, "a matter has come up that requires my attention. Please enjoy my hospitality and let my staff know if there is anything else you require." The slide show behind him ceased and the satin curtains were drawn shut once more. "I shall return shortly, and the auction will take place promptly at midnight, right on schedule."

He stepped down from the dais and headed briskly toward the nearest exit. Concerned guests accosted him with questions as he departed, demanding to know the source of the emergency, but Benoit politely brushed their queries aside. Within seconds he had left the parlor for parts unknown.

What's happening? Nadia wondered. As far she knew, the interruption was not of APO's making, unless Sydney was involved somehow. But her sister was supposedly deep in the bayous right now, searching for Kestrel itself with the aid of Terry Fujiwara. Had Benoit found out what she was up to?

Is Sydney in danger?

Nadia wasn't the only guest puzzled by the host's abrupt exit. Groups of puzzled terrorists murmured anxiously among themselves. Eavesdropping on various conversations, while slowly nursing her mint julep, she overheard a heated debate among the contingent from the Szekely Alliance, a violent Balkan separatist group. Sandor Kravac wanted to leave the plantation at once, convinced that the security of the gathering had been compromised, while his associate, a Serbian war criminal named Drago Popov, was still intent on taking part in the auction. Nadia guessed that similar debates were taking place throughout the parlor.

"We should take advantage of this timely interruption," she whispered to Weiss.

"Already on it," he replied.

Showtime, Weiss thought. Violating the self-imposed segregation keeping the various factions of guests apart, he sauntered over to where three members of the People's Liberation Brigade were huddled. "Jacob Raab of the Nth Wave," he introduced himself, extending his hand. "I must say I've always admired your organization's work. That bombing at the naval base was a thing of beauty, not to mention an inspiring blow against imperialist aggression. Such surgical precision!"

Chao Liang, acting commander of the PLB, regarded Weiss's hand coldly. He made no effort to shift the cocktail he was holding in his own right hand. "What do you want, American?" he asked warily.

"Just trying to build some bridges between potential allies," Weiss insisted. He took a step closer to Liang and lowered his voice. "Seriously, I wanted to warn you to stay on your toes. I have reliable intel that those turncoats from the PRF are up to something tonight." He tilted his head toward the representatives from the Proletarian Revolutionary Front, who were glaring at Liang and his cronies from the other side of the buffet table. "A word to the wise: Don't take your eyes off them for a second."

His vague allegations definitely got Liang's attention. "What sort of intel?" he asked intently. More than a decade of bitter conflict showed in his face as he glowered suspiciously at his rivals across the buffet table. "What are those treacherous curs plotting now?"

"I don't know the specifics," Weiss stated. He

took another step closer to Liang—and the man's cocktail. "Just that they're planning something big." As he spoke, he quietly detached a small, white faux button from the sleeve of his Armani jacket and hid it between his fingers. He joined Liang in contemplating the PRF contingent. "So who's the ugly guy with the bad hair?"

"Wolfgang Reinholz," Liang snarled, his voice dripping with scorn. In fact, Weiss was fully aware that Reinholz had personally ordered the drive-by shooting that had killed Liang's favorite mistress. "A coward, collaborator, and renegade!"

"You don't say?" While Liang stared daggers at his nemesis, Weiss deftly dropped the "button" into the man's drink, where it dissolved instantaneously. "He certainly looks the type."

Confident that his sleight of hand had gone unnoticed by both Liang and his confederates, Weiss began to back away casually from his new-found acquaintances. *Pretty slick, if I do say so myself,* he congratulated himself. *Great-great-uncle Houdini would approve.*

Weiss was indeed a descendant and namesake of the legendary stage magician, a fact of which he was inordinately proud. He seldom missed a chance to perform a little legerdemain on the job.

"Well, I'm glad we had this little chat," he said amiably to the PLB crew as he headed back toward the buffet table. He gave Liang a knowing wink. "Just remember, you didn't hear anything from me."

"Understood," Liang replied. He took a sip from his drink, and Weiss resisted the temptation to smile.

The bombing he had gushed about earlier had taken the lives of more than 180 victims, 57 of whom were civilians. It had taken all of Weiss's acting skills to conceal his revulsion while chatting amiably with Liang.

What happened next would be only a fraction of what the ruthless terrorist deserved.

Weiss could hardly wait.

It won't be long now, Nadia thought.

She watched as Weiss strolled away from the PLB and proceeded to pile a small mountain of barbecued shrimp onto a plate. Had he successfully pulled off his part of the maneuver? She couldn't ask him directly, since in anticipation of the tight security neither of them was wired for sound. Plus, for the next few minutes it was wisest that they stay away from each other, just in case Liang's associates put two and two together.

All she could do now was wait and have faith in her partner. *I shouldn't doubt him,* she thought guiltily. As he had proved in Guatemala and elsewhere, despite his breezy manner, Weiss was an extremely able operative. *He knows what he's doing.*

Sure enough, within moments of Weiss's departure Chao Liang suddenly stiffened in shock. His cocktail glass slipped from his fingers and shattered upon the hardwood floor. Liang clutched his throat and his voice emerged as a raspy croak. "Reinholz!" he blurted out, before collapsing to the floor in convulsions. His eyes rolled back until only the whites could be seen. His limbs jerked spasmodically. Foam sputtered from his lips.

Nasty but effective, Nadia thought, observing the effects of the toxin. *Just as the techs at APO promised.* Recoiling instinctively, she reminded herself of all the lives Liang and the PLB had destroyed. *Payback is long overdue.*

Liang's collapse threw the party into an uproar. One of Liang's colleagues, Anwar Nouri, hurled accusations at Wolfgang Reinholz and the other members of the PRF, who indignantly declared their innocence.

Cassandra Spiros, Liang's second-in-command, dropped to her knees beside her fallen commander in a desperate attempt to keep him from biting or swallowing his own tongue. Broken glass crunched beneath the tread of numerous feet as hotheads from both factions lunged at one another. Benoit's security guards ran forward to break up the fight, abandoning their posts at the exits.

"Bastards!" Nouri shouted at the PRF as the burly guards struggled to hold him back. "You'll pay for this!"

"Lying scum!" Reinholz shouted back, from behind the hefty shoulders of his own bodyguard. "What sort of clumsy trick are you pulling? This won't keep us from claiming Kestrel."

Liang continued to thrash around wildly on the floor, as though possessed by a voodoo spirit. His nails scraped at the polished hickory boards until his fingers were raw and bloody.

That's my cue, Nadia thought. Amid the tumult it was easy to bump into another guest, effectively spilling the remainder of her mint julep onto the front of her dress. "Oops! *Lo siento,*" she murmured before sidling toward an exit. There were at least two unwatched doors available, but instead she headed straight for the only door that was still being guarded by one of Benoit's hired goons. By coincidence, the watchdog in question turned out to be her old friend, the overenthusiastic frisker.

We meet again, she thought slyly. *All the better.*

"Excuse me," she said to him, dabbing ineffectively at her cleavage with a cocktail napkin. The combination of lace and spilled bourbon produced a semi-see-through effect that served to yank the guard's attention away from the ruckus elsewhere in the parlor. "I'm afraid I've had a bit of an accident. Perhaps you can show me someplace where I can straighten up a bit?"

To his credit, the guard actually hesitated. Tearing his gaze away from the translucent lace sheath, he glanced uncertainly at his comrades on the floor. Nadia could tell he wasn't sure where he was most needed.

She decided to make it easy for him. "Please," she entreated, batting her eyes and laying a gentle hand upon his arm. She gave him a thousand-watt smile. "I'd be ever so grateful."

That did the trick. A grin broke out on his tanned Cajun features as lust won out over his better judgment. After all, hadn't Benoit instructed his staff to take good care of his guests? "Come with me, *mon cheri*," he said, offering her his arm, which she graciously accepted. "I know just the place."

He led her out of the parlor into the foyer, then up a grandiose stairway to the second floor. She leaned against him as they climbed the steps, letting him feel the warmth of her body. She ran her fingers along the smooth oak balustrade.

At the top of the staircase he reluctantly let go of her arm and pointed at the third door to the left. "That's the master bathroom," he explained. He stood watch outside the door. "I'll wait here until you're through."

Where's the fun in that? she thought. "You'd better come in with me," she said throatily. Her eyes smoldered in an unmistakably seductive manner. She posed in the doorway of the bathroom, resting her hip against the doorframe. "I might need help getting this soggy dress off."

The nameless guard couldn't believe his luck. Eyes gleaming, he looked both ways to see if anyone was watching, then hurried forward. "You bet!" he exclaimed, grinning from ear to ear. "Whatever you want, baby, I'm ready!"

"Just what I like to hear." She stepped aside to

let him enter the sumptuously decorated bathroom. Locking the door behind her, she remembered his invasive hands groping her earlier this evening. "Nothing like mixing a little pleasure with business, I always say."

A roundhouse kick dropped him to the cool Italian marble floor. Before he could recover or cry out, she snatched a Turkish cotton towel from a rack and wrapped it around his throat like a garrote. She dug a stiletto heel into his back and twisted the knot at the back of the towel until he was gasping for breath. She waited until his face started to turn blue, then loosened the noose just enough to let him breathe.

"No more games," she told him. All the flirtatiousness vanished from her voice. "Benoit is holding a prisoner here. A black man, roughly fifty years old. Where are you keeping him?"

The guard's voice came out as a strangled squeak. "I don't know what you're talking about," he gasped.

"Wrong answer," Nadia said. She tightened the expensive cloth around his neck. *Fun's fun,* she thought, *but I'm running out of time.* "Where is the prisoner?"

"Why should I tell you?" the guard said defiantly.

He was stubborn, if not particularly bright. "Who the hell are you, anyway?"

"My name doesn't matter," she told him. She ground her heel into the small of his back until he yelped in agony. "What you need to know is that I am an invited guest at a soiree thrown exclusively for terrorists and mass murderers." She tightened the towel another notch. "Trust me, I've killed people a lot more innocent than you."

As she'd hoped, her menacing performance put the fear of God into the helpless guard. "The smokehouse!" he blurted out. "He's in the smokehouse out back!"

That's more like it, Nadia thought. Letting go of the towel, she slammed the guard's head into the bathroom floor, rendering him senseless. Then, for good measure, she extracted her inhaler from her purse and sprayed it in the man's face. The concentrated knockout gas would guarantee that he remained down for the count for at least another hour or so. *Pleasant dreams.*

Or not.

Deciding that turnabout was fair play, she groped beneath the man's jacket until she found the Smith & Wesson tucked into his shoulder holster. She checked the clip to make sure it was fully loaded.

"Thanks," she told him. "This will do just fine."

Opening the bathroom door a crack, she made sure the coast was clear, then slipped out of the room and down the hall. She could still hear angry voices yelling in the parlor below. From the sound of it more than just the PRF and PLB were up in arms; the entire reception seemed to have dissolved into pandemonium. Colliding bodies slammed into one another or hit the floor with a crash. Shouts and curses, in a variety of languages and accents, echoed off the venerable walls of the mansion. Terrorists, mobsters, revolutionaries, and spies demanded explanations, restitution, and revenge. Expensive glass and crystal could be heard shattering against marble.

How about that? Nadia thought, impressed by the free-for-all her partner had apparently unleashed. *Who knew terrorists couldn't play well together?*

Weiss met her at the foot of the stairs. "There you are!" he said in a hushed voice. Apparently the rest of the guards were too busy trying to contain the chaos in the parlor to keep track of every guest's whereabouts. "I wouldn't go back in there," he said, gesturing toward the untended doorways. "That place is a zoo!"

Where is Benoit during all this? Nadia worried. *Or Maya Rao, for that matter?* She scoped out the empty foyer, on guard against the arrival of any unwanted company. *What sort of crisis is keeping Benoit busy—and how long it is likely to last?*

"We have to hurry," she told Weiss urgently. She dropped the pistol into her purse. "I know where Dixon is!"

Alone in the smokehouse, Dixon struggled to escape from his constraints, yet neither the meat hook nor his shackles gave an inch. He pressed the soles of his feet against the brick wall behind him and strained until his arms felt like they were being stretched upon the rack, but to no avail. The humidity, combined with his exertions, left him drenched in sweat. Perspiration dripped from his face. His muscles ached. His mouth was as dry as dust, and he felt dizzy from dehydration.

I can't give up, he told himself. Maya could return at any minute, and then he'd once again be facing the prospect of permanent brain damage, assuming Maya was telling the truth about the insidious effects of the zombie powder. He had no reason to doubt her, however, and even less of a desire to experience the phenomenon firsthand. *I need to escape this place before I find out the truth one way or another.*

He could only hope that Sydney and Fujiwara were faring better than he was. If Kestrel could be recovered safely and kept off the black market, then his ordeal would not have been in vain. He remembered all the victories he and Sydney had scored over the years, all the innocents they had protected, and drew comfort from the knowledge that he had fought the good fight till the end. That counted for something.

But he wasn't ready to call it quits just yet. *Just a short pause,* he thought, sagging against the wall of his cell. *Then I'll try to break free again.*

Sounds from outside the smokehouse caught his attention, and he lifted his weary head. He heard footsteps approaching the brick shack, followed by a brief conversation between a man and a woman. Was Maya back already? Dixon didn't think so; the woman's voice sounded familiar, but he couldn't

quite make it out. Seductive laughter penetrated the
thick oak door. Somebody appeared to be having a
better night than he was.

There was a hiss, as from an aerosol spray, then
the unmistakable sound of a body thudding to the
ground. Keys rattled in the lock and the door swung
open.

Who is it now?

Nadia Santos, dressed in a gorgeous evening
dress, rushed into the smokehouse. "Dixon! Thank
God!" She hurried over to him and went to work picking the lock on his cuffs. He smelled bourbon and mint
leaves. "Are you all right?" she asked him urgently.

The cuffs sprang open and Dixon dropped onto
the dirt floor. Grimacing, he lowered his arms for what
felt like the first time in ages. He wiggled his numb
limbs in order to restore their circulation, ignoring the
painful pins-and-needles sensation this produced.
"Well, enough to get out of here," he told her.

A feeling of pride and vindication washed over
him. He *knew* his fellow agents wouldn't leave him
behind.

Nadia helped him out of the smokehouse and
onto the moonlit lawn of a large Southern estate.
Benoit's plantation, he guessed. Eric Weiss was

just outside the door, bending over the unconscious body of a guard. The same guard, presumably, whom Nadia had put out of commission a few minutes earlier. Weiss removed an automatic pistol from the fallen sentry and jumped to his feet.

"Dixon!" he said happily. "Good to see you, man." He turned to Nadia and pointed across the lawn at a distant structure. "The garage is over this way. We should be able to commandeer a limo and get the heck out of here."

Sydney's sister retrieved her own gun from her purse. "Sounds like a plan," she said. "Let's do it."

The two young agents each took Dixon by an arm and started to guide him toward the enormous garage. "Wait!" he protested. "Maya and Benoit were headed off into the bayous. I think they're going after Sydney." He grimly stripped the last pieces of latex from his sweaty face. In the distance, beyond the plantation's outbuildings, the Mississippi River sluggishly made its way past the grounds of the estate. "Maya said something about a pier."

We're not done here yet, he realized. Not while Maya and Benoit were hunting for intruders in the nearby swamps. "Forget the limo. We need a boat."

CHAPTER 14

THE BAYOU

"You were right!" Sydney told Terry. "Kestrel's right beneath us. We found it!"

She climbed back into the skiff, excited by her discovery at the bottom of the lagoon. Water streamed down her body onto the floor of the boat, but she didn't bother to towel off; she wasn't done swimming yet. She carefully put down the speargun, making sure the safety was still set.

"Thank God!" Terry exclaimed. He let out a massive sigh of relief, as though an enormous load of guilt had just been lifted from his shoulders.

"Maybe this is finally almost over!"

I hope so, Sydney thought, still worried about Dixon. She immediately contacted Sloane via her cell phone and informed him of their success at locating Kestrel. "Terry has a plan for getting the plane out of here," she explained. "You'd better put Marshall on the line too." She definitely wanted Marshall's input on the technical aspects of Terry's scheme.

"Good work, Sydney," Sloane replied. "Let me summon Marshall."

Sydney waited until both men were ready, then handed the phone over to Terry. He gulped nervously and cleared his throat before retrieving a compact electronic device from a Ziploc bag. The gadget resembled an ordinary pocket calculator, complete with a digital display and a numerical keypad.

"Meet Fido," he said with a touch of embarrassment. "I call it that because I built it to fetch Kestrel, so to speak." He waited for a laugh, which was not forthcoming. "Er, it's actually an electronic override device I designed specifically for an opportunity like this. Once it's affixed to the hull of the UCAV, directly above the plane's cybernetic brain,

Fido will download new instructions into Kestrel's navigational system, directing it to fly to the nearest local airfield, which just happens to be about fifteen miles away."

Sydney eyed the device skeptically. "Is this really going to work? No offense, but we're talking about a plane that's currently sitting at the bottom of a swamp."

"Trust me," Terry assured her. "I studied the specs for Kestrel practically until my eyes bled. It's perfectly capable of a vertical takeoff, plus it's been expressly designed to fly through sandstorms, blizzards, radioactive fallout, you name it. A little swamp water isn't going to hurt it."

Sydney recalled her initial briefing on Kestrel, back at APO headquarters. Terry's glowing description of the UCAV's abilities corresponded with what she'd been told then. *Maybe this isn't such a far-fetched idea after all?*

"Right now Kestrel's in hibernation mode," he continued. "All you have to do is wake it up. One quick, low-altitude flight later, and Kestrel will be at the airfield, ready to be picked up by the powers that be."

He seemed pretty confident, which Sydney

hoped was a good sign. She took the phone back from Terry. "You got all that?" she asked Marshall and Sloane. "What do you think?"

"It should work, theoretically speaking," Marshall hedged. "I mean, I'd love to take the gadget apart first and see exactly how it works before committing, but the whole idea behind Kestrel *is* that it's supposed to be able to fly itself, so you should be able to tell it where to go, just like programming your VCR . . . or TiVo, if you prefer. Plus, we're talking about VixNut1—that is, Fujiwara—here, so I'm inclined to give him the benefit of the doubt. I mean, he's already hacked into Kestrel once before, you know?"

Sloane cut into Marshall's rambling analysis of the situation. "I'm convinced," he informed Sydney. "We can't risk the possibility of allowing Benoit to move the UCAV before we can get a salvage team in there. For all we know, he's already got it programmed to fly to a different location on command." Sydney could practically hear the gears in Sloane's brain turning as he thought ahead to his next moves. "I'll notify Hayden Chase to secure the airfield. Proceed with the operation at once."

Easy for you to say, Sydney thought. *You don't*

have to go swimming with the gators again. She saw the logic behind Sloane's decision, though. "Understood," she told him. "What's the word on Dixon?"

She thought she heard Sloane sigh impatiently at the other end of the line, like there were more important things Sydney should be concerned with at the moment. "Nadia and Weiss have infiltrated Benoit's estate in search of Dixon. I hope to have more information shortly. In the meantime Kestrel remains your top priority."

Aye, aye, Captain, Sydney thought acidly. She was relieved to hear that her fellow agents were looking for Dixon—she had great faith in both Nadia's and Weiss's abilities—but she still resented chasing after an expensive piece of hardware while her partner remained unaccounted for. *What if they're torturing him at this very minute?*

There was nothing to be done about that now, however, except complete her mission as expeditiously as possible. She nodded at the device in Terry's hands. "So, how does this work?"

"It's a simple, four-step process," he insisted. "Very user friendly. First, you need to attach Fido to the hull, near the nose of the plane, where the cockpit would be if it had a cockpit." He indicated a button on the keypad. "Press here to magnetize Fido to clamp it to the ship. The display screen will light up when it establishes the interface with Kestrel's navigational controls.

"Second, you need to download the new instructions. I've already keyed in the proper coordinates. All you need to do is press this button and wait for the new program to download completely, which should take about five minutes or so.

"Third, you need to set the timer to give us enough time to get clear of the ship before it takes off. Maybe sixty seconds or so? Use your own judgment. I'm sure you've done this sort of thing a lot more than I have!

"Fourth, and finally, hit the plus key to start the countdown. Then swim like hell away from the plane." He looked up from the device to make sure Sydney was listening. "Got that?"

Sounds simple enough, she conceded. She reviewed the key commands one more time just to make sure she had them down. "Okay," she said. She attached Fido to a leather cord, which she secured around her neck. The lightweight mechanism bounced against her chest. "Here I go again."

Armed once more with her searchlight and speargun, she dropped over the edge of the boat and into the water. This time the sudden coolness came as less of a shock; it was a beautiful night for swimming, if you didn't mind worrying about ambushes and alligators.

As before she kept her eyes peeled for any approaching gators. So far, though, the intimidating reptiles appeared to be keeping their distance. Maybe that gooey repellent wasn't as useless as she'd feared it was.

She maintained a tight grip on the speargun nonetheless.

Confident that she knew where she was going this time, she swam straight down to Kestrel. She kicked herself along the length of the sunken aircraft until she was directly above the nose of the UCAV, then carefully removed Fido from her neck. As instructed, she magnetized the override device and placed it against the cool metallic skin of the aircraft. A lambent glow greeted her eyes as the display screen came to life.

So far, so good.

She pressed another button on the keypad. A muffled hum vibrated through the water, suggesting that the download had begun. Was Fido actually talking to Kestrel? The digital display began tracking the progress of the download in luminous green percentages.

Five percent.

Ten percent.

Fifteen percent.

Sydney hovered above the readout, paddling to keep herself in place. The download seemed to proceed with agonizing slowness, even though she knew that, objectively, less than a minute had passed. She wondered how many firewalls and other cyber defenses Terry's program had to overcome before imprinting itself on Kestrel's brain.

Twenty percent.

Twenty-five percent.

The roar of powerful engines suddenly filtered down through the watery depths. Alarmed, Sydney looked up to see the arrival of two speed boats churning up the surface of the lagoon fifteen feet above her head.

Who? she asked herself anxiously, afraid she already knew. *Maya and Benoit. Who else could it be?*

And Terry was all on his own up there.

For a moment she wondered what had alerted

Maya and Benoit to their presence in the bayous.
Had she and Terry triggered some sort of concealed
electric eye or alarm? Or had Maya simply anticipated their next move?

The muffled report of gunfire instantly ren-
dered all such questions unimportant. Terry was
clearly under attack. Was he managing to hold off
the bad guys with Sydney's Beretta, or was he
already wounded and dying?

Now what do I do?

Torn, she glanced back down at the digital display
on the override device. Forty-five percent. The download was nearly half complete. Ideally she should
finish reprogramming Kestrel before going to Terry's
rescue. Technically she didn't need the hapless computer genius anymore. All she needed to do to complete her mission was launch Kestrel, then quietly
swim away beneath the concealing waters of the
bayou. Chances were, she could get away scot-free.

That's what Maya would do, she realized.

But I'm not her.

Leaving Fido to complete the download on its
own, she swam stealthily back toward the surface,
extinguishing her searchlight in favor of the moonlight that grew steadily brighter as she kicked her

way upward, speargun ready. The keels of the newly arrived speedboats sliced through the water above her, circling the unmoving skiff at breakneck speed. Sydney carefully evaded the paths of the enemy boats, coming up beneath the skiff before veering off to the starboard side of the boat. She hoped the white water stirred up by the racing powerboats concealed the telltale bubbles rising up from her rebreather.

Her head bobbed to the surface in the shadow of the skiff. Waves generated by the violent passage of the speedboats lapped against her. Hoping to avoid being spotted, she stayed submerged from the nose down, paddling gently in the choppy water as she swiftly took stock of the situation.

It wasn't good.

Two high-powered speedboats—one black, one dark purple—raced around the perimeter of the lagoon, blocking off all escape routes. Rooster tails of surging foam and spray trailed after the zooming vessels. Brilliant yellow *vevers* were painted on the sides of the boats.

Sydney spotted Benoit standing in the back of the black powerboat, holding on to a rail with one hand and an AK-47 assault rifle with the other. A name inscribed near the prow identified the vessel as the *Baron Samedi*. A gun-wielding henchman stood across from Benoit; Sydney recognized him as the glass-eyed guard from La Maison du Vodou. A third thug manned the controls of the boat.

But where was Maya?

It took Sydney a second to spot her nemesis, who appeared to be in command of the purple boat. Maya's craft was named *Maman Brijit,* after the baron's wife, a powerful spirit in her own right. *The lord of the dead and the queen of black magic,* Sydney noted, recalling her voodoo lore.

Sounds like Benoit and Maya to me.

Gas fumes stung her eyes, even through her scuba mask, and she paddled around the side of the skiff until she could get a glimpse of the engine. Her heart sank as she saw that the motor was riddled with bullet holes. Black smoke rose from the ruined engine, while gasoline spilled out into the lagoon, spreading across the surface of the water in an iridescent film. Sydney had to raise her head above the water in order to keep the gas away from her face. The caustic fumes invaded her throat.

No wonder the skiff was dead in the water.

From her vantage point she couldn't actually see Terry, but to her relief she heard him crouching upon the floor of the skiff, firing back at Benoit and Maya. Alas, he was no marksman; his shots missed the powerboats, which were zipping past way too fast for him to take aim. It would be a stroke of luck if he actually hit something.

Sydney wasn't sure she'd fare much better, even if there were time to climb into the skiff and take the gun herself.

Which there wasn't.

Think, Sydney! she urged herself. Floating in the water, surrounded by Maya and Benoit's miniature armada, she felt helpless. *But I can't just leave Terry here! There must be a way to save him, too.*

Benoit fired a warning shot over Terry's head, then put down the AK-47 long enough to pick up a bullhorn. "Give it up, my friend. You don't stand a chance. Throw away the gun, or we'll blow you to pieces." The bullhorn amplified his Haitian accent and supernaturally deep voice. "Use your brain, Mr. Fujiwara. Do you truly want the alligators to feast on your flesh?"

"Okay, okay!" Terry hollered back, barely audible over the roar of the speedboats. To her dismay

Sydney heard the Colt hit the water with a splash, then sink out of sight. "Please don't kill me!"

Sydney couldn't blame Terry for surrendering. The enemies had superior numbers, arms, and boats. What other choice did he have? He was an inexperienced computer geek, not a field-rated CIA agent.

It's up to me to save him.

"An excellent decision, Mr. Fujiwara!" Benoit congratulated Terry. He signaled the boat's pilot to bring the *Baron Samedi* to a stop a few yards in front of the skiff, while the *Maman Brijit* continued to circle the edge of the lagoon. "Up on your feet!" Benoit ordered. The sign of Damballah glittered in silver upon his chest.

"Hang on!" Terry pleaded. "Just give me a nanosecond!"

Sydney heard him stand up awkwardly in the skiff, which rocked beneath his feet. She saw the upper part of his body rise above the side of the boat. His empty hands were raised high above his head.

Could Terry trust Benoit to spare him? Sydney had her doubts. Still unseen by Maya and the others, she released the safety on her speargun.

"Mersi," Benoit thanked Terry in Creole. "But such cooperation comes too late, I'm afraid. You've

proved far more trouble than you're worth, Mr. Fujiwara." The *gardes* on his face added to his menacing appearance. "Besides, I confess I still bear some ill will toward you for enjoying the embraces of my woman. A strategic necessity, to be sure, but not one I'm inclined to overlook."

He raised his rifle. . . .

"No!" Sydney cried out, reacting instantly. She swung the speargun upward and squeezed the trigger. An elastic power band snapped forward, propelling the metal spear through the air.

The shaft impaled Benoit in the chest, just missing his amulet. His eyes widened in shock as he saw the spear protruding from his body. He clutched the shaft with both hands. Bright arterial blood gushed from his mouth.

His men stared in frozen horror at their boss. *"Houngan!"* Glass Eye exclaimed. "Oh, crap!"

"Radegonde, Baron Samedi . . . ," Benoit intoned, calling upon the spirits who appeared to have forsaken him. Was he shocked that his protective scars had proved no match against a loaded speargun? "Gede-Loraj!"

He toppled over the side of the speedboat into the water.

One down, Sydney thought. The recoil from the speargun had nearly dunked her, but she let go of the weapon and grabbed on to the side of the skiff. Benoit's men were still stunned by the sudden death of their leader, but that wasn't going to last long. And there was still Maya to contend with. . . .

"Terry!" she shouted urgently. "Get in the water . . . now!" As long as he was stranded in the crippled skiff, he was a sitting duck. *I hope to God he knows how to swim!*

The terrified hacker didn't need any further encouragement to get out of the line of fire. He threw himself gracelessly over the side of the skiff, hitting the water with an enormous splash. Sydney readied herself to dive after him in case he started to sink, but to her relief his head quickly bobbed up beside hers.

"Ohmigod!" he gasped. Water streamed from his soaked black hair. "I thought I was dead for sure! You saved my life!"

"Don't thank me yet," she said. The odds were still against them. "Just follow my lead, and I'll try to get us out of this mess."

But how?

Benoit's body floated facedown in the lagoon.

Retrieving her spear was not an option, so she let the weapon's tether slip from her wrist and drew her knife instead. Blood spread from Benoit's corpse, staining the dark water red.

The freshly spilled blood attracted the attention of the gators on the shore. To Sydney's distress the deadly reptiles stirred restlessly. Scaly bodies slid into water, their powerful tails driving them toward the center of the lagoon.

Damn! Sydney thought. The approaching gators were the last thing she needed right now. *As if Maya and her goons were not bad enough!*

Speaking of whom, the *Maman Brijit* came around to where the Indian assassin could see Sydney and Terry clinging to the side of the skiff. Her face contorted with fury at the sight of Benoit's body drifting in the water. "You stupid bitch!" she shrieked at Sydney over the roar of her boat. "I should have killed you years ago!" She raised her rifle and yelled at the men on both boats. "Get them! Don't let them escape!"

The guard on the *Baron Samedi* snapped out of his daze. Along with Maya, he opened fire on the dog-paddling figures in the water. The deafening blare of the guns sounded much louder than they had from fifteen feet below. Bullets splashed into the water, missing their targets by inches. Hot lead ignited the spilled gasoline. Flames erupted atop the water, spreading rapidly.

"Dive!" Sydney shouted at Terry. She tugged on Terry's arm. "Under the boat!"

She dipped her head forward and dived beneath the cascade of gunfire. A bullet grazed her right arm, drawing blood, but she kept swimming until both she and Terry had taken cover beneath the bottom of the skiff. Gunshots blasted through the thin aluminum, proving that the boat provided meager protection at best. It was only a matter of time before the bullets found them.

Terry's cheeks bulged from trying to hold his breath in. Sydney tapped him on the shoulder, then passed the mouthpiece of her rebreather over to him. He gratefully accepted the apparatus, sucking down the precious air before handing it back to Sydney.

Swirling crimson tendrils entered her field of vision. *Crap!* she thought, glancing down at her stinging arm. Blood spilled freely from the bullet wound, streaking the murky water around them.

So much for my surefire gator repellent!

Despite all her training, Sydney found herself

at a loss as to what to do next. Guns, gators, fire . . . she and Terry were in deep trouble. And all thanks to Maya's treachery!

She peered down into the shadowy depths below her. Had Fido finished downloading the new coordinates into Kestrel? If so, it might be possible to launch the UCAV and thereby complete her mission, even if there was no way for her and Terry to survive.

Unless . . .

A wild idea occurred to her, but before she had a chance to think it through, she was suddenly distracted by the sound of *another* boat rushing into the lagoon.

Reinforcements for Maya?

The furious barrage of bullets suddenly abated, replaced by the din of gunfire being exchanged above the water. *What in the world?* Sydney thought. The only explanation was that Maya and her men had come under attack.

But from whom?

I need to know what's happening, Sydney decided. She tapped Terry and pointed upward. He gave her a puzzled look but nodded in assent; if nothing else he certainly trusted her more than he used to. *Let's hope his faith is not misplaced.*

They shared the air from the rebreather once more, then swam underwater away from the bullet-ridden skiff. Taking the lead, Sydney peered upward, searching for a gap in the bright orange flames spreading above them. An open patch of clear water presented itself, and she kicked toward the surface, hoping that Terry was following right behind her.

Her head broke through into the smoky air above the lagoon about four yards away from the skiff, which was taking on water from numerous bullet holes. She looked around hastily. Terry's head surfaced beside her. "What is it?" he asked anxiously. He choked on the acrid black smoke. "What's going on?"

"That's what I'm trying to find out," she said.

A chaotic scene met her eyes. Brilliant orange and yellow flames surrounded the sinking skiff, licking the surface of the water. Black smoke billowed upward. The smell of burning gasoline assaulted her nostrils. The rat-a-tat of automatic gunfire echoed throughout the bayou.

But who was firing at whom?

A high-speed airboat had invaded the lagoon

and was chasing after the original two speedboats, which were firing back at the newcomer, completely ignoring the two swimmers for the moment. There seemed to be three figures on the prop-powered vessel, one manning the pilot's seat while the remaining two blasted away at the voodoo boats with automatic pistols. The enormous propeller at the rear of the airboat sent it racing around the lagoon.

Sydney squinted at the newcomer as it rushed past her, trying to get a better look at its passengers. For a moment she couldn't believe her eyes.

Dixon was at the controls of the airboat, with Nadia and Weiss providing the firepower. They charged aggressively at the enemy speedboats, while zigzagging to avoid hostile fire. Sydney watched as the airboat came up behind the *Baron Samedi,* careening off the starboard side of the sleek black powerboat before veering away to come around again. From the front of the airboat Nadia flung a red plastic gas can attached to a burning rag. The improvised grenade arced through the smoky air before hitting the deck of Benoit's boat, where it exploded on contact. An ear-splitting boom rocked the bayou.

That's my sister, Sydney thought proudly. Bizarrely, Nadia and Weiss looked like they were dressed for the Oscars instead of a firefight in a swamp. Earmuffs protected them from the titanic roar of the airboat, which seemed to be louder than the other two boats combined. *Where did they get that thing?*

A tremendous fireball consumed the *Baron Samedi*. Fragments of charred wood and steel rained down upon the lagoon, along with what remained of Benoit's two men. The shock of the explosion sent foot-high waves rushing across the once tranquil surface of the lagoon, lifting and dropping the two swimmers in turn.

Fortunately Terry was too terrified to get seasick. "Who *are* these guys?" he asked in confusion. A fresh wave smacked him in the face, and he spit out a mouthful of swamp water.

"The cavalry," Sydney said.

With the *Baron Samedi* destroyed, the conflict in the lagoon became a one-on-one battle between Dixon's boat and Maya's. The two crafts jetted around the bayou at high speed, trying to get behind each other without presenting their flanks to the opposing vessel. Smoke and flames added to

ALIAS

the tumult, with the burning wreckage of Benoit's black boat bobbing atop the waves.

Sydney's skiff, on the other hand, had already disappeared to the bottom of the lagoon.

We're not out of the woods yet, she realized. Although the arrival of Dixon and his fellow agents had taken the heat off of her and Terry for the moment, there were still the flames—and the alligators. Her gaze was irresistibly drawn to Benoit's drifting corpse and the bloody water in which it floated. Even as she watched, the lifeless body was dragged under by huge saurian jaws. Swimming gators snapped and hissed at one another as they competed for choice morsels of human flesh. Scaly black tails whipped the gore into a crimson froth.

Daunted by the feeding frenzy, some of the less combative gators steered away from the pack in search of easier game. Steering clear of the smoking wreckage and gasoline, they zeroed in on Sydney and Terry, drawn by the fresh blood leaking from her wounded arm. Their dorsal scales crested above the waves as they glided through the water toward the swimmers.

Terry saw the gators approaching and started to freak out. "They're coming!" he whimpered, his eyes

328

wide with fear. Judging from his ashen complexion, the bad guys' bullets were far less intimidating than the prospect of being devoured by a not-so-distant relative of a dinosaur. "They're going to eat us alive!"

"Maybe not," Sydney said. A desperate gambit had popped into her mind right before Dixon and the others arrived on the scene; now it was looking like their only chance.

Paddling away from the gators, she quickly explained her scheme to Terry, who gaped at her as though she had lost her mind.

"Are you crazy?" he blurted out. "Is there a bug in your wetware?"

She shrugged. "You got any better ideas?"

Terry watched the hungry alligators draw nearer. There was no way they could outswim the aquatic reptiles. Gunfire and racing powerboats made the banks of the lagoon unreachable.

His gaze darted speculatively between the knife in Sydney's hand and the snouts of the oncoming gators. *Forget it,* she thought. *This isn't a Tarzan movie. I can't fend off a pack of alligators with just one knife.*

Terry's brain must have reached the same conclusion. He swallowed hard.

"Let's do it," he said.

With no time to lose, they swam back down to where Kestrel lay submerged. Terry's eyes widened at the sight of the futuristic-looking aircraft, and it dawned on Sydney that he had never actually seen the UCAV before. She prayed it wouldn't be one of the last things he ever saw.

Now that they had committed themselves, she couldn't help wondering if Terry had been right the first time, that she had gone completely insane. *Too late to worry about that now,* she resolved. *It's do or die . . . literally.*

Paddling above Kestrel's nose, they each refilled their lungs from the rebreather before checking the display on the override. DOWNLOAD COMPLETE, Fido reported, which meant their reckless plan was still on track.

The next step was to set the timer. Figuring the gators weren't far behind them, Sydney keyed in forty-five seconds. *That should give us just enough time to get into position,* she calculated, then she glanced over her shoulder to see if Terry approved. He looked positively green, his Adam's apple bobbing up and down like a yo-yo, but he gave her a hesitant thumbs-up sign.

All systems go. She activated the timer function on her waterproof wristwatch and synchronized it with Fido. Then she took a deep breath from her mouthpiece and pressed the oversize plus key on the override gadget, initiating the launch countdown. The luminous green numerals immediately starting counting down, in sync with her wristwatch: 00:45, 00:44, 00:43. . . .

She and Terry rushed to get into position, kicking off in opposite directions. She swam for Kestrel's starboard wing, which jutted away from the hull of the UCAV at roughly a forty-five-degree angle. Grabbing on to the leading edge of the wing, she laid herself flat against the streamlined metal appendage. The wet steel felt cold to the touch.

Was Terry in place on the other wing? Sydney lifted her head to check, only to see a sixteen-foot-long alligator diving straight toward the defenseless computer whiz. The gator's jaw gaped open, exposing rows of conical teeth that could easily strip the flesh from Terry's bones. Unarmed, he didn't stand a chance against the voracious predator.

Damn! Sydney thought. This escape plan was getting more complicated by the second. . . .

She ran the blade of her knife across her forearm, spilling fresh blood into the water. As she
hoped, the crimson libation distracted the gator
from Terry, so that it turned in the water and came
swimming toward Sydney instead. She tried to
remember that this was indeed what she had
intended.

Although ungainly on land, the hungry gator
cruised at her through the water with alarming speed.
Its massive jaws gaped open, hungry for Sydney's
vulnerable flesh. Unless everything worked out just
right, there would soon be a whole lot more of her
blood clouding the water.

But Terry might still get away, she thought.
That's the important thing.

Take that, Maya!

At the last second, right before the gator struck,
Sydney spun around so that her back faced the
monster. The reptile's jaws closed on the rebreathing apparatus strapped to her back, its teeth scrap-
ing against the metallic gas canister and harness.

Letting go of the mouthpiece, Sydney released
the straps and wriggled free of the unit. She kicked
away from the frustrated gator, who snapped and
clawed at the tangled apparatus in its mouth.

But for how long?

If I were Roy Scheider in Jaws, she thought, *I'd blow that oxygen tank apart with a flare gun.*

Unfortunately all she had was a knife.

That would have to do.

Turning around in midstroke, she dived for the confused gator below her just as the angry reptile shook the rebreathing unit from its jaws. Sydney swam onto the gator's back, pressing herself against its hard, bony scales. The creature's rough hide scraped against her skin. She wrapped her left arm around its neck and held on as tightly as she could.

Don't let go! she shouted silently at herself. *For God's sake, don't let go!*

Enraged by the weight upon its back, as well as by the hot mammalian blood tantalizing its senses, the gator spun about wildly, trying to dislodge its unwelcome rider. Sydney clamped her legs around the beast's sides in order to keep from being thrown from her perch—and into snapping range of the furious gator's jaws. Bubbles streamed from her nose as she raised the knife in her free hand.

She knew better than to try to force the knife through the gator's scaly hide. Instead she tightened her grip on the blade and drove it right into one of the creature's slit yellow eyes.

Carbon steel sliced into the reptilian orb, lodging deep in the socket. Cold blood gushed past Sydney's fist. The gator roared in agony and flailed about violently. Its thrashing tail struck Sydney like a bullwhip, knocking her off the gator's back. Her own blood mingled with the gory juices spewing from the gator's skull, where her lost knife remained firmly embedded. The billowing gore clouded the lens of her scuba mask, and she yanked it from her face to see what was happening.

Half blinded and in pain, the gator seemed to lose interest in munching on Sydney. As she kicked away from the animal, however, she was horrified to see at least five more gators diving toward her.

Oh, hell.

Her cheeks bulged. Her lungs ached. She was running out of air . . . and time.

How much longer before Kestrel launched?

Then, finally, she got a lucky break. The blood-crazed gators turned on their wounded compatriot, clawing and biting at Sydney's victim in an orgy of crocodilian cannibalism. Ignoring Sydney entirely, they tore into the injured gator, churning up the scarlet water until all Sydney could see was a tangle of tails and webbed claws.

She didn't wait to see how it turned out.

Exhausted, and shaking from the adrenaline rush, Sydney checked her wristwatch. How much time did she have before takeoff?

Eight seconds to go!

Sydney swam with all her might, putting everything she had into reaching the wing of the UCAV before it left without her. Desperate kicks and strokes propelled her through the water until she could see the leading edge of the starboard wing right in front of her. Her lungs screamed for oxygen, and her legs ached with every kick, pushed beyond endurance, but she couldn't rest for so much as a heartbeat. A thunderous noise rose from the bottom of the lagoon, Kestrel's powerful jet engines coming to life. The reverberations grew louder as the UCAV revved for takeoff.

Her fingers stretched out desperately and she felt cold metal beneath her touch. One last kick brought the wing within reach, and she grabbed on to the forward edge with both hands.

Made it!

Now for the hard part . . .

She didn't need to look at her wristwatch to know that time had run out. VTOL thrusters roared beneath Kestrel's wings, and the sunken aircraft rocketed upward, the sudden motion slapping Sydney's outstretched body against the top of the wing. She gritted her teeth and hung on for dear life, hoping that Terry was doing the same.

One moment they were fifteen feet underwater. The next they were blasting from the surface, straight up into the sky. Sydney had half expected to smash into either Dixon's or Maya's boat as they took off from the lagoon, but for the second time that night luck was on her side. Kestrel rose unobstructed above the bayous.

Was Dixon still chasing Maya? Sydney wished she could see, but the UCAV's rapid ascent flattened her against the surface of the wing. With effort she turned her head to one side in order to keep from having her face pressed into the unyielding metal.

Their vertical liftoff took only seconds. Sydney had no way to gauge how high they had climbed, but she heard a change in the engines and knew that Kestrel's flight was only just beginning. The UCAV leveled off, then surged forward at unbelievable speed.

A gale-force wind blew against Sydney, tearing at her hair and clothing. Her eyes were squeezed tightly shut, her fingers wrapped around the edge of the wing so hard that her knuckles turned white. The rushing wind instantly dried her hair and skin, but Sydney was in no state to appreciate this convenient side effect. Kestrel's extreme acceleration left her fighting to maintain her precarious perch, even as the massive forces tried to dislodge her. If she let her grip slacken for even an instant, she knew, she would go flying off into the sky like chaff in the wind.

What was I thinking? she asked herself in disbelief. This was far and away the craziest stunt she had ever pulled, counting the time she bailed out of a crashing 747. Her only consolation was the knowledge that even if neither she nor Terry survived the trip, at least Kestrel was returning to its rightful owners.

She just hoped the plane was worth dying for.

CHAPTER 15

THE BAYOU

The sudden appearance of the UCAV startled Dixon so much that he almost ran the airboat aground. One minute he was chasing Maya's purple speedboat around the lagoon, while Nadia and Weiss traded gunfire with the passengers aboard the other boat, and the next he was gaping in amazement as Kestrel burst from the water and rose up into the sky. His eyes widened as he glimpsed human figures clinging to each of the aircraft's wings. One of the figures he identified at once.

Sydney? He couldn't believe his eyes. *What in the world do you think you're doing?*

He could tell from their shocked expressions that Weiss and Nadia had seen Sydney too. Weiss said something, but Dixon couldn't hear him over the noise from the giant propeller spinning behind him. Beside Weiss at the front of the airboat, Nadia clapped a hand over her mouth at the sight of her sister ascending upon the wing of the UCAV. She looked completely shocked.

A second later Kestrel took off over the bayous, carrying Sydney away from them at unfathomable speed. Dixon looked away from the sky to see a grassy bank dead ahead. He pulled back hard on the steering stick and accelerated into the turn so that the airboat veered sharply to the left, narrowly missing the shore.

That was close, he realized. No matter what sort of danger Sydney was in, he needed to focus on what was right in front of him. For better or for worse her fate was out of his hands for the time being; now all that mattered was piloting the airboat.

And catching Maya Rao.

He spotted her across the smoking, alligator-infested surface of the lagoon. She and her men appeared to have been equally transfixed by Kestrel's spectacular departure, but she snapped out of it quickly. She barked a command at the driver of her boat, and the *Maman Brijit* banked to the right and took off for the mouth of the lagoon.

She's making a break for it, Dixon guessed, *now that she's lost Kestrel for good.* He didn't blame Maya for cutting her losses, but she would have to do better than that if she wanted to get away from him. Sydney wasn't the only who had a score or two to settle with Maya Rao. *I'll chase her halfway down the Mississippi if I have to.*

The powerboat zoomed out of the lagoon into the winding canals and tributaries beyond, leaving spray and white water in its wake. It zigzagged back and forth between the shores of a sluggish outlet, making it hard for Weiss and Nadia to get a bead on the fleeing vessel. Maya and a henchman fired back at them from the rear of the speedboat in a futile attempt to discourage pursuit.

Dixon opened up the throttle and the airboat raced after the *Maman Brijit,* planing across the surface of the water. Nadia and Weiss crouched at the front of the boat, shooting at Maya and her cohorts whenever they thought they had a clear shot.

They had stolen the boat from Benoit's own dock. Dixon wasn't surprised that Maya and Benoit had chosen the flashier powerboats, but that may have been a mistake on their part. Maya's purple craft was faster and quieter, but the prop-powered airboat was better for navigating the verdant wetlands. Unlike the *Maman Brijit,* which had to stick to the water, the airboat was an all-terrain vehicle, capable of traversing land, water, and everything in between.

That may give us an advantage, he thought.

A lucky shot, from either Nadia or Weiss, nailed Maya's fellow gunman, who tumbled backward onto the floor of the purple speedboat. That left just Maya and the pilot to deal with, provided the agents could catch up with them. *Where is Benoit?* Dixon wondered. He had not seen anyone matching the arms smuggler's description on either Maya's boat or the one that Nadia had blown up with the flaming gas can. *Did I just miss him, or did something happen to Benoit before we arrived at the lagoon?*

He would have to ask Maya—once he had her in custody.

The airboat was going nearly sixty miles per

hour, a dangerous speed for these twisty bayous, but Dixon was not about to let up on the throttle now. The controls responded ably to his touch, and he mentally congratulated the missing Benoit on the quality and maintenance of his craft. The massive propeller sucked in the air in front of them, creating a wind against his face. The spinning blades gave them plenty of thrust.

But was it enough to catch Maya's powerboat?

Up ahead the meandering channel took a leisurely bend around a protruding wedge of land. Dixon saw his opportunity. The *Maman Brijit* was forced to follow the curve, steering clear of the shore, but Dixon opened up the throttle another notch and the airboat cut right across the land, its polymer-coated hull effortlessly sliding across overgrown willows and dense thickets of needlegrass. Dixon's seat jumped beneath him as they hit the water again on the other side of the wedge, right behind the *Maman Brijit.*

He could feel the spray from Maya's boat against his face.

We're gaining on them!

Looking ahead, he saw that the bayou joined a larger canal at the point of a sandy delta topped with drooping cypresses. Levees had been built up along both sides of the canal, hemming them in. The high embankments were lined with concrete as a precaution against flooding.

His heart sank as he spotted what looked like a clear straightaway, which would give Maya a chance to pull away from them again, perhaps for good. Then his anxious eyes lit upon a fallen cypress lying across the path of the canal.

It was a dead end!

We have them, he thought triumphantly. But would Maya surrender without a fight?

Probably not.

He watched with concern as the purple speedboat executed a tight U-turn in front of the obstruction and came zooming back at them like a torpedo. To his surprise the powerboat seemed to be making no effort to avoid the other vessel, but was instead heading straight for the prow of the airboat. Dixon suddenly found himself in a high-velocity game of chicken.

As the *Maman Brijit* rushed toward them, Dixon saw Maya Rao standing at the front of the boat, holding a gun to the terrified pilot's head. She made eye contact with Dixon and smiled coldly, as if daring him to try his luck against the speedboat.

A bullet from Nadia's gun hit the windshield of the powerboat. Cracks spread like spiderwebs across the once transparent screen, rendering it instantly opaque. Dixon could no longer see Maya or the pilot—and vice versa.

And yet the powerboat kept on coming, on a collision course with the airboat. At the prow, Weiss cast a nervous look in Dixon's direction, as if unsure just how far the older agent was willing to push this. Nadia crossed herself instinctively.

The hell with it, Dixon thought, scowling. He wanted Maya, but not enough to sacrifice all three of their lives. *I have my children to think of.*

At the last second he shoved the steering stick forward, sending the airboat veering to the right. The side of the boat careened against the embankment before stabilizing back on the water. The impact sent Nadia and Weiss sprawling to the floor of the airboat, landing in a tangle of limbs, but Dixon managed to keep the boat from capsizing as he hastily circled around to see what had happened to Maya.

Have we lost her again?

He heard a crashing noise and spun around in his seat in time to see the purple speedboat lose control and zoom straight up onto the delta, barreling through the tangled reeds on its way toward a looming cypress draped in Spanish moss. The boat hit the tree head-on, then exploded in a red-hot ball of fire that ignited the hanging moss, turning the venerable cypress into a gigantic torch, with the crumpled remains of the *Maman Brijit* quickly lost in the smoke and flames. Within seconds an inferno raged atop the delta, filling the night sky with billowing black smoke.

Dear God, Dixon thought. He eased off the throttle and the airboat gradually slowed to a stop a safe distance from the flames. An eerie silence fell over the canal, broken only by the crackling fire and the horrified gasps of the agents on the airboat. Weiss helped Nadia to her feet, and the three of them stared in shocked silence at the blazing conflagration.

"Wow," Weiss said finally. "What a way to go."

Is that it? Dixon wondered. Had Maya Rao finally paid for her innumerable crimes, or had she somehow managed to jump clear of the boat in time? It was hard to imagine that anyone could have survived the accident, but stranger things had happened, especially in the shadowy world he and his colleagues lived in. *We thought Sydney was dead for two years. . . .*

He drove the airboat up and down the bayous until the craft was nearly out of gas, but they found no trace of Maya Rao.

Living or dead.

The flight lasted less than ten minutes, but it felt like an eternity. Sydney couldn't feel her fingers anymore. Despite the balmy temperature, the wind generated by Kestrel's acceleration had chilled her to the bone. Her teeth chattered, and the left side of her face felt like it was permanently welded to the cold steel wing beneath her. One of her swim fins came loose, and the rubber flipper was torn from her foot. Only the weight of her body kept both pieces of her swimsuit from joining the flipper.

I can't last much longer, she realized. Any minute now she was going to lose her grip on the wing and go flying off into oblivion. God only knew where her body would finally hit the earth or if it would ever be found. *I might end up as a snack for the alligators after all.*

For a second she wondered if she would see her mother on the other side. There were many questions she wanted to ask Irina Derevko. *Why did you arrange to have me killed? Did you ever, at any moment, really care about me at all?*

Perhaps she would finally have those questions answered.

Sydney was almost ready to give up when she felt the plane beneath her tilt slightly downward. Kestrel was descending already, only minutes after taking off. Its engines slowed and the wind against Sydney's body began to abate, negligibly at first, but then enough to give her hope. If she could just hang on for a few more moments. . . .

She forced her eyes open long enough to see a paved runway, surrounded on both sides by acres of soggy marshland. The tiny local airfield seemed to be rushing up at her with heart-stopping speed. She braced herself for impact as Kestrel hit the tarmac with a bone-jarring jolt that caused Sydney to bounce violently against the metal wing. The shock knocked the breath from her lungs, but she didn't let go of the wing's cold metal edge until the coasting UCAV came to a complete stop. Even then she had to force her fingers to unclench.

She collapsed face-first onto the wing, as limp as one of the rag dolls sold at La Maison du Vodou. Her heart was pounding like a ritual drum, and like a newly awakened zombie, she couldn't believe she was alive. *We did it!* she thought exuberantly. *We survived!*

Or rather, *she* had survived.

What about Terry?

Despite an overwhelming sense of fatigue, she lifted her head and looked to her left. Her heart nearly leaped out of her chest as she spied the petrified hacker still clinging to the opposite wing. His eyes remained tightly shut and his white knuckles were still wrapped around the edge of the metal.

Sydney laughed out loud. "It's okay, Terry!" she called to him ecstatically. "You can let go now!"

"What?" Terry cautiously opened his eyes. He looked around warily, as though not yet convinced that they were safely on the ground. Slowly he released his grip on the wing. "Is it over?" he asked Sydney uncertainly. "Really over?"

"Pretty much," she assured him. Now that she'd had a moment to catch her breath, she couldn't help wondering what was happening in the secluded lagoon, which was now many miles away. Were Dixon and Nadia and Weiss still exchanging fire with Maya and her thugs, or had the onetime bandit queen made a break for it? Knowing Maya, Sydney couldn't imagine her sticking around after Kestrel made its spectacular exit. Deprived of her prize, Maya would surely try to escape to fight another day. The only questions was, would she make it?

I guess that's up to Dixon and the gang now, Sydney concluded. She wasn't sure she had enough strength left to tangle with Maya, even if the slippery assassin were right in front of her. *I've done my part, at least for the moment.*

"Agent Bristow? Is that you?"

A jeep came rushing down the runway, pulling up beside the motionless UCAV. Men and women in dark suits and sunglasses jumped from the jeep and ran toward them, anxious expressions on their faces. *CIA or Homeland Security?* Sydney wondered idly. Either way Hayden Chase had obviously arranged a suitable reception for Kestrel, just as Sloane had promised. The agitated agents seemed more than a little surprised to find two unexpected passengers sprawled atop the top secret aircraft's wings.

"Agent Bristow!"

Sydney knew she should probably climb down from the wing and identify herself. She needed to hand Kestrel over to its new babysitters and update Sloane on the status of the operation. Come to think of it, she probably needed to have her bleeding arm looked at too. Not to mention the scrapes and scratches she'd received from the gator's scales. There was still much to do, including the inevitable debriefing back at APO and the final decision as to what to do with Terry.

First things first, she thought.

Sydney allowed herself the luxury of quietly passing out.

Mission complete.

LOS ANGELES

"Well, you'll be glad to know that Kestrel has been shipped back to White Sands for further testing," Hayden Chase declared. The CIA director was making one of her rare visits to the APO bunker. "Obviously there's still some work to be done before the UCAV is securely hackerproof."

The agents had convened in Sloane's office for a final update on their recent operation. Sydney was relieved to note that everyone was more or less intact. Her father was limping some and a temporary crutch was leaned up against his chair, but he was expected to recover fully. Dixon looked absolutely normal; you'd never guess that he had been drugged, beaten, strung up, and nearly zombified.

"What about Terry?" she asked. She had not laid eyes on the intrepid computer whiz since a couple of Feds at the airport hustled them away to safety, taking Terry with them to God knew where. She hoped the government hadn't come down too hard on him because of his involvement with the Kestrel heist. He had risked his life, after all, to get the UCAV back where it belonged.

Chase smiled slyly. "Mr. Fujiwara has been 'persuaded' to assist the CIA in testing the security of various vital computer systems. Don't worry," she assured Sydney, "he's being kept quite comfortable in an undisclosed location, although his computer usage is being closely monitored. If you don't believe me, ask Marshall. I believe he's been in touch with Fujiwara via e-mail."

"Oh, yeah!" Marshall confirmed. "Vixnut1—I mean, Terry—has been great about letting me pick his brain about quantum encryption and a few other ideas I've been playing around with. I'm putting together a whole new bag of tricks!" He doodled on a legal pad as he spoke, no doubt devising some ingenious new bit of op-tech. "But I still can't convince him that I don't know anything about Roswell."

"Tell me about it," Chase said, sighing wearily. "He keeps asking to be transferred to Area Fifty-one."

Sydney couldn't hold back a grin. *Sounds like Terry is adjusting okay,* she concluded. Certainly his current situation sounded a lot less terminal than the fate Maya and Benoit ultimately had in store for him.

"Any word on Maya?" she inquired. Dixon had told her about the fiery demise of the *Maman Brijit,* but Sydney still didn't believe that her duplicitous partner was really dead. She had known too many supposedly dead people who came back when she least expected them: her mother, Emily, Allison Doren, even Sloane himself. *I'll believe Maya's dead when I see her body—and maybe not even then.*

Chase said nothing to overcome Sydney's doubts. "We found some carbonized human remains at the site of the crash, but nothing that we can definitely determine to be Maya Rao. The canal has been dredged and Benoit's known addresses raided, but Maya's precise status remains a question mark."

Figures, Sydney thought. In her heart she knew

that she and Maya Rao were bound to cross swords again. *At least I managed to rescue Terry as well as the UCAV, which is more than Maya would have done.* She realized now that despite their similar talents, she and Maya were completely different where it mattered most: in their hearts.

Sydney glanced across the lounge at Vaughn, who caught her look and replied with a devilishly attractive smile. Barring any unexpected threats to national security, they were supposed to go on a double date with Weiss and Nadia that evening. Some new Vietnamese place Weiss kept raving about, followed maybe by a show at Mann's Chinese Theatre. There was a new romantic comedy out, which was just what Sydney was in the mood for.

A warm feeling came over her, one that not even Sloane's odious presence could dispel. It was hard to imagine Maya Rao enjoying a moment like this or looking forward to an evening out with family and friends. Had she and Benoit truly loved each other, the way she had pretended to love Terry? Sydney doubted it; in the end people like Maya cared only for themselves.

Two of a kind, my foot, she thought. *Next time I'm stopping her for good.*

Greg Cox is the New York Times bestselling author of numerous Star Trek novels, including To Reign in Hell and The Eugenics Wars, Volumes One and Two. He wrote the official novelizations of the movies Daredevil and Underworld, as well as many other books and short stories based on such popular series as Buffy the Vampire Slayer, Roswell, Spider-Man, X-Men, Batman, Iron Man, and Xena: Warrior Princess.

He lives in Oxford, Pennsylvania.